Murder
on a
Queen

John Simpson &
Robert Cummings

Dreamspinner Press

Published by
Dreamspinner Press
5032 Capital Circle SW
Ste 2, PMB# 279
Tallahassee, FL 32305-7886
USA
http://www.dreamspinnerpress.com/

Murder on a Queen

Cover Art by Adrian Nicholas
adrian@cometfactory.com

ISBN: 978-1-61372-669-3

Printed in the United States of America
First Edition
August 2012

eBook edition available
eBook ISBN: 978-1-61372-670-9

I dedicate this novel to my mother, who fought a horrible battle with lung cancer and lost. The world has lost a wonderful, talented person, and heaven has gained a beautiful angel to watch over us all.

—Robert Cummings

Chapter 1

IT WAS a beautiful morning in Tampa, Florida. Richard Cosgrove rolled toward his wife, Jessica, and placed his hand on her shoulder. He pulled himself closer to her warm body, inhaling the rich aroma of the beauty cream she wore to bed every night. Richie gave her a gentle kiss on the neck and hugged her tightly.

"Morning, sleepyhead," he said as he kissed Jessica's neck and playfully nibbled on her earlobe. Jessica stirred as her husband's attention woke her.

"Good morning, honey, happy anniversary," Jessica said as she opened her eyes slightly and turned toward Richie. This was their twelfth wedding anniversary, and Richie had been planning today for over a month.

He grabbed the small silver bell from the nightstand and rang it to let his staff know it was time to begin the festivities. The live-in maid and butler walked into the room and went to work. Helena opened the blinds to let the sun shine into the room as Enrique placed the breakfast trays in front of Jessica and Richie. After serving breakfast, Enrique set a vase containing a dozen pink roses on Jessica's nightstand.

"One for each year, babe, I know roses are your favorite. Thank you, Helena and Enrique. Great job as always," Richie said as he and his wife began eating their breakfasts.

"Thank you, Rich. They're beautiful!" Jessica exclaimed as she pulled a rose from the vase and inhaled the intoxicating scent. Jessica placed the rose back in the vase and put her right hand under the covers, caressing Richie's inner thigh as a thank-you for the surprise. Richie felt desire swelling in his groin as his wife moved her hand higher and squeezed his manhood.

They finished breakfast and Richie called the servants back to remove the trays. When Richie and Jessica were alone again, they celebrated the morning of their twelfth wedding anniversary by making love.

"God, you're an animal in the morning. Come help me," Jessica exclaimed as she got out of the bed and motioned for her husband to follow her to the shower. For an hour, the happy couple celebrated over and over under the fast-flowing stream of water. They continued to make love until Richie had very little energy or stamina left.

Richie exited the shower and wrapped himself in a towel. He looked at his wife through the steamy mist that hung in the air and smiled. Jessica's long, fiery-red hair accentuated her Irish beauty. Richie thanked God every chance he got for making him lucky enough to land this ex-Playboy Bunny as his wife. Jessica had looks and the brains to match. She had him wrapped around her little finger, and he knew it.

"My God, you look amazing!" Richie said as Jessica emerged from the shower. She stepped toward him, and he enveloped his bride in the soft Egyptian cotton towel.

"Thanks, hon. You're not so bad yourself," Jessica said with a wink and a quick kiss on her husband's cheek.

"We're a pair of tens, and you know it, babe," said Richie, smiling.

"So… besides the clichéd breakfast in bed and flowers, what grandiose schemes do you have for me today?"

"Well, after we get dressed, I was going to take you to the spa and have them spoil you rotten until lunchtime. The rest is a surprise."

"I do that all the time. I want to do something exciting today."

"Okay. You surprise me this year, then."

"I like that."

"But keep in mind we have the party tonight so we can't go too far."

"I told you I didn't want that stupid party. I want to take the jet and head out to the Keys for the day," Jessica said as her face started to take on the same tint as her hair.

"Honey, you know my employees look forward to this party every year. I can't just skip it."

"So once again your work is more important than your wife? Even on our anniversary!" Jessica picked up a hairbrush and threw it at Richie before she stormed out of the bathroom.

"Jessica… that's not what I said at all," Richie said in a futile attempt to quell his wife's Irish temper.

Richie knew that if he didn't give in to Jessica she would be miserable for at least a week. He looked at his reflection in the bathroom mirror and sighed in resignation before he walked back into the bedroom and picked up his phone. He entered the number for his events manager, and after several rings a man answered. Richie cut him off midsentence.

"Hey, Kevin, how's it going today?"

"Great, Rich. Happy anniversary to you and the missus."

"Thank you. We appreciate that a lot coming from you. I've got some bad news for you, though."

"Uh-oh, what's wrong?"

"Jessica and I aren't going to be able to make it to the party tonight."

"Is everything okay? Is there something I can do?"

"No, there's nothing anyone can do, really."

"Well, I'll call the guests and cancel the festivities. I'm pretty sure everyone is going to be crushed. They love this yearly shindig."

"I didn't say that you had to cancel the party. I just said me and the wife can't make it tonight. You can still have the party. I just need you to give everyone my regrets."

"Okay. I'll see what I can do, sir. You're going to have four hundred very sad people."

"Four hundred and one, Kevin. You forgot to count me."

"Well, I hope everything works out okay. Try to enjoy the rest of the day, sir."

"Thanks." Richie hung up the phone and threw it onto the bed. Then he sighed and walked over to his closet to select his clothing for the day.

Jessica was standing outside of the bedroom door, eavesdropping, during the phone call. She heard her husband cancel their appearance at the party, and she smiled in satisfaction at getting her way yet again.

She reshaped the smile into a pouty frown and lowered the front of her towel just enough to expose the top of her cleavage before she walked into the room with her eyes on the floor.

Richie saw her reflection in his closet mirror, "Okay, Jessica, just to prove to you that you are the most important thing in my life, I canceled our appearance at the party and my next call is to the pilot so he can get the jet ready."

"No, I can't do that to you, babe. I lost my temper for no good reason, and I'm sorry. This party means too much to you, and I don't want to spoil it."

"I don't understand," Richie said, furrowing his brow as he turned around to face his wife.

Jessica raised her gaze from the floor and looked her husband in the eyes. She walked over to him and embraced him, giving him a kiss on his cheek. She began to button Richie's shirt as she spoke to him.

"I'm sorry. It's just that you're always so busy with those stupid hotels that I feel neglected sometimes. I try my best to hide it from you, but sometimes it gets to be too much for me to handle."

"Sweetie, you know you're the most important thing to me," Richie said as he removed her hands from his buttons and brought them to his face.

"Sometimes I don't *feel* like I'm the most important thing, that's all."

"I just told four hundred of my employees and their families that I would rather spend my anniversary alone with my wife than with them. I would also like to point out that I did it on a moment's notice. If that doesn't say I love you, then I have no idea what will."

Jessica led Richie over to the bed, and they sat down on the edge together.

"I know keeping your father's legacy alive is important to you and that's why you spend so much time on the hotels, sweetheart. I learned to accept that twelve years ago," she said.

"Twelve years ago my father left me three beachfront motels with four bungalows. I fixed them up and reinvested in the business and look at where we are now! We live in a five-million-dollar house with a staff of five, and let's not forget everything else we have. It takes sacrifice to have things like a private jet on call and four-hundred-person anniversary parties."

"Ever since you started to expand the business, you're never home. You're on the road going to different properties, and you're like a stranger. I think you should hire someone to do that for you so we can have more time together," Jessica said with a halfhearted smile.

"We've been through this, Jess; I'm not turning over control of the company that my father started to some stranger. This has been and always will be a family company. My father always told me to never take on a business partner because they always screw you in the end."

"I think you're being just a little bit paranoid. It's those little things that remind me of why I love you as much as I do."

Jessica hugged Richie with all of her might, and then they stood up.

"So, Jessica, what is it that you want to do today?"

"Sweetie, whatever makes you happy makes me happy. Let's go to the spa like you planned, and then we can get ready for the party tonight," Jessica said, knowing that Richie would rather be skinned alive then caught dead in a beauty spa.

"The spa is for you, babe. I'll be here taking care of some business, waiting for you to come back all relaxed and extra beautiful, as if that were possible."

"You're so sweet to me. I couldn't love you any more right now if I tried."

Jessica squeezed her husband as hard as she could and went over to the closet to pick out and change into her spa clothes. Richie rang the little silver bell to call Enrique. When Enrique arrived, Richie asked him to have Carl bring the car around so Jessica didn't have to wait when she came downstairs. He also informed Enrique that the rest of his plans for the day had been cancelled except for the party.

Enrique acknowledged his new orders.

As Richie and Jessica left the room, Helena came in and began to clean.

Once their employers were out of the room and out of earshot, they began to gossip.

"He has all that money but no brains, I swear to God," Enrique said in a hushed tone.

"No kidding. She shows him her pouty face, and he'd jump off a bridge if she asked," Helena replied.

"Who cares? As long as the checks clear every week, I don't care," Enrique said as he put a smile on his face and walked out of the bedroom.

Enrique and Helena had a long history with the Cosgrove family. They had worked for Richie's father back when he had bought the first motel. They'd stayed with him as he expanded the business to three motels on the beach, and Richie's father had rewarded them whenever he could afford to.

Truthfully, Richie's father had rarely showed a profit from the business, but what he lacked in wealth he made up for in happiness. The three motels kept him busy for ninety hours a week, but he always made time for his son. When a man Richie's father had hired to manage the three motels stole $50,000 from him, he decided that he would never again hire an outsider and kept the business a family affair from that day forward.

When Richie was old enough to help with the business, his father hired him as a front desk clerk. Richie learned very quickly, and his father recognized the boy's business sense, promoting him to manager within a year. Richie worked hard to learn the ins and outs of running a motel, and after two years, his father had enough faith in him that his parents took their first vacation in fifteen years. Richie felt a deep sense of pride the day his father informed him that he trusted him enough to manage the business by himself for a month. He promised his father that he wouldn't let him down.

Richie's parents went to London for a month. While riding on a tour bus, a motor vehicle accident claimed their lives. When Richie learned of their deaths, he was devastated and vowed to keep the promise he made to his father. Richie was the only known relative, and he inherited the family business in its entirety.

Richie poured himself into the business to avoid dealing with the loss of his parents. He ran the hotels as he thought his father would if he were still alive. The motels began to thrive in a way Richie's father had never envisioned.

Richie met Jessica while he was surveying a new property for acquisition. Jessica was staying at the hotel for a Playboy Bunny event that was taking place in St. Petersburg. He fell completely in love with the gorgeous, fiery redhead, and they were married six months later.

After Richie married Jessica, he worked even harder on the hotel empire so he could impress her with expensive gifts and a lavish lifestyle. After eight years of marriage, Jessica came to resent the fact that Richie spent more time with his hotels then he did with her and told him she wanted a divorce. After a three-month separation Jessica came back, saying that she loved him too much to leave him. Christopher Powell, Esq., a family friend, had been the communications link between Richie and Jessica. He had been a friend of Richie's since high school, and he seemed to be determined to keep Richie and Jessica together. In the four years since the separation, there had been no further problems, and Richie and Jessica appeared to be a very happy couple.

JESSICA sauntered down the staircase wearing a sexy black dress. She was greeted at the bottom by her adoring husband.

"You have fun at the spa, honey. I'll be counting the seconds while you're gone," Richie said teasingly.

"Oh, please." Jessica gave him a kiss on the lips and walked out the door to the waiting car.

Carl was the Cosgroves' driver and bodyguard. Richie had hired him after receiving threats against his life. Carl had performed above and beyond the call of duty on several different occasions, and Richie had decided to keep him around permanently. He opened the door for Jessica as she was sending a text message. She got into the car without acknowledging Carl's existence. As the car began to move, Jessica rolled down the window and waved goodbye to her husband before she turned and faced Carl.

"Carl, I need to stop at the Powell law firm before we hit the day spa."

"Yes, ma'am."

Jessica closed the privacy window between her and the driver as she sent another text message. She knew she would be late to the day spa so she called and informed them of the delay. The spa's receptionist told her that it wasn't a problem and moved her appointment to a later time. Richie spent thousands of dollars a year on his wife at this particular day spa, so they were always happy to work around Jessica's schedule.

After a twenty-minute ride through light traffic, Jessica arrived at the Powell law firm. Carl stopped in front of the building and exited the vehicle to open the door for his employer's wife.

"Thanks, Carl," Jessica said dismissively as she got out of the car and walked to the entrance.

"Should I tell your husband we're going to be late coming back, ma'am?" Carl asked politely.

"No, Carl, you should not. We've talked about this before, so stop trying to be cute. If you like your job, you're going to sit here and wait, like a good little boy. If anyone asks, say that traffic was really bad," Jessica said coldly. "Oh, and, Carl, don't forget that little nondisclosure agreement you signed when my husband hired you," she finished as she walked toward the entrance.

"I fucking hate that bitch," Carl muttered to no one in particular.

Jessica knew she didn't have to worry about Carl opening his mouth to her husband. Richie had made it very clear to him that any violation of the nondisclosure agreement would void his contract. The fact that Carl was paid triple the rate he had received as a dignitary protection specialist, combined with the fact that there was less risk in this job than any other he had performed, made him very content to stay put.

"Good morning, Beth. Where is he?" Jessica asked the law firm's receptionist.

"He's in his office waiting for you, Mrs. Cosgrove," Beth said with a fake smile.

Jessica walked past the receptionist's desk and down the hallway to Christopher Powell's office, where she opened the door without bothering to knock.

"Mrs. Cosgrove, good morning. It's great to see you as always," the attorney said in his most professional tone.

Jessica closed the door and locked it.

Attorney Chris Powell had already called the front desk and informed his receptionist that he was not to be disturbed once Mrs. Cosgrove arrived.

As Chris stood up, Jessica dropped her handbag to the floor. Chris quickly closed the gap between them, and they embraced. They kissed passionately as Jessica's hand wandered below Chris's waistline to his cock. She could tell that Chris was very excited to see her. She gave his cock a slight nudge with her hand, and then Chris broke free of the embrace.

"I can't stand it anymore, Chris. I want you inside me." Jessica paused for dramatic effect.

"You know my rule about the office. We have to be careful right now. If anyone was able to produce evidence of our little affair, it could ruin the whole deal and land us in prison."

"I understand that, Chris. I watch TV too!"

"Would you like a drink?" Chris offered as he walked over to his small office bar.

"I could sure use one."

"Well, I keep the Grand Marnier just for you, my dear."

"My favorite."

"So what's on your mind, Jessica?" Chris asked as he opened the large brown bottle of orange-flavored liqueur.

"Oh, I don't know, maybe the payoff after four years of waiting? When are we going to do this?"

"If it wasn't for his dad having a half brother, we could've sealed the deal already. If Richie dies, the inheritance could be contested by a relative that Richie's never even met. That would leave us with almost nothing, sweetie. Besides, like you said, you watch TV. They always look at the spouse first in a murder investigation," Chris said as he handed her the drink.

"Aren't you worried about your office being bugged?" Jessica asked as she took a sip.

"You watch too much TV! Attorney-client privilege, my dear. Besides, no one suspects anything, so why would they bug my office?"

"Your receptionist acts weird when I come in. Are you sure she isn't suspicious?"

"She'll mind her own business if she knows what's good for her." Chris raised his glass and tapped it against the rim of Jessica's. They made a silent toast as they finished their drinks.

"I need you to take Richie for a walk on the beach in front of the hotel tonight. Be there at eight o'clock sharp."

"Why? What are you going to do?" Jessica inquired leaning forward.

"*I* am not going to do a thing. I'll be at the party celebrating your anniversary. Just have him on the beach at eight o'clock."

"Am I going to get hurt?"

"If you come away unscathed the cops will definitely think something's up. You're going to get a few scratches and bumps that will make it more believable. Don't worry. I've used these guys before, and they're professionals."

"No scars or I swear I'll kill you myself!"

"Oh, come on, now, do you think I would scar the hottest woman I've ever known?"

"For eight hundred and fifty million dollars? God knows."

"You forget, my dear, *you* are the one with medical power of attorney. Without you nothing gets done, so just act terrified and make sure he doesn't bring his gun to the party."

"Oh, please. I told him I hated those things, and after my little tantrum he stopped carrying one altogether."

"You're such a manipulative little thing, aren't you?"

"Little ole me?" Jessica said in a heavy Southern accent. She stood and then headed toward the door.

Chris grabbed her from behind and turned her around for one more kiss. Jessica gave him a ten-second embrace and then checked herself in the mirror.

"Shit!" Jessica exclaimed.

"What?" Chris asked.

"I forgot my makeup kit in the car, and you smeared everything."

"Just wipe it all off and put your glasses back on. No one will notice anything," Chris said as he handed Jessica a handkerchief.

As Jessica emerged from Chris's office, Beth informed her boss that Richie Cosgrove had called about a half hour before and that it was urgent. Chris thanked Beth and went into his office to call Richie.

Carl sat in the car watching the entrance for forty-five minutes before Jessica emerged from the office. Carl moved the car to the entrance and then got out and dutifully opened her door. Jessica had her sunglasses on and didn't bother to make eye contact with him as she got into the vehicle.

Carl noticed that Jessica's makeup was gone but would never say anything due to fear of retribution or termination. He closed the door and got back into the driver's seat of the car. He lowered the privacy screen as Jessica started to reapply her makeup. "To the spa, ma'am?" Carl asked as he looked at the woman in the rearview mirror.

"Yes. Go." Jessica raised the privacy screen again and locked it in place as she finished reapplying her makeup.

Carl shifted the car into drive and began the trip to the spa. It had been three years since Carl had discovered that something was going on between Jessica and Chris Powell. Carl had once tried to inform Richie of his wife's comings and goings, but Richie had stopped him and reminded him of the nondisclosure agreement. Carl had never again attempted to treat Richie as anything more than an employer.

RICHIE closed the door after waving goodbye to his wife and then headed for his office. He had a lot of work to do and very little time to get it done before he had to spend the afternoon appeasing his wife. The spa would take two to three hours, and then Jessica would be back at the house monopolizing his time.

In the office, Richie logged onto his company's private network and reviewed the overnight receipts. After fifteen minutes of reading the night clerk memos, he picked up the secure line and dialed Chris Powell's office. Richie had to take care of a pending litigious matter against one of his Miami properties and needed to talk to his lawyer.

"Good morning, Powell Law Firm. How can I help you?" said a woman with a pleasantly professional voice.

"Good morning, Beth. It's Richard Cosgrove."

Beth was silent for a second before she answered. "Um, good morning, Mr. Cosgrove. What can I do for you?"

"I need to speak with Chris. I dialed his direct line, but the call was rerouted to you."

"Mr. Powell is in a meeting right now, Mr. Cosgrove. Can I take a message?"

"I'm not paying a fifteen-thousand-dollar-a-month retainer to have my calls rejected by my lawyer. I would like to speak with him right now," Richie said sternly.

"Mr. Powell has the 'do not disturb' on right now. Calls do not go through, and I'm not allowed to go into his office until he takes it off."

"Look, I don't care if he's banging somebody across his desk. Go in there and tell him I want to talk with him right now or I'm coming down there to speak with him in person."

"There's no need for that, Mr. Cosgrove. Please don't shoot me. I'm just a messenger," the receptionist replied.

"I'm sorry. It's been a pretty crappy day so far, Beth. It's my anniversary, and I only have a little time to take care of business before the wife gets back, so it's kind of urgent that I speak with him now."

"I'll relay the message for you, Mr. Cosgrove. That's the best I can do right now. She won't be much longer." Beth realized her slipup and quickly tried to recover. "The client won't be much longer."

Richie noted that the woman's voice had sounded apprehensive when she used feminine pronoun.

"I knew it was some floozy! I've known Chris since high school, and the only time he blows me off is for a woman."

"As soon as his meeting is over, I'll dial your number and hand him the phone, I promise. Oh, and happy anniversary."

"Thanks, Beth, goodbye."

Beth hung up and placed her head in her hands. Everyone suspected that Chris Powell was having an affair with Jessica Cosgrove, but no one knew for sure. The office staff only knew that Chris Powell and Jessica Cosgrove were awfully friendly for their relationship to be of a strictly professional nature.

Richie hung up the secure phone and looked down at the list of things he had to accomplish today. It was the beginning of the quarter, and he needed sales figures for budgeting so he dialed his business headquarters to speak with his accountant.

The phone was answered by a flamboyant-sounding male. "Cosgrove Hotels, how I may direct your call?"

"Hey, Troy, it's Richie."

"Good morning, Mr. Cosgrove, sir. Happy anniversary. My partner and I are looking forward to the party tonight."

"Glad to hear it. Could you patch me through to Louie, please? And tell your boy Jason I said hello."

"I will, Mr. Cosgrove. I'm putting you through to Lou now."

Several clicks later, Richie was connected to his chief accountant.

"Hey, Richie, how are you this morning?" Louie asked.

"Good, I'm just calling to check on last quarter's figures. I've been waiting for a week. Give me some good news, Lou."

"Sorry, I'm fresh out of good news. Unfortunately, it's all of the bad variety. I've been preaching to you for ten years now about restructuring how you run this monster of a company. You're getting slaughtered in taxes. Revenues of one hundred and twenty million a year put you in the top tax bracket."

Going public with his company would put some of the authority in other people's hands, and his father had instilled a serious fear of that in him when he was a child.

"Don't start with the corporate restructuring bullshit again. My father—"

Lou cut Richie off midsentence.

"Your father ran three tiny motels on a small beach outside of Tampa. You're running a total of fifteen five-star establishments all over the country as well as those same three motels. Thankfully those are great write-offs every quarter, but that's a small light shining in a deep dark tunnel. With the amount of spending you've done in the last year, we'll be lucky to still be in business five years from now."

"So talk bottom line to me here, Lou. What were my losses this quarter?"

"Three million, and those aren't really business expenses, either. They fall under your personal expenditures."

"Well, I'm not exactly hurting here. I can afford to have a good quarter and a bad quarter. It all evens out, right?"

"Not really. You really need to hire a business manager to help you handle this stuff. I'm afraid that you're going to lose it all if you're not careful."

"Hey, you're my accountant. Just count the money and let me know what I have left in the bank, thank you very much."

"Could we at least look at dropping the timeshare on that stupid jet? That alone costs two hundred and fifty thousand a year."

"I'll consider it. Any other good news to cheer me up with?"

"Nope, I've given you all I have. Did you call that investors group back yet?"

"How did you hear about that?"

"You're asking a guy who lives and breathes finance how he heard that the largest hotel investors group in the US was interested in the Cosgrove brand? Seriously?"

"Well? How?"

"My buddy works for them, and he gave me a call to see how receptive you'd be to an offer. I told him that it never hurts to talk."

"Don't you ever do that again! I wondered why they would call out of the blue after all this time."

"Do what?" Lou asked, knowing he was in some serious hot water for discussing things behind his boss's back.

"These properties are not and never will be for sale. If you ever get another call like that again, your answer better be an immediate and absolute no! You signed a nondisclosure agreement with me when I hired you."

"It's not like that. My friend Phil called me at home two weeks ago, and we were just talking about our families when the hotels came up in conversation. Phil had heard that you might be looking to get out of the business."

"Well, wherever he got that little tidbit of information, it's absolutely false. I'm not getting out of this business nor selling any of the properties."

"I'm sorry I mentioned it, and it won't happen again, Mr. Cosgrove. I promise you that."

"Just e-mail me those figures soon because I have to take a look at them and do some budgeting." Richie hung the phone up with a little more force than usual.

He had been offered three billion dollars for the hotels and brand name and had turned them down flat without a blink of the eye. The thought of selling any of the hotels felt like a betrayal of his father's trust.

Richie was looking at the next thing on his to-do list when the phone rang. He let it ring five times before he decided to answer it. He felt as if he needed to take a breath before setting about his next task, but he leaned forward and picked up the receiver.

"Hello."

"Hey, Rich, it's Chris Powell. Beth told me that you called and that it was urgent. What's up?"

"How in the world does a guy as butt ugly as you get so many women?" Richie asked his old high school buddy.

"I have a twelve-inch dick and lots of money."

"Bullshit, I used to play baseball with you. I saw it in the shower and you're lucky if that cock of yours is two inches when it's hard, pee wee."

"So you called me to break my balls about cock size?"

"No, I called you about the lawsuit against the Miami property."

"Like I said three times last month, it's a meritless case. The woman hired some schmuck local lawyer hoping for a payday because you have two dimes to rub together. We have this beat, so stop worrying about it."

"Her son fell off an eighth-story balcony because the railing wasn't secured properly. How in the hell is that meritless?"

"If you admit to fault in this incident, you're going to open the floodgates for lawsuits and bankrupt the whole operation. You'll be lucky to be working as a night clerk at an Econo Lodge in Clearwater after it's all said and done."

"The kid's a quadriplegic for the rest of his life, for Christ's sake. You're telling me there's nothing we can do for her or the kid?"

"Sure, if she wants to settle, but her lawyer is advising against it and won't even return my phone calls regarding the matter."

"I just can't sleep thinking about that poor kid and how fucked up his life is now. He's sixteen, and his life is screwed up beyond belief because of two screws on a railing."

"Look, if they want to take this to court, they can go right ahead. The window was sealed so no one would be able to go outside onto that balcony. There were signs on the windows warning against trying to get to the balcony, and he ignored them. The kid broke the window to get to the balcony and decided to lean on the decorative railing, which—surprise, surprise—broke. We have video of him damaging the property to gain access to the balcony. They have no case. Let me handle this, Rich. It's what I do. I'm here to protect you, buddy."

"I appreciate it. I just feel bad about the whole thing."

"It's all under control. I won't need you for the hearing next week, so you can take that off your schedule. I'll be at the party tonight, but I'll have to cut out early. And I'll be out of the office for the next couple of days."

"Well, at least I'll get to see you at the party for a bit. Where are you going?"

"A funeral in Maryland."

"Oh my God, your sister didn't die, did she?" Richie asked with genuine concern.

"No. Her adopted son Ray got killed in Rock Creek Park."

"Killed?"

"Yeah, it turns out Ray was a gay hooker, and he got killed while meeting someone in the park. Apparently, whoever it was tied him to a table and beat him to death. I don't know too much more about it, but my sister's really torn up, and I told her I would come to the funeral if it would make her feel better."

"Did they catch the guy?"

"I didn't ask her a lot of details. I can't believe he was prostituting right under her nose after she let him stay there after he turned eighteen. She said she failed him, and that's why he turned to drugs.

"How old was Ray?"

"I'm not sure. I think he was in his early twenties or late teens. Way too young to die, that's all I know."

"My condolences, and have a safe trip. Keep in touch."

Richie hung up and crossed Chris Powell off his to-do list. He began to send out e-mails to his hotel managers regarding new operating policies and lost track of time. About an hour later, he heard the car pull up outside and knew Jessica was back from the spa.

Well, time to clock out, I guess, Richie thought as he rose to go and see his fresh-from-the-beauty-spa wife.

Richie came down the stairs just as Enrique opened the door for Jessica. Jessica's face was glowing, and she seemed much happier than when she left to go to the spa.

"The spa was a fabulous idea, baby. I feel like a million bucks."

"Well, you look like a billion to me." Richie leaned in to kiss Jessica.

Jessica gave Richie a quick kiss on the lips and then continued up the stairs to change into more comfortable clothing. She knew that she would be back in formalwear soon enough.

As she walked up the steps, she heard her husband following her. She stopped and turned around to look at her smiling husband.

"Richie, honey, I'm going to go lie down before the party. Enrique, could you wake me in two hours, please, and see that I'm not disturbed until then."

The smile faded from Richie's face, "Okay, sweetheart, I'll see you later. Guess I'll go finish up my e-mails." At the top of the stairs, he turned toward his office as Jessica went in the opposite direction to the bedroom. The bedroom door closed and was locked from the inside.

Jessica waited just inside the bedroom door until she heard the office door close. Once the door closed and she was alone, a smile spread across her face. The thought of the money that would be hers in less than a month was inebriating.

She had waited four years for this day to come, and now she only had to get through tonight, and in another month she would be a rich woman.

Two hours later, Enrique knocked on the bedroom door, per Jessica's instructions. She was already awake and had started to get ready for the anniversary party. Richie was in his office and heard Enrique performing the wake-up call. He got up from behind his desk and walked to the bedroom. Enrique passed by as Richie exited his office.

"Wow, you're getting ready really early. The party isn't until seven thirty, honey," Richie said as he walked behind his wife and gave her a hug.

"I want to look my best for you, baby. You're always so excited to have these large employee parties, so I figured I would start getting ready so we wouldn't be late."

"Sounds good to me. I'm going to do a few laps in the pool, and then I'll be up to shower and get ready."

Richie placed a small box wrapped in pink silk on the stand next to Jessica. Her face lit up as she grabbed the box.

"Oh my God, you didn't!"

"Open it up and find out."

Jessica unwrapped and opened the box. Inside was a white platinum necklace with a three-karat heart-shaped emerald. Surrounding the emerald were twelve diamonds.

"Oh my God, I can't believe you remembered," Jessica squealed.

"How could I forget your reaction to that necklace when we were in Italy? You were so excited I thought they were going to call the cops."

"Thank you so much! I'll give you your gift after the party. I'm not wearing any panties, and I think it's about time we made that beach fantasy come true." Jessica leaned in and kissed her husband.

Richie embraced Jessica but noted that she was not squeezing back as hard as she usually did. He ignored the odd feeling in his gut and let her go. Then he grabbed a towel and changed into his swimming apparel.

As Richie exited the room, Jessica put the necklace on and stared at herself in the mirror. Richie smiled at his wife's happiness over the gift and left her to go swimming.

At seven o'clock, Carl pulled the car around the back of the hotel where the party was being held. The obviously happy couple arrived at the hotel ballroom a little early. The guests would be arriving soon, and Richie liked to greet them personally.

Chris Powell was the first guest to arrive. He had a blonde-haired woman on his arm who looked as if she might be higher maintenance than a Ferrari.

"Chris, good to see you." Richie extended his hand.

Chris introduced Richie and Jessica to his date for the night. "This is Claire Desmond."

"Miss Desmond. Mr. Powell, a pleasure as always," Jessica said politely.

"Mrs. Cosgrove, ravishing as always," Chris replied.

"I'm going to get a drink. I'll see you two lovebirds later," Chris said as he and his date walked away from the couple to allow them to greet the rest of the guests.

The rest of the party guests had arrived by seven fifty, and Richie got on stage and gave his customary welcome toast. Everyone clapped when he finished, and the waiters began to serve the appetizers.

Richie and Jessica took their seats at the head table as the guests of honor. Jessica looked at the clock on the wall, and saw she had four minutes to get Richie onto the beach.

Jessica leaned over and whispered in her husband's ear. "I just wanted to remind you that I don't have any panties on and that there's no one on the beach right now."

Richie became instantly hard as his wife stroked his leg. The thought of getting caught having sex was just as arousing as the act itself.

"You go first, and I'll follow in two minutes."

Jessica got up from her seat and walked to the beach. Two minutes later, Richie did the same. They met at the rear of the hotel and started their search for a spot in the sand.

Chapter 2

"LIEUTENANT, you know that I love the Homicide bureau and working with Pat. It's just I think if I let this opportunity to get promoted pass me by, I might regret it. It will haunt me like the decision not to join SWAT," Hank said as he sat in Lieutenant Capparell's office.

"I've known you since you were a wet-behind-the-ears rookie, Capstone. I think you're a fantastic detective, and the Homicide bureau would really hate to lose you. To be honest, I was surprised you passed on joining the SWAT unit," replied Capparell as he sat on the edge of his desk looking down at Hank.

It had been almost five years since Hank Capstone had joined the Prince George's County police force, and he had always wanted to be in the middle of the action. Working as a homicide detective presented its own set of unique challenges, but the position in the Narcotics unit was a promotion to a leadership position and the work was a lot more exciting than investigating homicides.

Hank had passed up the opportunity to join the SWAT team so that he and his longtime partner Pat could continue to work together. After the Albright case, there had been very little adrenaline associated with being a homicide detective.

"I haven't told Pat that I was thinking of transferring to Narcotics yet. I'm just considering it at the moment, Lieutenant."

"If you're in here asking me for a letter of recommendation, it must be under some serious consideration."

"True, but I haven't put in any paperwork yet, and the test isn't until next month. I have time to weigh my options. It's just that I'm torn between the pros and cons of Narcotics work. I want to make a definite decision before I talk to Pat."

"Well, don't wait until the last minute, Hank. I know Pat wouldn't want to hold you back from a promotion, but I'm sure he doesn't want you to just dump this on him and run away."

"I know. I just feel really bad about breaking up the band."

"Well, divorces are always messy, Capstone," the lieutenant said with a chuckle.

"Very funny, Lieutenant."

Hank stood before walking out of the lieutenant's office. He had a lot to think about. As he went back to his desk, he worried that Pat would have the same reaction to this news that he had when Hank wanted to join SWAT. They didn't talk or hang out for a week, and even when they did manage to get together outside of work, it was tense until Hank withdrew his application. He smiled at his partner as he reached his desk.

"What was that all about?" chided Pat St. James. "Did another old lady file a complaint about your lack of driving skills?

"Oh, please, you've dented more county cars than I will for the rest of my career. I had to see Capparell about a letter," Hank responded without looking up.

"A letter for what?" Pat asked, only half paying attention as he filled out a supplemental report to their latest case.

"I'll tell you tonight at dinner. Right now just isn't a good time."

Hank chewed his bottom lip, hoping that his partner would drop the subject. He knew that Pat wasn't going to be satisfied with the answer he had just received once what he had said sunk in.

"Dinner? Oh my God, I forgot about dinner tonight! Dean and I have to go to his parents' tonight for their anniversary," Pat said, looking at the ceiling.

"I thought Dean wasn't on speaking terms with them?"

"Nah, they kissed and made up, so it's all good."

"Thankfully Shawn never had those types of problems after his parents accepted him. I don't have to worry about the in-laws like you do."

"I don't let them get to me. I'm happy as long as Dean's all right with the situation."

"Well, we can do our usual Friday night dinner at Isabella's next week, but you're buying the first round of drinks since you're standing us up tonight, Mr. St. James."

"Deal! You can have all the water that you can handle that night, and it's on me, buddy," Pat said as he returned to his typing.

"Yeah, right. I'm drinking Cristal and Dom Perignon by the bottle since it's coming out of your pocket."

Pat shook his head and decided not to answer Hank's latest tease. After this many years doing the job together, they knew how to get on each other's nerves just enough for it to be fun.

The lieutenant's door opened, and he emerged holding a piece of a paper in the air.

"St. James and Capstone, you're up on the rotation, and I have two bodies for you." Lt. Capparell motioned for the boys to come into his office to get briefed. Pat and Hank logged off their computer terminals and headed over to the lieutenant's office, where Pat pulled out his notepad as Hank closed the door to the office.

"Patrol just called in a homicide by firearm down near the university section. According to the watch commander, it looks like a possible murder-suicide. Two male victims; both are white and in their early twenties."

Lieutenant Capparell handed Hank the piece of paper with all of the victims' information and the address of the crime scene. Pat and Hank emerged from the office and went over to the coat rack. They grabbed their coats and radios as they headed out door.

"I hate these murder-suicides because there's not really much to do. No tracking down the bad guy, no tense interviews, and no action," Hank said to his partner.

"You'd prefer to have a psycho nut that tracks us down and almost kills our husbands on a daily basis?" Pat asked with a furrowed brow.

"No, it's not just that I like the chase. It's my favorite part of this job—the cat and mouse kind of games."

"Holy shit! We make detective in record time, homicide detectives, no less, and you're still not happy with how things are! I can't believe what I'm hearing!"

"Our probationary year as detectives was a lot of undercover stuff, and I really enjoyed the adrenaline you feel just before the bust."

"That was chasing hookers, when we weren't busy doing everyone else's busy work. You would think that's fun, wouldn't you?"

Hank avoided making eye contact with his partner. This conversation might lead to Pat putting the clues together and making the day a living hell from that moment on.

Pat walked to the driver's side of the car and was about to open the door when something in his mind clicked.

Hank had opened the passenger's side door, and he froze for a second as he saw Pat turn to him with his mouth agape. Hank knew that look. It happened whenever Pat connected all of the small details into a clear picture. Hank turned his head to make eye contact, and his stomach wrenched into a knot.

"So that's the letter you were talking about." Pat cocked his head to the side and broke eye contact with Hank as he entered the vehicle.

"What do you mean?" Hank inquired with false indignation.

"You come out of Capparell's office and tell me you were in there about a letter. You've been griping about no real action at work just like you did when the SWAT opening came up. You transferring out to Narcotics, aren't you?"

Pat started the car and put it in drive after Hank secured his safety belt.

"This is not how I wanted to tell you. I wanted to be outside of work when we discussed it."

"Discussed it? What is there to discuss? It sounds like you have your mind made up, and you've already put things in motion… *partner*." Pat stressed the word "partner" as if he were spitting the word at the dashboard.

"It's not like that, Pat. I haven't done anything yet—"

"Yet?" Pat interrupted.

"Yes. *Yet*. It was just something I was kicking around in my head, and the notion of chasing drug dealers around and raiding houses had more appeal than staring at dead people and watching their families cry."

"And what? You were going to tell me on your last day with the Homicide bureau?"

"Hey, it doesn't say anywhere that I have to run my decisions by you! We're partners, not lovers."

"That's for sure, and apparently we won't even be partners anymore because you can't handle the boredom. Some guys beg for this assignment, and you just want to go where there's more action. I thought that this action crap was out of your system with the whole SWAT conversation."

"Oh, you mean when you talked me out of joining the team because you can't stand not seeing me every day?"

"Yeah, wonder if your boy likes his job or not?" Pat asked rhetorically.

"What the fuck does that mean? So now you're going to threaten my husband because I'm not doing what the great Pat St. James says?"

Pat was so involved in the heated exchange of words that he failed to see the stop sign posted at the intersection. He went through it at a high speed and almost caused a three-car wreck. Pat pulled off to the side of the road and looked in his mirror to see if any cars had crashed. None of the cars that were forced to skid to a stop had collided, and it appeared that everyone seemed content to blare their horns and be on their way.

"This is why I didn't want to say anything to you, Pat. You get so unreasonable when I make a decision without discussing it with you first that I just figured I would wait until we were away from work to tell you. I sure as fuck hoped that Shawn—who loves you like a brother—would be left out of this!"

Pat sighed. He knew that he could sometimes be a little shortsighted when it came to Hank or his other friends. Pat always wanted to be the protector and make sure nothing bad ever happened to them, but he was slowly realizing that he had no control over the universe.

"Let's just stop talking about this for now. You do what you think is best, and I'm still your friend regardless of what your decision is. We can have a few beers while we watch the Eagles game at your house on Saturday, and talk about this."

"Beer and arguments should be better than the game."

"Stop it. I'm just worried about you, buddy. Besides, you're the one breaking up the band, Yoko!"

Pat and Hank continued their journey to the crime scene, where they got right down to business... or so Hank thought.

Pat parked the car outside of the yellow crime scene tape, and they exited the vehicle without saying a word to each other.

The medical examiner from the coroner's office had arrived before Pat and Hank. David Collins worked for the coroner's office and was a trick from Pat's life pre-Dean. He walked up to the two men and said, "Nice of you guys to finally show up."

"Hey, Dave. Sorry, we almost got into an accident on the way here so we were delayed."

"Congratulations are in order, I hear," Hank said as he patted David on the shoulder.

"Yep, I'm done with college and med school for good. I graduated last month, and when I play doctor from now on, it'll be for real," David said with a grin.

"Great to hear, good for you, buddy. So what do you have on the menu for us today?" Pat asked, ending the exchange of pleasantries.

"I heard patrol call over the radio for a coroner, and I was stuck in traffic two blocks from here. I used my lights and came directly to the scene. The victims have gunshot wounds. One male has a hole in the head that looks to be a forty or forty-five caliber. The other was shot in the chest. The head wound seems to have powder burns, but the blond guy's chest wound doesn't, so I'd say he was shot from more than seven feet away. The victims appear to be in their early twenties and both have their wallets. When patrol looked for ID, they said they didn't notice anything missing. Money and credit cards are intact. The patrol officers have their IDs, and they're checking for addresses for the next of kin. Between us, the taller, heavier-set white guy was always on the Bear Finder app on my phone, so I know he was gay or bi."

"Did you get his name?" asked Pat.

David pulled out his notes. "Jesse Kovalick, age twenty-three."

"All right, sounds good. I see crime scene processing is here, so, Hank, you go get the information on the victims from the patrol officer, and I'll go talk to the witnesses," Pat said coldly.

"Yes, sir, Detective St. James."

Hank shot Pat a warning glare in order to communicate extreme displeasure regarding his high-handed demeanor. Hank walked over to the patrol officers who were standing near the barrier tape. Hank knew one of them from a veterans' organization they both belonged to.

"Hey, Boyle, how's it going?" Hank asked warmly as he extended his hand to the patrol officer.

The patrolman made a quick mock salute and snapped to attention. "Detective, sir!"

Hank returned the salute and said, "At ease, soldier. So what kind of information do you have for me, Boyle?"

"Two gunshots, and we only found one gun so we're thinking a murder-suicide. From what the witness told us, the whole thing may have been a lovers' quarrel," Boyle said.

"Lovers' quarrel?" Hank asked.

"Well, one of them was a known homosexual. Dispatch pulled some information from the system indicating that he'd been cited more than once for open lewdness. The other victim is a pretty little blond boy, so when you do the math, it adds up to boyfriends fighting. It looks like there's only one gun, so I was thinking murder-suicide. The head wound is a contact shot because I can see the powder burns. The other one has no burns, so I'm thinking the one guy shot the other and then killed himself."

"Wow, Boyle, all that without so much as reading a medical report or any scene reconstruction whatsoever. I think you'd better stop reading Sherlock Holmes books, buddy."

Boyle curled his lip and squinted, and he decided not to respond to Hank. Instead, he returned to his position near the crowd control line.

Pat walked over to Hank and the patrolman after speaking with three witnesses who had heard the gunshots.

"You're just making friends all over, Capstone, aren't you?" Pat said.

Hank ignored Pat's remark and returned to the task at hand. "What did you get?"

"Well, two of the three witnesses heard at least three gunshots, but Dave says he can only account for two."

"Did crime scene find any shell casings?"

"Only one so far, and it's from a forty-five caliber handgun," Pat said, looking at his notes.

"So possibly there's an unaccounted-for shooter and maybe a missing gun."

"That's what I'm thinking too. So what's the plan?"

"I'm going to go check a few of the local stores and see if they have any external cameras in this alleyway. Hopefully someone caught a glimpse of these guys and what happened," Hank said as he looked around at the rooftops in hopes of spotting a video camera.

"Good idea. I'm going to start tracking down the families of the vics so we can make notifications and start digging into backgrounds," Pat said without looking up from his notebook. Then he walked away without another word.

Hank stared at Pat for a second in hopes of getting a look of acknowledgment from his friend, but Pat didn't so much as nod in Hank's general direction. This was not how Pat and Hank conducted themselves at crime scenes, and Hank knew that there was a storm brewing underneath Pat's calm exterior.

Pat had always been a bit more introverted and emotional than Hank, but today he was displaying an extreme case of passive-aggressive behavior, and it was starting to get under Hank's skin.

Pat walked over to the car and opened the passenger door. He got into the car and sat motionless for a few moments, feeling numb inside. Logging onto the vehicle's mobile computer terminal, he typed the names of the victims into the NCIC computer. As Pat went about his police duties, a sense of betrayal filled the numb void. The more he thought about Hank's actions, the more he believed that Hank was trying to leave him. Pat sat back in the driver's seat and sighed, then he removed his cellular phone from his pants pocket and punched in Dean's number.

The phone rang twice before a cheerful Dean answered, "Hey, babe."

"Morning, Dean, how's work?" Pat asked as he put the Bluetooth earpiece on and typed the rest of the information into the terminal.

"Okay, mister! What's wrong? After two years of marriage, I know your voice gets like this when something's eating at you, so out with it."

"I just felt like I needed to talk to someone and see how their day was going. I have two dead guys on the ground, and sometimes I just like to talk to the living."

"This isn't about dinner tonight, is it? We have to go to this dinner or they won't talk to me for another five years."

"Is that such a bad thing?" Pat managed a halfhearted chuckle.

"Yes, it is! Now don't be trying to find a way to get stuck at work so I have to go to this dinner alone!"

"It's not the dinner, honey. Like I said, it's just work crap."

"Isn't that what your work boyfriend is for, dear?"

"Ha ha, very funny, Mr. Dean. You know you're the only one that matters to me, and I'd never leave you, so knock it off with the work-boyfriend stuff."

"Okay… sorry… geez, Mr. Grouch," Dean mocked.

At that moment, the computer terminal indicated that an important piece of information had been located in its database.

"I know what that sound means. Be safe out there and I love you," Dean said as he hung up the phone. Dean knew that when his husband was at work he might have to hang up at a moment's notice. So Dean always tried to be the one to end the call so Pat wouldn't feel bad.

The computer terminal flashed the words *Wanted for armed robbery*" across the screen. Pat hit the print button and removed the small curled-up wanted poster. On it was a picture of the man who was currently lying dead with a bullet in his chest.

Pat exited the police cruiser and walked over to the medical examiner.

"I have something to show you, Dave," Pat shouted across the crime scene.

The medical examiner looked up and lifted his bloody gloved hands to show Pat that he was busy, and Pat would have to walk over to him if he had something to share.

Hank was canvassing the neighborhood for surveillance video when he heard Pat holler to the medical examiner. He hurried back to the crime scene to see what Pat had found that was so important.

The masked medical examiner stood up as Pat walked over to him. Hank arrived just as Pat had finished speaking with the medical examiner.

"Hey, Pat, what's up? Did you find something?" Hank asked. He knew that Pat heard his question, but Pat turned around and walked back to the car without a word.

Hank called out Pat's name once more. He was rapidly reaching his boiling point and had taken just about enough of Pat's behavior. It would have been very unprofessional for Hank to explode at the crime scene, so he took a deep breath and swallowed his anger. Hank knelt down to speak with David, who was again tending to the body.

David summoned a crime scene technician with the wave of a bloody gloved hand.

"So what did you guys find, Dave?" Hank asked, masking his displeasure with the current working environment.

"Well, this guy lying at my feet has a warrant for armed robbery, so I'm going to have my favorite female crime scene technician, Dana, do a gunshot residue test on his hands. I'm thinking he may be the shooter."

Dana came over to the body, and David instructed her to do an angle of shot test and a gunshot residue field test.

"You think he was the aggressor?" Hank asked.

"Honestly, I don't know yet. There's a lot more to do before I can give you a complete scenario. What I do know is that you and Pat need to remove whatever is up your asses because everyone here is starting to feel really uncomfortable."

"What are you talking about?" Hank asked, feigning ignorance.

"Oh, please! The dead guys could feel the tension between you two right now, and I'm sure they would get up and walk away if they could," David said.

"Sorry, it's just been a tough day for both of us, but the problem will be addressed," Hank said blushing slightly.

Dana opened her examiner's kit and removed several sizes of caliber probes to stick into the wound. The first rod was too large, so she switched to a forty-caliber sized probe, and it too failed to fit the dimensions of the wound. Dana pulled out the nine-millimeter probe, and it fit perfectly.

The angle of the entry wound showed that the victim had most likely been standing when he was shot and that he was shot by a person standing to his left. Dana then conducted a gunshot residue test. As she blotted the victim's hands with paraffin wax, Hank was writing down everything said by the examiner and his technician.

"Would you like us to field test it, Hank?" Dave asked.

"You'll do the official one back at the morgue, right?"

"Absolutely, this will just be faster than waiting for my report."

"Yeah, give it a shot."

Pat saw David and the crime scene technician using the angle rods and speaking to Hank, so he ended the call he'd been making and walked over to the body.

"Hey, Pat, what did you find out with the background check on NCIC?" Hank asked as he stood up to look Pat in the eye.

"This one's wanted for armed robbery, and the other one is a local college student. That's all I have for now. What do you got?" Pat asked as he stared down at the body.

"What? I didn't quite catch that because of all of the noise around here. Could you come over here for a second so we can trade information out of earshot of the public?" Hank motioned for his partner to follow him.

"One second, I need to do something first," Pat replied as he knelt beside the body.

David could sense more trouble brewing and decided to step in as Pat's friend and as a professional. David had become reacquainted with his old hook-up buddy during the Albright case, and he knew that Hank could be bullheaded—especially when he was upset. The medical examiner tapped Pat on the shoulder and closed his clipboard.

"Pat, Hank, come here. This is important." David said as he motioned toward the large van with the word CORONER emblazoned on the side.

Pat stood and followed David. Hank paused, and then followed David and Pat into the van. Before David closed the rear doors, he shouted instructions to his head crime scene technician.

"Dana, process the other guy, and then we'll start moving them. What do you have for me, Dave?" Pat asked.

"I have two detectives acting like children," David said as he tossed his clipboard on the desk.

"Excuse me?" Pat said angrily.

"Save it, Pat, I don't work for you, and I'll call your boss for two other detectives if whatever the hell is bothering you two doesn't stop right here and now in this van."

"What are you talking about?" Pat asked.

"I don't know, Pat. What the hell am I talking about? You two don't seem to be talking a whole lot on scene, and you're not sharing notes, let alone coordinating. I hate to say it, but you're not acting like grown men, and neither of you is acting like a detective." David knew that Pat was the main part of the problem, but Hank was by no means innocent.

"It's just a personal issue, Dave," Hank said. "We're sorry it got brought out on scene."

"Don't apologize for me," Pat said. "I have nothing to be sorry about. Now, if this little counseling session is over, I'm going to go back to work... if that's okay with you two." Pat brushed past Hank without saying "excuse me."

"Fine. I'm calling the lieutenant to send someone else down here," David said as he began to punch in the number.

Hank placed his hand on the phone and said, "Whoa, Dave, you can't do that to us."

Pat turned around and scornfully spat out, "Fine, Dave, do whatever the hell you want! Capstone won't be with the division much longer anyway. They'll have to assign me a new partner to work this case as it is."

"I thought this issue was dead," Hank replied. "If that's what you want, I'll call Capparell and tell him to send Rodriguez or someone else if you like. Hell, I'll see if Flanders could come out of retirement since you seem to have a higher opinion of that drunken asshole than you do of me."

"I never said that."

"You might as well have, because I can't get important information out of you on scene, and now you're saying you don't want to work a case with me because I won't be here. Seriously, what the fuck is your problem, man?"

A look of understanding came over Dave's face.

"Guys, I'm glad you're making progress in the back of my van, however, we still have a scene to finish processing. I'm not going to make that call, but I'll tell you this: if you two weren't my friends, I would have made that call twenty minutes ago."

"We appreciate that, Dave, and we're sorry," Pat said, beginning to feel sheepish.

"All right, partner, we took down a governor, and we took down a serial killer, so I think we can go out there and solve this one in time for you to go to Dean's parents for dinner." Hank extended his hand as a sign of truce.

"I'm sorry," Pat said. "Let's get to work. We can talk about everything else off duty." He pulled Hank in for a hug and patted him on the back.

David was known for his gallows humor and for breaking the tension with a joke, so he jumped in and said, "Oh, you guys," as he gave them a big, fat, sweaty bear hug.

"Okay, then... awkward," Hank said as the hug took several seconds longer than necessary.

The boys straightened up their clothing and left the van much more focused than before.

Officer Boyle walked up to the three men as they emerged from the back of the van.

"Hey, detectives, watch command just called and said there's a little Asian guy who just turned himself in for shooting the blond boy. He was even nice enough to bring the gun with him to the station."

"Thanks, Boyle," replied Hank.

"Dr. Collins, can you and the techies finish up processing the scene and sketching it for us?" Pat asked the medical examiner.

"Yep, the uniforms and I have a handle on things. Don't forget my notes!" David said as he removed the carbon copy from underneath his original. He handed Pat a form with the angle rod results, and Dana came over to give them the GSR results, which indicated that the dead man had fired a weapon recently.

"Don't forget, Pat, you guys still owe me a dinner from the last time I had my guys clean up." David smiled.

"Don't worry about it. I'll think of something soon, buddy," Pat said, as he and Hank walked toward their car.

"It looks like a nine millimeter," Pat said as he read Dana's notes.

"For the blond guy?" Hank asked.

"Yeah, so it's a forty-five caliber contact shot on the other guy's head, and a distance shot with a different gun on the blond boy."

"Hey, Boyle! Before we go, I forgot to ask you something."

Boyle walked over to the car.

"What's up, Hank?"

"Where were the wallets when you got here?"

"The blond kid's was in his pocket, and the other was on the ground near his feet."

"So there goes the murder-suicide angle. It's starting to look like robbery to me. Thanks, Boyle."

The patrol officer mouthed the word *fuck* as he realized he had failed to recognize a major clue prior to making a determination.

Hank winked at the patrolman and got into the passenger side of the car. The engine roared to life, and the detectives departed the scene.

As Pat was pulling out of the alleyway, Hank said, "Try not to kill us this time, buddy."

Pat turned his head and shot Hank a look as he raised his middle finger.

"Sorry, Pat, I'm on my period this week so you can't finger-fuck me."

"Wah wah wah," Pat replied as he turned his attention back to driving.

It took twenty minutes to get back to headquarters using their lights and sirens. They went inside and reported to the watch commander.

"Hey, Sarge, where's that guy who confessed to the shooting?" asked Hank.

"Dang Quoc Nguyen is sitting in the interview room. We have a nine millimeter in the temporary lockup. I ran the numbers, and the gun is registered to Nguyen," replied the watch commander.

"Thanks," Pat said.

Pat and Hank removed their coats and hung them in the room where a two-way mirror allowed observers to see and hear the interview process. They looked at the suspect seated at the table.

"That guy is five foot nothing if he's lucky."

"Not to mention he's, like, a hundred pounds soaking wet," Hank observed.

"Don't you have a fetish for Asians?" Pat teased.

"Yeah, but one of my turnoffs is people who might shoot me," Hank said as he opened the door.

The slight-framed Asian boy held his head in his hands and didn't move when the two detectives entered the room. Pat and Hank exchanged looks, and Pat decided to take the lead on this interview.

"Hey, buddy, wake up!" Hank said, slamming his notebook on the table.

"I'm not asleep," the suspect said in heavily accented English.

"Then do me a favor and look at Detective St. James, please."

"Why you people aren't listening to me? I have gone through my story six times already," the Asian man said in an exasperated voice.

"Well, my partner and I are the ones who count, so go ahead and make it seven or eight," Pat said in an unemotional voice.

Nguyen sighed and raised his head. His eyes were swollen and red from crying, and his shirt had blood splattered on it.

"My friend Jesse Kovalick and I were walking down that alley, and that blond jerk jumped out and demanded our wallets. He had a gun, and when Jesse refused to give his wallet up, the guy shot him."

"Hold on there, partner," Hank chimed in.

Pat knew what questions Hank was going to ask because he had the same ones. The guys had worked a rhythm into their interrogation method, and it usually paid off royally.

"Partner? My name is Dang, not partner!" the man said between stifled sobs.

"Okay, Dang it is. What were you two doing in that alleyway in the first place?" Pat asked, tapping his pen on his notepad.

"So it's our fault for getting robbed because we walked into an alley?"

"I didn't say that. Calm down, Dang. You don't want to make this a hostile environment. I'm curious as to why you two would go into that alley, that's all."

"Jesse and I were close friends, and it was my birthday, so we were headed to Starbucks so I could get my favorite drink. That alleyway is a shortcut through the block."

"Which Starbucks?" Hank asked.

"The one across the street from the alley."

Pat wrote down the information as he formulated the next question.

"Okay, so you're walking in the alleyway on your way to Starbucks with your good friend on your birthday. So then what happens?" Pat asked as he leaned back in his chair.

"I told you. That blond guy jumped out with a gun and demanded our wallets. Jesse had his in his hand when he changed his mind. Then the guy shot him." Dang paused for breath. "Why didn't you just give him your wallet, you stupid asshole?" he wailed.

Pat and Hank could see that the direct approach wasn't going to work on this one, so they decided to shift gears. It was time for the old good cop/bad cop routine. Hank would make a rude comment or ask a hostile question, and Pat would swoop in to show empathy for the interviewee.

"So you and your buddy were in some back alley where you shoot the guy and get away with your wallet and the gun. Something just isn't right with your story, buddy, so start telling the truth or get ready for a murder charge," Hank exploded.

"What? Fuck you. I came in here to straighten this out, not get accused by ignorant jerks!" Dang jumped from his seat.

Pat got between Dang and Hank, and as nicely as possible, asked Dang to be seated. As Dang complied, Hank shot a threatening glance at the Asian man. The routine was working.

"Look, I'll level with you, Detective St. James. Me and Jesse have been dating for a year. It was my birthday, and he wanted to take me to Starbucks and get me my favorite drink. I had class in an hour, so I suggested we cut through the alleyway. That blond guy jumped out from behind the dumpster, put the gun against Jesse's head, and demanded our wallets and jewelry. Jesse was never one to get bullied, so he told the guy no. The guy racked the slide on his forty-five—"

"Wait… racked the slide?" Pat interrupted.

"You know, to put a bullet in the chamber. I'm not an idiot. I was on my high school shooting team." Dang folded his arms.

"Sorry, it's just that most civilians don't know that kind of lingo. Go on," Hank said as he sat down in the corner of the room.

Dang ignored Hank's statement and continued to address Pat.

"I yelled at Jesse to just give him the damn wallet! Jesse threw the wallet on the ground."

"Okay, so how did you shoot this guy if he had a gun on your boyfriend?" Pat inquired.

"The scumbag bent down to grab the wallet, and the gun went off."

Tears formed in Dang's eyes as he relived that moment.

"Keep it together for me just a few more minutes, okay? What happened then?" Hank said in a caring voice.

Dang was confused by Hank's sudden kindness. He wiped the tears from his face and stood up.

Pat and Hank stood up as well. "What are you doing?" Hank asked.

"I'm going to show you what I did."

"Okay, just don't jump around too much," Pat said as he backed away.

Dang put his hand into his pocket and pulled it back out with his fingers held in the shape of a gun.

"I pulled out the nine millimeter that I carry for protection and shot at him twice. When the second round hit him in the chest, he fell down, and I checked on Jesse, but I could tell he was dead and that's when I ran away." Dang sat back down.

"Do you have a permit to carry, Dang?" Hank inquired from a standing position.

"Yes, I'm a naturalized citizen from Vietnam. I'm here legally, and I have a permit that is in my wallet."

"Where did you get the gun?" Pat asked.

"A gun shop. Jesse bought it for me when all those people were turning up dead in the parks."

"So it's your gun, you have a permit, and you shot the guy because he shot your boyfriend, and you were afraid that he would kill you next, right?" Hank asked.

"Yes," Dang stated emphatically.

"Okay, then, write it up on this statement form, and we'll be back in shortly," Pat said as he handed Dang a pen.

"No problem."

"Listen, Dang, you held it together very well out there. Just make sure you talk to a counselor, okay?" Hank said as he patted the man on the shoulder, and then both detectives walked out of the room.

The Asian man was very confused by Hank's mood swings but it didn't matter because he had a funeral to attend.

The watch commander walked into the observation room after knocking on the door.

"Hey, Sarge, what's up?" Hank asked.

"The medical examiner left you a message at the desk." The sergeant handed them the note and then walked out of the room.

"Thanks," Hank said as the door closed.

Hank read the message aloud. "Found the other two empty casings in the gutter. You're welcome. See the photos and findings I've e-mailed you. I'll be doing the autopsies tonight and sending you the reports in a day or two. Dave Collins, Chief Medical Examiner."

"Can't believe we missed that, partner," Pat said, as he started to wonder what else they might have been missed if Dave hadn't pulled Pat's head from his ass.

"Do you want to call the DA's office, or do you want me to do it?" Hank asked.

"I'll do it, and the paperwork is all mine today. Sorry I was so pigheaded," Pat said.

"I'm sorry you found out that way. Let's go tell Capparell this looks like a case of self-defense," Hank said, holding the door open for his partner.

The boys walked up to Homicide Division feeling much better than they had three hours ago. As they walked, Pat ran through his mind what it would be like to work in Homicide without his partner. Worse yet, who would he get stuck with as a replacement? By the time they got to Capparell's office, Pat's mood had soured again. He knocked on the door, and the lieutenant waved them in.

"What's up? You get a confession?" Capparell asked.

Pat and Hank sat down in the chairs in front of the lieutenant's desk, and Hank began to speak.

"It's looking like a case of self-defense and not homicide. Well, let me clarify a bit. The blond victim was actually the bad guy and committed homicide by shooting victim number one. Suspect one shot victim/suspect number two after watching his boyfriend, victim number one, get gunned down during an armed robbery. What the bad guy didn't count on was that one of the holdup victims was legally packing a nine and paid the price when he shot victim number one. Nguyen got scared and took off for the hills."

"Why run if you're clean?" Capparell asked.

"Dang Nguyen is a naturalized citizen from Vietnam, and I'd imagine over there you don't actually sit down to tea with the local cops to explain two dead bodies and hope to walk out in one piece. Fear and instinct took over until he could calm himself down and come in to explain it all."

"So you guys believe this Dang is telling the truth?" Capparell asked.

"It all fits," Pat said in a low voice.

Capparell looked at Pat and then at Hank and back at Pat again.

"Pat, what's eating you? You look like you're pissed off at the world!"

"Nothing," Pat replied. "Just glad we got a solution to this homicide so quickly, thanks to Dang coming forward. We'll follow up and verify that Dang was in fact victim number one's boyfriend. Once we check the facts, we'll close the case."

Capparell wasn't quite buying the response but let it go. He figured if there was a problem between his two detectives, they were big boys and could work it out. After all, they were best friends as well as partners.

"All right, submit your final case report when verification is complete. Then we'll run the entire case past the DA to get his okay for closing it out as justifiable homicide."

Hank and Pat nodded and left the office, but before the door could completely close, Capparell yelled, "And work your problem out!"

Hank looked over at Pat as they headed toward their desks.

"Ya hear that? Work the problem out!" Hank said.

"Hank, my only problem is the way you were trying to sneak out on what I thought was a winning team. No one can touch our record, no one. We rose up together and covered each other's backs, and then you're making arrangements to go to Narcotics behind my back!"

"So what's the answer, Pat? Do you want me to just forget career advancement and stay tied to your apron strings for the rest of our time here? Can't you police without me being at your side?" Hank asked, turning red.

Pat looked up, hurt obvious in his eyes. "I told you I'd do all the paperwork on this. You can either go home or follow up on what Dang gave us. I'm headed down there to get his written statement and cut him loose. Do what you want."

Pat got up and left the office for Interrogation. Hank sat there shaking his head as he realized that their friendship was on the line. They had been each other's best man at their weddings. Pat's lover, Dean, employed Hank's lover, Shawn. They had saved each other's lives in the line of duty. All of that was being threatened by Hank's desire to move on from the Homicide bureau. The thought of cancelling his plans had crossed his mind on more than once, but he refused to pass up an opportunity just because Pat was mad.

Pat entered the interrogation room and picked up the completed statement. He sat down and read it from beginning to end. When he was done, he looked up at Dang.

"This is all true?" he asked, raising an eyebrow to see if he could catch any indication that Dang was lying.

"Yes, all true."

"Okay, Dang, here's the story. We're gonna let you go for now while we check out your statement. If it checks out, then we'll run it all by the DA and close the case out as justifiable homicide on your part. We should have an answer fairly soon on whether or not the DA will present the entire case to a grand jury. Chances are that as long as your story checks out, you won't be indicted. If this went down the way you say it did, you have my deepest sympathy and that of my partner, Detective Capstone."

"Thank you, Detective St. James. What about my gun?"

"We have to hold on to that until the DA gives us the okay to release it. Be patient for a few days, and you should have it back. Again, I'm sorry for your loss."

"I did not expect that from the police. You guys are always homophobic and laugh at the gay community."

"All things are not as they appear," Pat said, and then he escorted Dang out of Interrogation.

When he got back to the office, Hank was gone. There was a note on his desk saying that he had gone home. Pat tossed the message into the trash can and began the first of three reports that had to be done immediately. It was just after four thirty when Pat remembered he had to get home to join Dean for dinner at his parents' house. He definitely wasn't in the mood for making nice, but he knew that if he missed that dinner he would have hell to pay at work and at home. That he *knew* he couldn't handle.

Chapter 3

AT SIX o'clock, Pat's cell rang, and he saw that it was Dean.

"Hi, honey," Pat answered.

"Are you still at work? It's getting late, and we're due at my parents' house in Chevy Chase in one hour!" Dean said in a slight panic.

"I've got exactly two paragraphs to type before I sign the reports, and I'm outta here. Could you pull out a fresh shirt for me? I'll change downstairs, and we'll split. We'll take the cruiser and we'll be on time, I promise."

"Okay. Will a blue shirt be okay?"

"Yeah, whatever you think works, hon, now let me get this done so I can get outta here."

"See you shortly," Dean said and hung up. Pat worked fast to get the final paragraphs typed and then signed the document, hoping he'd gotten everything right. He had no time to reread what he had typed, and he tossed the reports at the in basket on the lieutenant's desk as he ran out of the office.

WHEN Pat walked into his house, he found not only a fresh shirt but also his best suit lying over the sofa along with dress shoes and a different tie.

"Hi, honey, sorry this is so rushed. Guess you want me to change everything?" Pat asked.

"Yes, you've been working and sweating in that suit all day. Strip and put on fresh underwear and all the rest. I'll get you a soda, and then we're gone."

As Dean was getting him a drink, Pat stripped off his clothes and then started to redress. He had to admit, the feel of clean clothes ramped up his mood somewhat. There was nothing like slipping on a fresh pair of underwear.

When Dean walked back in, Pat had almost finished dressing. Pat checked his watch and saw that they had just enough time to make it to dinner.

"Thanks for the change of clothes. I feel better already."

"Rough day, hon?"

"Shitty day is more like it. Huge fight with Hank, and I don't wanna talk about it, or I'll get all pissed off again. We definitely don't need that before going to your parents' house."

"You fought with Hank? God, what now?" Dean paused. "Okay! I won't push, but I want to know after we leave Chevy Chase."

Pat drank down the 7Up, put on his tie, combed his hair, and then they went out the door after setting the alarm. Pat had to push the speed limit a little to make sure they weren't late, but Dean knew that his husband was a good driver and that other cops would recognize a police detective's car.

At exactly five minutes to seven, they rang the doorbell of Dean's parents' front door.

The dinner, while cordial, was a bit formal. There was obvious tension between Dean and his parents over his coming out, and they were also uptight that their son had brought his husband with him. This was the first time that they had met Pat, and they were not impressed. The fact that Pat was a homicide detective did nothing to allay Dean's parents' sense of propriety. He was, after all, nothing more than a policeman, and definitely not in their class.

Two and a half hours later, Dean and Pat said goodbye and left. Once they got into the car, Dean vented his reaction to the visit.

"If I never go back there again, it'll be too soon. How dare they look down their noses at you because you're a cop! If it weren't for cops, people like them wouldn't be safe in their ivory towers! I won't forgive them for how they acted toward you and that's final!"

"Calm down, honey. It's not like they made me leave by the servants' entrance or anything. They obviously hoped that you'd be with a doctor, a lawyer, or some other highly paid professional. Me, I'm a public servant. For them, that's a bit too blue-collar."

"That's bullshit! They're fucking snobs, and I'll have none of it. You're my husband, a fact they won't even acknowledge. They refer to you as my companion, like you were some sort of dog!"

Pat barked and laughed. "Honey, for you, I'd be anything you wanted and that includes being your puppy!"

It was Dean's turn to laugh, and the tension had eased by the time they arrived home.

PAT and Dean got out of their clothes and went down to the living room in their underwear. Whenever possible, they hung out in their skivvies for the ultimate in comfort.

Dean brought drinks in and sat down next to Pat.

"Now, are you going to tell me what's going on at work? Is it Hank? And if so, what is it he's doing to tie you in knots?"

"I really don't wanna talk about it," Pat said sourly.

"All the more reason that you should. What could you two possibly fight about? If you're fighting over some piece of ass that you both want, split him! Just don't let me or Shawn find out!" Dean snickered.

"God, I wish it was as simple as that." Pat sighed and then smiled at Dean. "Besides, you know you're enough for me, and unless you were in bed with me and this piece of ass, it wouldn't happen. Are you sure you wanna hear about this?"

"Of course I do, you blockhead! Hank is your best friend and like a brother in more ways than one. His lover, who we both adore, works for me at the bank. So I'd say yes, I want to hear about it."

"You asked for it. I found out today that Hank has been planning on breaking up our partnership by taking a job in Narcotics. He never even bothered to ask me what I thought. We've been a team since we were rookies. We've made departmental history with one of the most sensational busts to ever occur, and yet I was kept in the dark."

"Well, I'm sure you both sat down like adults and talked it out. Is he angry with you? Angry enough to terminate your partnership?"

"We didn't actually talk much about it. Frankly, it got in the way of our job today on a double homicide and other people noticed. We embarrassed ourselves and others, including the coroner. Even the lieutenant noticed and ordered us to work our problems out. But how can we work it out, Dean? One of the major reasons I love going to work in the morning is that I know I'll be working with my buddy. I trust him with my life after what we've been through. If he leaves, they'll assign a replacement and I could end up with a screwup. I deserve better, damn it!" Pat said.

"Okay, I can see how that would upset you, but he must have had a reason for doing it this way."

"He says that he didn't want me getting upset over the whole thing. Well, news flash, I'm upset. Then, as the day wore on, he said he'd chuck the whole idea of a transfer if it would make me happy! What right do I have to tell him not to make a move that he thinks is good for his career? He doesn't seem to realize that Homicide is the best assignment in almost any department. It leads to promotions a lot faster than any other division."

"He gave you no reason why he wanted out of Homicide?"

"Oh yeah, he gave a reason, if you can call it that. He said he wanted more action because 'Homicide is boring!' Can you believe that? What better job for a cop then bringing killers to justice? Families of victims as well as the victims deserve that, and he wants to chuck it to go play with junkies?" Pat made a disgusted face.

"Honey, you're going to ruin a friendship and more than likely two. Do you really want to lose Hank and Shawn over this? Think about it. In the not too distant past, Shawn was shot in this very room, and I came close to being killed. You and Hank killed a serial murderer and saved us. We've got so much history together. There must be a way to work this out. Would you consider going with him to Narcotics?" Dean asked.

"The department doesn't usually move personnel by pairs. We're not Starsky and Hutch. Besides, I'm happy working in Homicide. It was an honor to be assigned there. The department moved us there together in the hope that we would rise to the top of that field. I just don't know."

"Sounds like to me you both should get away from the job and talk this whole thing out. But remember, hon, Hank has the right to make his own career decisions, just as you do. He gave up joining SWAT for you once upon a time. Is it fair to ask him to give up another assignment that he wants because you don't approve?"

Pat didn't answer. He took a sip of his drink and laid his head back on the sofa. Dean put his hand on Pat's thigh and nuzzled into his armpit. When Pat was down and upset, it affected Dean in a very negative way, and cuddling comforted him.

HANK finished this fourth beer in an hour as Shawn crawled up alongside him. Shawn knew that Hank was very upset over work, and apparently it had something to do with Pat.

Finally, after prying and prodding, Shawn got the story from Hank.

"Pat was a dickhead today, and I was miserable the entire shift. He's pissed off because I was arranging a transfer outta Homicide and into Narcotics. I think he was just pissed because I didn't get his okay first. You should have seen him today on a homicide scene. We hardly spoke to each other, and we missed evidence that the coroner had to find for us! Toward the end of the day, when I thought we had gotten past this problem, it started to flare up again, and I took some personal time and came home early."

"I wanna make sure I understand this correctly. You were arranging a transfer to Narcotics, and you never mentioned it to Pat? Is that right?"

"Yeah. I didn't mention it because I didn't want days or weeks of what we had today. It's definitely affecting our job, and everyone around us knows it. I'm waiting for one of the boys to say we're having a lovers' quarrel or some shit like that, and I'm gonna go off big-time."

"This is ridiculous and has to be fixed. You two are practically brothers, and we're a tight group of four. Hell, I work for Pat's husband!"

"Oh, he brought that up too, which really blew my mind."

"If he did that, you two must have been really angry with each other. Pat's not petty, and it sounds to me like he was throwing anything he could to hurt you. No, this has to change, whether or not you go to Narcotics. Don't you think our friendship is more important than what division you work in? Narcotics is an important job too, and I'm sure he'd agree. Hell, both of you should go over there!"

"He won't leave Homicide. He thinks that's the most important assignment in the detective bureau and that Narcotics is dirty and dangerous."

Shawn perked up when he heard Hank say it was dangerous.

"Is Narcotics more dangerous than Homicide?"

"Sure it is. In Homicide, you get dead people, and you look for who killed them. Narcotics is an entirely different ballgame."

That did it for Shawn. He instantly decided he didn't want his husband going to Narcotics. The wheels began to turn in Shawn's head as he tried to figure out how to keep Hank and Pat together, and his husband out of Narcotics. Maybe Shawn needed to have a talk with Dean.

"Are you two going to be able to work together tomorrow?" Shawn asked.

"Yeah, we've got follow-up work to do on the double homicide from today. That transcends this issue, and I hope Pat can get over it by tomorrow. Maybe we'll try and get out somewhere nice for lunch and talk, but I doubt it."

THE next day Shawn walked up the stairs to the executive floor of the bank where he worked.

"Good morning," he said to the secretary. "I'd like to see Dean, please."

"Do you have an appointment?"

"No, but I think he'll see me."

"Look, Shawn, I've told you this before. You can't just walk up here and expect to waltz on in to have a chat with the boss. You have to have an appointment," the secretary said.

"Look, he'll see me. Either tell him I'm here requesting a quick conversation, or I'm just gonna walk into his office."

Like a peacock with ruffled feathers, she responded testily, "You'll do no such thing. You just wait right there while I see if he can fit you in."

"That's all I wanted in the first place."

"Sir?" the secretary said as she put her head in the door of Dean's office. "Shawn from the loan department is here, but he doesn't have an appointment. Shall I tell him to make one? Oh, I see, very well."

"You may go in," she said and went back to typing a letter without looking at Shawn.

Shawn smiled as he entered Dean's office.

"Good morning, sunshine," Dean said as he crossed the room to give Shawn a hug. "What brings you here this morning?"

"First, your secretary is a bit of a bitch, isn't she?"

"No, not really. She's just doing her job. You didn't have an appointment, and therefore you violated protocol, which in her book is an executable offense. So what can I do for you?"

"In case you don't know it, our husbands are at each other's throats, and it's dangerous. I think it's up to us to defuse the situation before it gets out of hand. Did Pat talk to you about work last night?"

"Yes, he did, and I agree with you. It sounds very serious to me. Seems Hank wants to go one way, and Pat sees it as a betrayal of their friendship and love. I don't see what we can do about it, though," Dean said, frowning.

"I know exactly what to do if you'll okay the plan and go along with it."

"Let me hear it."

"The four of us need to get away on vacation. It's been a while since any of us took any real time off from our jobs, and we need to get those two together where they can't run from each other and avoid talking about their issues. So here's my plan. I looked it up and found that the *Queen Mary 2* is sailing from Los Angeles to Australia in three weeks. It goes via Hawaii, and we can take a plane back home after we hit Australia. The cruise is sixteen days, with an overnight in Hawaii. The long stretch of water is between Hawaii and Sydney. They would have to talk to each other, and we'd be in a strictly social setting. The tension of work would be gone for the time we're on the ship, at least.

The fact that the *Queen Mary* was where we had our honeymoon can't hurt either! What do you think?"

"I think that I hope you use those problem-solving skills for the bank! It's brilliant, and I vote yes. I'll okay an extended vacation for you. I'll say it's necessary to relieve post-traumatic stress disorder associated with the bank robbery. I'll see if we can get a suite on the ship that has two bedrooms. These cruises sell out fast, so I'm hoping that they still have something available. The price might be outrageous, so I'll cover the cost of a suite for all of us."

"Hank would never go for that part of it, I'm afraid," Shawn replied.

"Then he doesn't have to know. I'll tell him that we got the cabin through the bank at a reduced rate, and you two can throw in the money for a regular cabin. Will that work?"

"Yeah, that would work. How do we do this?" Shawn asked.

"I managed to get close to their lieutenant after the hostage incident. I'm going to call him to see if he'll let them off for that long to repair their issues. If he green-lights us, I'll make the reservations."

"Great!"

"Now you get back to your desk and work your cute little butt off so that the bank can afford to be without you for over two weeks."

"Yes, sir!" Shawn said, getting up and heading for the door. As he passed the secretary, he gave her a smile and winked at her.

Dean walked out to talk to his secretary and had a word with her. "Look, Shawn doesn't need an appointment to see me. So if he shows up, just let me know he's out here waiting."

"Yes, sir," she replied.

Dean went back into his office and began to think about the cruise idea. It was important that he and Shawn at least try to make sure that their husbands' close friendship weathered the current storm. Hank's transfer would end four friendships, not one, if they let it.

He picked up his phone and dialed his favorite travel agent.

"Scott? Dean here. How've you been?"

"Great! Was just thinking about you and that hunky husband of yours yesterday and wondering why I haven't heard from you lately. Is there something I can do for you?" Scott asked.

"Yeah, there is. Can you get us a two-bedroom suite on the *QM2* that's sailing from LA to Sydney in three weeks? It would be Pat and I, and Hank and Shawn."

"Let me pull up Cunard right now and see what they have. You guys are cutting it a little close," said Scott.

"I know we are. It's important that we have a two-bedroom suite," Dean emphasized.

"Ah, here you go. Leaving LA exactly three weeks from today. They do have a Queen's Grill two available. It has an upstairs bedroom with a downstairs sofa bed. Would that do?"

"Yes, grab it while it's there and then get back to me with a price."

"Okay, be right back," Scott said with glee, thinking of the huge commission he'd make.

Dean tapped his fingers on the desk as he thought about the problem between his husband and his husband's best friend. He grew concerned about the three weeks between the present and when the cruise would sail.

"Dean, the fare for the four of you would be $122,000, plus airfare back home. Shall I begin the registration?"

Dean nearly choked. "No way! For a little over two weeks?" he asked in shock.

"Well, I could get you a lesser suite but remain in the Queen's Grill category. Would you like me to do that?"

"Hell yes! Bring it down to less than fifty thousand at least!" Dean said as he wondered how he'd hide the cost of the vacation from Pat.

Scott came back on the line. "How's forty thousand sound?"

"A hell of a lot better than the first figure. Where are we? Down in the engine room?" Dean joked.

"Actually, you guys would be in a Queen's Grill suite five. It's far smaller than the first option, but you would have a queen-sized bed and a sofa bed. Will that do?"

"Yes, book it and send me an e-mail. You have my credit card information?"

"Yes, I do. Do you want me to process it upon confirmation?"

"Yes, and let me know all the stuff we have to do prior to sailing."

"Thanks, Dean. It's a pleasure doing business with you."

Dean abruptly remembered he needed to give Shawn a price for the fare, one that would be less than the actual amount but would save Hank's pride. "Oh, wait. I also need a price for an ocean-view cabin for the same cruise."

"I doubt there are any left, but I still have it up on my screen. Let's see, the cheapest ocean view would be just over three thousand dollars per person."

"Okay, thanks, Scott, I appreciate the information, and forget about the ocean-view cabin; just book the Queen's Grill suite five."

"Okay, but if you know someone who wants an inside stateroom in the lower decks let me know. There's a large gay group on the ship, and they've had a few cancellations."

"I think we're set, Scott, thanks," Dean said, as he hung up the phone.

Forty thousand was a lot of money, but it sure beat over one hundred thousand. Dean decided to put off getting a new car until next year so he could pay for this cruise. He reminded himself he'd get a few dollars from Hank and Shawn to apply to the fare.

Dean dialed Shawn's number.

"Hi, boss," Shawn answered.

"I booked a cabin for us on the Queen. If you're sure you guys are going to want to pay part of it, the amount would be six thousand plus air home. If that's too much, I can cover whatever you're short. Does that work?"

"That's a lot, but I'll talk to Hank tonight."

"Okay, that means I have to tell Pat tonight. I was kind of hoping to spring it on them, but if we have to do it this way, let's go for it. We'll be home tonight if you need backup!" Dean said with a laugh.

"Gotcha. I'll call you tonight either way."

THAT night when Pat came home, he was met at the door with a Grey Goose screwdriver and his husband wearing nothing but blue silk boxers and a smile. Pat was both aroused and on guard at the same time.

"Hello, honey, welcome home," Dean purred.

"Thanks," Pat said as he closed the door and took off his jacket and shoulder holster. "What are you up to now?"

"Up to? Nothing, darling, just glad to have my man home. Now let's go sit down and be comfortable," Dean said, pulling off Pat's tie and unbuttoning his shirt halfway.

They sat down on the sofa, Pat eyeing his husband up and down. He took a sip of his drink and then put his glass down on the coffee table.

"Out with it, Dean. You're not playing Mrs. Cleaver for nothing."

"Not at all. I just wanted you relaxed while I tell you what I arranged today." Dean inched closer to Pat.

"I knew it. What have you gotten us into now?"

"Nothing bad. I've arranged for a vacation for us to get away from all of this. You are entirely too tense and upset and you're fighting with your best friend. So I arranged for our vacation today and paid for it. It's nonrefundable."

"Why is that?"

"Because we sail in three weeks, and it's within the no-refund period. So we can go and have fun or stay home, be miserable, and lose the money."

"Go where and when?" Pat asked, growing more worried the more he heard.

"I thought we could do something completely different, so I booked us a suite on the Queen's Grill level on the *QM2*, sailing from Los Angeles to Sydney. It will take sixteen days, and then we'll fly home. As a bonus, there's a large gay group aboard so there will be some gay activities."

"What! How the hell am I going to get over two weeks off from work without sufficient notice? You just wasted a lot of money because you didn't check with me first!" Pat yelled.

"Relax, honey—you have the time off," Dean said, smiling sweetly.

"And how would you know that?"

"I talked to your boss, and he's given you the time off," Dean replied sheepishly.

"You did what? You called the lieutenant about my vacation?" Pat yelled again.

"Yes, dear, and you know it's for your own good. Put in a leave slip tomorrow for these dates," Dean said as he handed Pat a piece of paper with all the details on it.

"I can't believe you called my boss! Where do you get off doing that?" Pat asked angrily.

"Honey, I've been talking with Capparell since Albright busted in here and tried to kill us, and we've become rather close. Now, stop with the huff and puff act and drink your drink. You want to take me upstairs and fuck the anger out?"

Pat shook his head in amazement, and then he picked up his drink and guzzled it down. He stood up, grabbed his husband by the hand, and pulled him up the stairs to the bedroom.

"You asked for it, and I'm gonna give it to you, bucko! You'll be lucky if you can walk tomorrow!"

"Go ahead. Threaten me with a good time!" Dean replied, sporting an erection in his shorts.

THE conversation at Hank's went along the same lines, with Hank hauling Shawn off to the bedroom to take his punishment for making plans without consulting his husband first. Shortly afterward, the sounds of a spanking came from the Capstone bedroom, along with much giggling.

What neither detective knew was that his partner would be on the same cruise—not to mention the same cabin. Shawn called Dean after playtime, and the two spoke quietly together.

"Okay, I got Hank to agree to the cruise. I didn't tell him that it would be the four of us, though. When should we spring that on them?"

"The secret won't last more than a day at the most, and there'll be hell to pay if they find out on their own, so I think it's best we just tell them now," replied a sore Dean.

"Telling him about the first part of the plan was hard enough, I'm going to need some ice for this," Shawn said as his shoulders slumped, and he gazed toward the ceiling.

"Dear Lord, Pat just fucked the living hell out of me for fun and as punishment for scheduling the vacation without talking to him first. Not sure I can take another round!" Dean said.

"Lightweight. I got spanked *and* banged! I'm sore on the outside and inside, but I know I can take another round." Shawn giggled.

"What are you giggling about out there?" Hank called out.

"Just talking to Dean," Shawn replied.

"Then I know something's up. Get your cute butt back in here!" Hank growled.

"My master calls!" Shawn said. "I'm gonna tell him the whole story now, so I suggest you do the same. Gotta go."

Dean smiled as he pictured Shawn's cute little ass upturned and being walloped by Hank. He hoped that his husband and Hank didn't talk about that little aspect of their relationship.

"Honey, I need to tell you something," Dean said as sweetly as he rejoined Pat in the bedroom.

"What now? Have you managed to get me the rest of the year off?" Pat asked with a raised eyebrow.

"Not exactly," Dean said as he moved in close to his husband.

"Out with it. I know a guilty look when I see it."

"You know this wonderful cruise we're about to take that's nonrefundable?"

"Yes, and…?"

"Well, in talking with Shawn, we decided it would be fun if we could all relive our honeymoon on this cruise. Doesn't that sound great?"

"Oh for fuck's sake! You and your little buddy just can't help but stick your noses into everything, can you? Hank and I have a rather serious issue we're trying to work out, and now you're gonna throw us together for over two weeks? Well, at least when he pisses me off I can go to our suite and slam the door. In fact, I might eat in there too!"

"Well, that might be a good thing, because Hank will be in there when you slam that door."

"What! You mean to tell me that the four of us are sharing a cabin? Is that what you're telling me?"

"It's a suite, not a cabin, and yes, that's what I'm telling you," Dean said.

"It'll never work. The job won't let us both go for that long; won't happen," Pat said with some satisfaction.

"It's already been approved, honey."

Pat sat up on the edge of the bed and buried his head into his hands. "Who the hell works down there, me and Hank or you and your little buddy?"

"It should make you feel good to know how important you are to the department," Dean replied.

"Tell you what. I want a buffer zone between Hank and me if we don't get our shit together. I'm not spending two weeks on a ship fighting," Pat said as he got up and left the bedroom.

Worried, Dean got up and followed Pat. He stopped halfway down the staircase and sat down when he heard Pat pick up the phone.

"Hey, it's me. Is there any chance you and Greg would be able to take a cruise with us in three weeks? We're on the *Queen Mary 2* to Sydney out of LA, flying home from Sydney."

"Wow, that's some trip. Is this a straight cruise? Because if it is, we aren't interested."

"As fate would have it, Mr. Brian, there's a large gay group on the cruise. There will be hundreds of queens on the Queen."

"A gay cruise is definitely something we'd be interested in. Let me talk to Brian and call back."

"Okay, I'll wait to hear from you," Pat said as he hung up. "You might as well come all the way down and grab me a drink!" Pat said loudly.

Damn. Dean stood up and then came down the stairs and went into the dining room, where the liquor was kept. He grabbed the bottle of Grey Goose, made a screwdriver, and took it into the living room.

"You know, hon, this is an expensive cruise. I'm not sure those boys can afford to get on board even if there are any remaining cabins," Dean lied.

At first Pat didn't reply, just sipped his drink. Then he looked up at the man he loved and smiled. He patted the cushion next to him, indicating that Dean should sit down.

"Did you know that Hank spanks Shawn when he's been naughty and as a prelude to sex?" Pat asked ominously.

"Oh, I don't believe that," Dean replied.

"Oh? I seem to remember you having no problem taking a belt to my ass because I screwed up big-time. Remember that?"

"Oh… well… that was different. You left me a note that said I could if I felt you deserved it."

"And you took full advantage of that."

"Why are we talking about this?" Dean asked.

"Just in case I decide you need a spanking. It's much better to get it out of the way instead of being mad at you for days or weeks."

The phone rang, saving Dean from responding.

"Hello? Hey, Brian."

"I'm shocked as hell, but he said yes. We'll put in for the time off tomorrow, and we'll call Dean's travel agent so he can hook us up with the same cruise."

"Hang on a second," Pat said.

Dean looked up.

"How much is our suite?"

Stammering, Dean finally answered, "Forty thousand, but that's for all four of us!"

Pat's mouth dropped open. Instead of exploding, he went back to Greg.

"Sounds like it's ten thousand apiece for the suite we're in, so I'd suggest you try for something that's not that insane."

"Holy hell!" Brian exclaimed. "Yeah, we won't be in any suite. We'll see if we can get a sleeping bag on the deck, and I'll let you know."

"Okay, let me know," Pat said and hung up.

"They're coming, but they're booking space on the deck instead of a suite," Pat said, chuckling.

"Yeah, it's rather expensive at the Queen's Grill level on any of the Cunard ships."

"I'm surprised that Hank and Shawn can afford it. They are paying, right?"

"Oh yes, they're giving me money before we sail."

"Well, I really hope your scheme works out. I don't wanna lose my best friend, but it's headed that way now."

"That's what Shawn and I thought too."

THREE days before the cruise, Pat arrived at the station early for his shift. Hank was already seated at his desk, typing away on his keyboard.

"Morning, Hank, ready for the cruise?" Pat asked as he took a sip of his coffee.

"I can't believe how much this cruise costs," Hank said without making eye contact.

"Well, it's a big ship with a five-hundred-person gay group on board, so I'm hoping it's as much fun as camp."

"Yeah, we had a blast that weekend, didn't we?" Hank said vaguely, showing that he was intent on finishing whatever he was typing. His typing rhythm seemed to increase the more Pat talked.

"Definitely was a good time. What are you working on?" Pat asked as he came around the desk.

As Pat got within visual range of the screen, Hank collapsed the window he had been working in.

"Just some paperwork I need to get done before we leave work today," Hank said.

Pat could see that Hank's forehead had become moist, and he was acting nervously.

"You mean your application for the Narcotics corporal test? They're due today, aren't they?" Pat spat out as he went back to his desk.

"Yes, it's the test application, if you must know," Hank said as he maximized the screen once again and continued typing.

"I already know you're leaving, Hank, so stop trying to hide it. I'm a big boy. I can handle it."

Hank stopped typing and swiveled his chair to face his partner. "Really? Then why do you bring it up every minute of every day?"

"I'm not looking for a fight. It's going to be a very long two weeks on this cruise if we're fighting the whole time."

Pat got up and went to the coffee machine, even though his cup was still fresh and half full. He dumped out the remainder of his coffee and washed out his mug.

Hank finished typing his test application, printed it out, removed it from the printer, and signed it. The only step left was to turn it in to the lieutenant, and then he would be eligible for the test.

Lieutenant Capparell had been watching the exchange through his office doorway. He couldn't hear everything, but he could tell from the body language that it was not a good conversation. His observation was disrupted when Sergeant Durkin knocked on the doorframe.

"What's up, Sergeant?" Capparell asked as he tried to look busy.

"Not much, Lieutenant. I have that paperwork for you. Are you feeling all right?" Durkin asked in concern.

"I'm fine. Why?"

"I was standing in your doorway for two minutes before I knocked, and you didn't even look at me."

"Impossible!" Capparell protested as he opened his desk drawer.

Durkin closed the door to the lieutenant's office before he walked over to the large leather chairs and sat down.

"What's eating you? You can't fool me, so out with it."

"What are you talking about? I have work to do, and I don't have time for a therapy session."

"How about lunch with a friend?"

"Sorry, I can't. I have a command staff meeting at twelve. We're doing lunch there."

"Okay, I'm just trying to help. I guess I'll go listen to those two have their little catfight out there," Durkin said as he stood up and jabbed his thumb toward the doorway.

"I don't get it, Durkin. Why would anyone want to leave Homicide for a Narcotics job? I feel like I'm failing as a supervisor somehow," Capparell said as he leaned back in his chair.

Durkin smiled. He knew that if he said the right thing Capparell would open up to him. Durkin sat back down and crossed his right leg over his left.

"I talked to Capstone about the transfer, and it has nothing to do with you. He wants to get promoted and do some running and gunning. He said he misses the chases and the action he had on patrol, and Narcotics is a great way to get back out there and do it."

"You get promoted much faster in Homicide, and it's a lot less dangerous here. He's young, so I guess the piss and vinegar hasn't run out of his veins yet," Capparell said as he rocked in his swivel chair.

"We were all like that once, you know that yourself. I'm thinking with all the recognition he got over the governor and the prostitute killings, he's feeling withdrawal from not being in the spotlight lately. As for St. James, well, he's just afraid of losing his best friend and partner, and I know what that's like."

"That's right. Who could forget Patrolman Jason Kutzer?"

"Well, there's a little difference between this thing and what went on with Kutzer. Kutzer's dead, and Capstone's just looking to transfer." Durkin started to play with his tie as he uncrossed his legs and shifted his weight around in the chair.

Capparell could see that Durkin was uncomfortable talking about his old partner, so he got up and locked his office door. He removed a small bottle from the office safe.

"What are you doing, Lieutenant?" Durkin twisted around to see what Capparell was retrieving from the safe. He could hear liquid being poured.

Capparell closed the bottle and replaced it in his safe. The small amount of amber liquid in the glasses he carried swirled as he walked over to Durkin and handed him one.

"We're on duty, Lieutenant. Do you really think this is a good idea?"

"You're not on the field rotation today, so you're doing office work all day. It took a serial killer task force to get me back out there, so I'm pretty sure we'll be fine. I'm not ordering you to do anything, but I think we could make an exception in honor of a fallen brother. Besides, it's a quarter shot of scotch, and it's older than you are."

Durkin closed his eyes and sniffed the scotch in his glass. It was against regulations to drink on the job, but Capparell's mention of his old partner brought forth a lot of emotions and thoughts that he'd buried deep years ago.

"To Jason." Durkin raised his glass, and the men slugged down the tiny bit of spirits. Capparell collected the glasses and placed them in his lower desk drawer.

"So that's what's bothering you, Lieutenant? That Capstone and St. James won't be together anymore?" Durkin asked as he enjoyed the mellow burn of the drink flowing into his stomach.

"I don't like where the whole thing is headed. They function phenomenally as a team. Together, they're the brightest couple of young cops I've ever seen. Hank's going to be a good narcotics officer, but he's a *great* homicide detective."

"We can't control what these young guys do. All we can do is offer them advice and hope they take it. That's all, then? Nothing else is eating at you?" Durkin said, knowing that his friend was holding something back.

"I'm sorry. I'm not allowed to talk about it right now."

"Is it private or professional?" Durkin said, leaning forward, concerned that his longtime friend might be ill.

"A little of both, actually. I'm tired of getting used to things only to have the higher ups play God and screw with me." Capparell stood and walked over to his door, unlocked it, and opened it. That was a signal that it was time for Sgt. Durkin to leave.

Capparell put his hand on Durkin's shoulder as the sergeant stood, and he handed him a stick of gum to cover any possible trace of alcohol on his breath.

Durkin walked out the door and went back to his workstation. He saw Hank get up from his desk and walk to the lieutenant's office with a piece of paper in his hand.

Pat glanced up and his stomach felt queasy as his friend and partner walked into the boss's office. This was the first step in the end of their partnership.

Pat knew that narcotics officers worked varying shifts and almost never had weekends off. He and Hank would be lucky to get together once a month—let alone for their weekly dinner with their partners. The pay raise Hank was after would only increase his salary by two thousand dollars a year, so Pat knew that Hank wasn't looking to get rich by transferring. Pat just couldn't wrap his head around his partner's determination to leave Homicide.

When Hank emerged from the lieutenant's office without the paper in his hand, Pat resigned himself to the fact that his partner really was going through with the transfer.

Pat chewed his bottom lip, feeling like he needed to get out of the office.

"Hey, Capstone, Dean just called. I have to run an errand. Would you mind if I took off for an hour or so?"

Hank was caught off guard by Pat's use of his last name, and he could see that Pat's eyes were watery.

"Yeah, no problem, partner. I got things covered on this end, and if the boss asks, you're out doing a follow-up for me," Hank said as Pat grabbed his coat and left. Hank sat down at his desk and thought about the effect that his desired transfer was having on their friendship.

THREE days later, the two couples went to the airport to take off for Los Angeles. Baltimore/Washington International was a nice airport and made it much easier than other airports to go through all the aggravation that flying entailed.

Everyone arrived at the airport at the same time, including Sgt. Durkin's stepbrother, Clay Wilkins, a friend of Brian and Greg's who had decided to join the cruise as well. Apparently, Clay had found a sugar daddy who let him play around on the side as long as he didn't take money from anyone else. For Clay, it was the best of both worlds.

Clay, Brian, and Greg had booked an ocean-view room large enough for three. The only problem was that they couldn't eat with Pat, Hank, and their husbands in the Queen's Grill.

Hank had taken the news pretty well, and knowing they had a cruise of that length coming up, things were a little better at work. They decided that they would work the issue out for good while on the cruise and away from their spouses.

Chapter 4

RICHIE'S head pulsated with pain. He tried to speak, but he couldn't open or close his mouth. There were large plastic tubes extending from his mouth to somewhere behind him. He began to panic and tried moved his arms around with no better success. He blinked rapidly but his vision remained blurry.

A loud beeping echoed in his ears as he became more aware of his surroundings. A blurry figure came into his field of vision and shone a bright light in his eyes. He closed his eyes tightly to stop the burning. His ears seemed okay, and he was starting to catch bits of the conversation around him.

"Mr. Cosgrove… feeling?" the hazy blue-clad figure said.

"Richard… fingers… Richard." This was a new voice, a feminine one. The beeping subsided.

Where the hell am I? Richie wondered.

He opened his eyes and blinked rapidly again in an attempt to clear up his clouded field of vision. After several minutes, he was able to see that the person wearing blue was a doctor. When Richie looked down, he saw that his hands were restrained by leather bands. His hearing was almost back to normal, but the tubes prevented him from speaking.

"Mr. Cosgrove, if you can hear and understand me, blink three times," the doctor said.

Richie blinked three times, and a nurse whispered to someone standing behind the doctor.

"Great, Richie, that's terrific. I'm Dr. Horvath, a neurologist here at Sacred Heart Hospital. I'm sure you have a ton of questions, and we'll get to that in a little bit, but first I have to make sure you're all right. If you understand me, blink three times again."

Richie was frustrated, and a wave of fear enveloped him as he realized that this was a hospital and that his wife was not in the room. He began to jerk his head around violently to see if she was behind him. The doctor asked him to calm down, but he ignored the doctor's orders and continued to scan the room for his wife.

A nurse removed a syringe from a cart and filled it with a clear liquid. She injected the fluid into an intravenous tube connected to Richie's arm. He started to feel very warm and comfortable just before he passed out.

Richie regained consciousness again several hours later. This time there were no tubes in his throat, and his vision and hearing were functioning almost normally. A security officer was sitting in a chair near Richie's bed, reading a newspaper.

"Hey there," the guard said as he folded the newspaper and stood up to signal the nursing station.

"What the hell happened? Where am I?"

"You're in a hospital, sir. When you woke up, you were freaking out so they had me come and sit with you," the young security officer said.

"Where's my wife?"

A male nurse entered the room and excused the security officer, who posted himself outside of the door.

"I'm not sure where your wife is, Mr. Cosgrove. We haven't seen her in a while," the nurse answered in an overly pleasant tone.

"What do you mean?" Richie was irritated by a response that held no real answers.

"Dr. Pelter will be in to speak with you shortly, so just sit back and rest until then. Here's your pill," the nurse said as he handed Richie a pill in a little white cup.

"What's this for?"

"It's to help with the pain and relax you while the counselor speaks with you."

"Counselor! Oh my God, my wife's dead!" Richie began to sob loudly.

"Mr. Cosgrove, I didn't say your wife was dead. You've been through a very traumatic event and it's a lot to take in, so the hospital sends a counselor to talk with you."

"She's alive? I need to call her!" Richie tugged at his restraints as hard as he could. "Get these things off me."

"You're going to hurt yourself, Mr. Cosgrove. Please don't make me give you another sedative."

"Richard Cosgrove?" asked the doctor who walked into the room. His nametag identified him as Dr. Kevin Pelter, Staff Psychiatrist.

"Yes, get these things the hell off me now. You guys are going to have one hell of a lawsuit for keeping me here against my will," Richie hollered as he finally gave up resisting his bonds.

"If I think you're emotionally stable enough after we talk, I'll consider removing those for you," the doctor said calmly.

"I want to know where my wife is and how I got here." Richie began to feel a fierce headache coming on, but a wave of warmth enveloped him and calmed his demeanor and brought the pain down to a manageable level.

"What the hell did you give me?" Richie asked in a groggy voice.

"A sedative and some pain killer. You suffered a very violent attack, Mr. Cosgrove. Do you prefer Mr. Cosgrove or may I call you Richie?"

"Attacked? What do you mean attacked?"

"You were brutally beaten. A friend brought you here seven months ago. He told the emergency room staff that you were found on the beach, bleeding profusely. Do you remember any of that?"

"Oh my God! How is Jessica?"

"Jessica's injuries were nowhere near as severe as yours. According to police reports, she said you fought the attackers."

"How do I not remember any of this, Doctor?"

"Our minds are designed to protect us from trauma. You're probably blocking the memories of what happened and maybe even some of what preceded the traumatic events. In time your memories may return, but you should be prepared to accept that they may not."

"Where is my wife?"

"One thing at a time, Richie. Right now let's concentrate on how you're feeling," the doctor said as he looked up from the file he was holding.

"Where is my wife? I have a right to know!" Richie said furiously.

"Your wife is alive and well, but let me explain a few things before we talk about her. All of the doctors at Sacred Heart, as well as the specialists that we brought in, believed that you would never wake from your coma. We believed that you would be in a vegetative state for the rest of your life. You see, your skull was fractured, and the damage to your frontal lobe was severe. Your jaw was broken in three places, and several vertebrae were shattered in your cervical and thoracic areas." Dr. Pelter opened the medical chart at the end of the bed and showed Richie the notes made by the emergency room staff. After a few minutes, he cleared his throat. "I'm hesitant to tell you this, considering your weakened condition, but I think you'll be less agitated if you have the facts, instead of speculation. I'm sorry to inform you that your wife divorced you two months after the attack."

"She divorced me? That's impossible! This has got to be a big misunderstanding," Richie said as his voice escalated up the scale.

"I'm sorry, but all of the paperwork is here in your file," Dr. Pelter said.

Richie felt a wave of nausea come over him, and he became dizzy and lightheaded. He hyperventilated and passed out.

A nurse rushed into the room to check his vital signs and found them normal.

"Let him sleep, nurse. I barely scratched the surface with this poor guy," Dr. Pelter said as he scribbled notes. Underneath the report was a newspaper article that read: "Cosgrove Hotels Sold to Nevada Investors Group for $850 Million."

The doctor left the room and told the security officer that he was no longer needed. The guard thanked the doctor and walked away. He removed a cell phone from his belt as he walked into a stairwell.

When someone picked up on the other end of the line, the security guard said two code words and then gave the message: "He's awake."

The person on the other end replied, "The money will be in an envelope at the security station by the time you get there." The line went dead.

RICHIE woke the next morning feeling groggy from the drugs. He rang the buzzer for a nurse, and when one arrived, he saw it was a different nurse than yesterday. She seemed very excited to see he was awake.

"It's a miracle, Mr. Cosgrove. I never thought I'd see you open those eyes." The nurse hugged Richie, who was taken aback by her demeanor.

"Thank you," he said.

"What can I do for you, Mr. Cosgrove?" the perky blonde asked.

"I need to use the bathroom, and I'm hungry."

"No problem. The doctor said you can have your restraints off as long as you weren't acting up this morning, so let me go ahead and take those off for you." She smiled as she fished in her pocket for the key to the leather restraints.

A large security guard stood watch outside the door, peeking inside just to let Richie know he was there.

"Don't worry, big guy. I'll be good today, I promise," Richie said mockingly.

The nurse ignored her patient's sarcasm and gave him instructions. "When you try to stand up, your legs are going to be very unstable. Lean on me, and we'll see if we can't shuffle over to the bathroom."

Richie sat up, and it felt as if he had never moved a muscle in his life. There wasn't any strength in his body, and he needed the nurse's help just to get up. She helped him out of bed without so much as grunting.

"You're a strong woman."

"Years of doing this job helps build core strength. I also eat lots of spinach, and I have my Wheaties every morning." The nurse chuckled, and Richie laughed.

After Richie finished his morning business, a physical therapist came to see him. Richie still had many questions regarding his situation, but every time he tried to ask someone, they referred him to Dr. Pelter. It was frustrating, but Richie did *not* want any more of the drugs they gave him when he got upset.

Over the next three weeks, Richie became stronger through his therapy, and he learned more about his divorce. Dr. Pelter finally revealed to him that he no longer owned the hotels, and Richie lost all control. He went into a full rage, and it took four security guards and two injections to restrain him. The doctors explained that Richie had sustained damage to the areas of the brain that controlled impulses and judgments, and that was why he was so easy to anger.

Richie had come to accept that he had been the victim of a brutal attack and the severity of the injuries had caused scarring to his body and mind. It would take time before he could fully process what had happened and for the cumulative effects of the attack to surface.

He didn't have access to the Internet in the hospital, and all of the numbers in his cellular phone were disconnected or out of service for some reason.

Three weeks after Richie woke from the coma, Dr. Pelter believed he was strong enough for one of the most vital pending matters. Dr. Pelter asked Richie to meet him at his office. This visit was different from the usual in that there were unfamiliar people in the room.

"Good morning, Richie," Dr. Pelter said, smiling warmly and shaking Cosgrave's hand.

"Who are these people, Doctor?"

"They had heard you were awake and wanted to help you get your affairs in order before you leave the hospital. These two gentlemen are attorneys," Dr. Pelter said, pointing at two men seated behind a table.

"Attorneys for whom? I already know she divorced me and sold the hotels. I don't have anything left, and I still don't know who the hell attacked me!" Richie shouted.

"Richie, Richie, relax, have a seat, please. Don't get all worked up."

Richie pulled a chair from under the table and sat, folding his arms and staring silently at the lawyers.

"Mr. Cosgrove, I'm Jeffrey Davis. I represent your ex-wife," the older attorney half rose and extended his hand, but it was refused.

"I'm David Phelps," said the other attorney. "I handled the sale of Cosgrove Hotels." He didn't bother to offer his hand after seeing how Richie reacted to Mr. Davis's overture.

"Wait.... What? Chris Powell didn't handle the sale of my properties? Explain why before I lose my mind and explode."

Uncomfortable with Richie's belligerence, no one answered. "Tell me how my wife can sell my hotels. I didn't leave them to her in my will, and she never owned any part of the business. So tell me exactly how someone with no rights to it sells everything my father and I built!"

Dr. Pelter stood. "Gentlemen, perhaps this meeting is more than Mr. Cosgrove can handle right now."

"Nah, Doc. I'm fine. Have a seat. This should be enlightening," Richie unfolded his arms and leaned forward.

"Are you sure, Richie?" Dr. Pelter said with concern for his patient.

"Okay, Mr. Divorce Guy, let's hear why I'm single now."

"To be quite honest, Mr. Cosgrove, no one expected you to recover from your injuries. It was believed that you would never regain consciousness, so Jessica decided to move on with her life."

"But not until she sold my properties and ran away with the money, right, Mr. Real Estate Thief?"

"I am by no means a thief. You signed a medical power of attorney almost five years ago. It stated that if you should become medically incapacitated, your wife would assume total power of attorney."

"I never signed a power of attorney. My accountant was to become the executor of my estate if anything happened to me, not my wife."

"Mr. Cosgrove, with all due respect, that was in the instance of your death. The document you signed gave your wife full power of attorney if you were incapacitated. As such, she decided to sell the properties, taking a one-time eight hundred and fifty million dollar payment from a group of Nevada investors."

"What? She sold what I built"—Richie began to hyperventilate—"and my father's legacy for pennies on the dollar!" Richie leaned back in his chair and ran a hand through his hair as he fought to calm himself.

"I'm not sure who her financial advisor was, but they gave her some very poor advice. Those properties are worth billions," said Phelps.

"Oh you think so, smartass?" Richie could feel his right eye twitching, and his leg began to shake. "What about my house and cars? Do I have anything left at all?"

"Your ex-wife sold the hotels, the house, and all other property shortly before she divorced you. There was stipend left in a care fund for you."

"Well, how goddamned nice of her. How much is in it?"

"As of close of business yesterday, there was fifteen million dollars in the account."

"You're telling me that out of the billions of dollars' worth of real estate, and the savings that I had six months ago, I'm left with fifteen million dollars? Properties my father left me and that I built up to a thriving business are all gone, and all I have to show for them is a crust of bread that she left on the floor?" Richie shouted.

Jeffrey Davis stood. "Mr. Cosgrove, I can see you're becoming agitated, so we'll cut this short. I'm here simply to inform you that a divorce decree was issued four months ago, and you are to have no contact with your ex-wife whatsoever. If you try to contact her in any way, there will be severe legal ramifications."

The divorce attorney placed an official-looking piece of paper in front of Richie and exited the room before Richie could respond.

Richie's hands were shaking, and a severe headache enveloped his forehead. The lights in the room seemed extremely bright, and he could feel his heart trying to pound its way out of his chest. He felt light-headed and slipped off the chair as everything went dark.

Richie woke in his hospital bed. The clock indicated that three hours had passed since the meeting in the doctor's office. He sat up and tried to sort through the overwhelming emotions he felt over the loss of everything that meant anything to him.

He opened a file folder on the nightstand next to his bed. The manila folder contained the divorce decree and state-issued paperwork declaring that Jessica held his power of attorney. The paperwork regarding the property sale was bound together and much thicker. Jessica, acting as power of attorney, had sold all of his properties, including the original three left to him by his father. The real estate was disposed of for a fraction of what it was worth. Richie needed to get out of the hospital and piece together what had happened on the beach. If he could get a good lawyer, he might be able to fight the sale and get his properties back, but he knew it would be a long shot. He kept searching his memory, trying to remember when he had signed the medical power of attorney, but he could recall no details of such an occurrence.

Even after intensive psychotherapy, he was unable to recall any of the events after the morning of his anniversary.

The perky nurse who had been excited to see him open his eyes entered the room to give him his daily medications.

"Hello, Mr. Cosgrove, how are you this morning?" she said in the singsong manner that was her trademark.

"Well, to be honest, I've had better days, but things are looking much brighter now that you're here."

"Oh, you little devil you, knock it off. I'm married, mister," the nurse said as she shook her finger at him. She checked his chart, circled something, made a note, and then closed the file.

"Well, it seems this little bird is ready to fly the nest."

"Huh?" Richie said, confused by the analogy.

"I can see by the look on your face that you're ready to get out of here."

"Very observant, and you're right; I need to get out of this place."

"Well, I have some great news for you because your doctor has you scheduled for discharge tomorrow morning."

"Great to hear, I just wish I knew where I was going."

"I know. I heard all about it. So tragic, but you're a smart guy. I'm sure you'll be back on your feet in no time."

"Thanks, you've been great. I hope you don't get bored without me here to bug you."

The nurse leaned in and gave Richie a hug before she left the room. Several moments later, a flower deliveryman knocked on the door.

"Yes?" Richie said to the man who held a small flower arrangement.

"Are you Mr. Richard Cosgrove?" the deliveryman asked.

"What can I do for you?"

"Sign here, please," the man said, handing Richie a clipboard.

"Thank you. Do you know who sent these?"

"Oh, I bought those in the gift shop downstairs. I just wanted to let you know that you've been served. Have a good day," the man said as he handed Richie a legal-sized envelope.

"Goddamn process servers," Richie said in disgust as he snatched the envelope from the man's hand. He angrily tore open the envelope as he wondered what else could possibly happen to him.

The paper stated that his ex-wife had a restraining order against him, and that any attempts at contact would be met with immediate incarceration under state law. Richie threw the letter in the garbage and sat back. His eye began to twitch and his leg started to shake violently. He knocked over the bedside table and began to kick at the foot of the bed. The nurse that had befriended him rushed into the room and closed the door behind her.

"Mr. Cosgrove, if you don't calm down, they won't let you out of here. You need to calm down before someone calls security and you get locked up in the psychiatric unit."

Richie had not fully lost control. He heeded the nurse's warning and attempted to calm himself, with some success. The nurse walked over to where the table had landed and saw the envelope and receipt from the process server.

"I always thought something was up with that ex-wife of yours," the nurse said as she straightened up the room. "My ex-husband was a cheating son of a bitch who took me for everything I owned. Luckily, husband number two turned out to be Prince Charming, and we've been together for ten years. "

Richie had regained most of his composure and the headache had begun to subside.

"How often did she visit me when I was in the coma?"

"She only came one time when I was working, but I never saw her name on the visitors' log after that. She was a very nasty woman. All she wanted to know was if you were going to wake up or not. It was like she hoped you never would."

"Do you have any idea who else came to see me while I was in the coma?"

"I'm sorry, the only reason I remembered your ex was because she was a very rude and self-centered person. I tend to remember people like that so I can avoid them in the future."

"You said there's a visitors' log, right?"

"Yes, every visitor to patients in the long-term intensive care unit must be logged in and out."

"Is there any chance I can see who stopped by so I can thank them?"

"I guess so. I don't see any harm in it." The nurse opened the door to the room and disappeared for several minutes before she returned and handed Richie a sheaf of papers.

"I can't let you have the whole book because it can't leave the nursing station, but I made you copies," she said before she left him alone again.

Richie looked at the list of people who had visited him while he was hospitalized. In the first three months, the list of visitors took up twelve pages, but by the fourth, fifth, and sixth month the list barely filled a page. Jessica had only come to see him twice, and Christopher Powell's name was directly under hers both times.

One name stuck out like a sore thumb, and Richie was confused as to why the person would have visited him at all. The signature was a scrawl and illegible to anyone who wasn't familiar with it. Fortunately, Richie had seen Carl's signature on the back of his paycheck enough times to recognize it.

Why the hell would my driver visit me? Other than the interview and one or two conversations, we never shared so much as a shot of scotch, so why would he come see me? Richie wondered.

The next morning Richie was discharged from the hospital and escorted to the front door via wheelchair, per hospital policy. He stood and walked out the door into the hot Tampa air. Since he had no relatives to call and most of his friends had been work-related, he walked to a nearby payphone to call for a cab.

As Richie lifted the receiver to dial the cab company, a car horn beeped behind him, and he jumped. He turned around and saw Carl sitting in a sedan across from the bank of payphones. Replacing the receiver, he walked over to the vehicle.

"You scared the shit out of me, Carl. How've ya been?" Richie asked as he reached into the window to shake the man's hand.

Carl grasped Richie's hand in an iron grip and gave him a half smile.

"Figured you could use a ride. Why don't you hop in, Mr. Cosgrove?"

"Since I'm not your boss anymore, why don't you just call me Rich?"

"Okay, Rich, hop in, and I'll take you where you need to go."

Richie was curious how Carl had known he was being released today, but he trusted his former driver. As soon as Richie was in the car, Carl pulled away from the curb.

"So, Rich, how's life been since you woke up?"

"Not at all what I expected."

"You can say that again. I'm guessing you saw what she did to your hotels."

Richie shook his head in disgust. "Why are you here, Carl?"

"To give you a ride. Why else would I be here?"

"Don't bullshit me. I saw in the visitors' log that you checked in on me every so often. What's the deal?"

"Let's go get a drink," Carl said without looking at Richie.

Carl pulled into a parking space at a local Mexican restaurant, the kind of place where very little English was spoken and the staff was almost certainly made up of illegal immigrants.

"I hate Mexican food. Isn't there somewhere better we can go for a beer?"

"Not if you want to chat. Besides, the tacos here are amazing," Carl said as he shifted into park and turned off the engine. The men got out of the car, and when Richie stopped walking, Carl turned to him and raised his eyebrows.

Richie could feel the hair on the back of his neck standing up and his stomach churn. He had hired Carl because of Carl's extensive work experience in dignitary protection and physical security services. On the rare occasion that a disgruntled employee got in Richie's way, Carl quickly dealt with the threat. Richie couldn't imagine what this meeting was about, but he had a bad feeling.

"Hey, Rich, did you ever see that movie *The Matrix*?"

"Yeah, it's one of my all-time favorites, why?" Richie asked, still contemplating the wisdom of going into a dive restaurant with a man whose intentions were not clear.

"Well, this is the part of the movie where I offer you the two pills," Carl said. "You can come into this place with me and swallow some truth, or you can go over to that payphone and call a cab. Up to you, brother, but this is the only time I'm making this offer." He took off his sunglasses and walked into the restaurant.

Richie still wasn't sure what he was doing here, but Carl might be the only man that knew the truth about what had happened the night of his anniversary. There was so much to piece together that Richie had no idea where to begin. He might as well see what Carl had to say.

Richie went into the restaurant and saw Carl sitting in a corner, speaking to the waiter in Spanish. As Richie approached, he saw that there were already two beers on the table.

"You were that sure I was coming in?"

"Deep down at the core, Richard Cosgrove is the same as any other man. After life kicks us in the balls and runs away with everything, we all just stand there with a blank look on our faces, wanting to know what the fuck happened to us. From the scars on your head and face, I'm pretty sure that'd be the number one question on your mind too."

"Thanks for pointing out the scars, Carl, I forgot they were there for two seconds," Richie said as he rubbed the long scar on his forehead.

"From what I heard, she left you around fifteen million. That should be enough to get a really good plastic surgeon."

"How do you know what she left me?"

"I'll be honest with you, Richie. I would rather have a fat juicy steak any day instead of the crap they call food here, but these people keep their mouths shut so I can trust that whatever we talk about will never leave here. Ya get me?"

"All right, fine, out with it already," Richie said as his eye began to twitch. Carl was playing some sort of game with him, and he didn't like it one bit.

"You want to calm down? That twitch in your eye will give you away every time, Rich," Carl said as he took a large gulp of his beer. "The truth is I'm waiting for one other person before we can start chatting."

"You can have two beers waiting when I walk in, but you can't have this mystery person here when we arrive?"

"Patience, my friend. I had to gauge your reaction and see if you really wanted to know the truth. I wasn't going to out this person until I was sure it would be safe."

"Safe for what?"

"You'll know in a second. She just walked in." Carl stood, and Richie spun around in his seat. A short young woman stepped from behind a booth, where she had concealed herself. It was Beth from the Powell Law Firm. Richie knew her well from his visits to the office, as well as from her attendance at the yearly anniversary party.

"Hello, Bethany, great to see you," Carl said as he motioned for her to sit.

"Hello, Beth," Richie said with a sideways glance.

"Hello, Mr. Cosgrove, it's good to see you looking better," Beth said as she extended her hand over the table for Richie to shake.

"I'm feeling a lot better, thank you. What are you doing here?"

Beth looked at Carl and then pulled a bulky yellow envelope from underneath the sweater she was carrying. Carl took the envelope, and Richie watched him slide the small basket of nachos toward Beth. The secretary took an envelope from beneath the basket and put it in her pants pocket.

"Beth is here as a friend," Carl said as he smiled and took another mouthful of beer. "She had some information and was nice enough to get me a copy of it."

Carl motioned to the bartender for two more beers, and then looked back at Richie.

"Do you remember when you hired me, Rich?"

"Yes, it was three or four years ago, I think," Richie said.

"Close enough for government work. Up until six years ago, I did a little contract and consulting work with different agencies I won't name. After the little mix-up in Kandahar, I was let go and pretty much unemployable."

"Whatever happened there is irrelevant to me. I wasn't looking for a gate guard. I needed a professional to deal with the threats on my life. I remember seeing your resume and talking to a friend of mine who worked for that contract security place where you were employed. My buddy said you were more than what I needed, and I thought that the fit was perfect."

"Well, regardless, I couldn't find a job anywhere, thanks to blacklisting by a couple of agencies. I was at my lowest point and broke. I had nowhere to go when you called me out of the blue and asked to meet me. Thanks to you and your very well-paying job, I was able to get back on my feet. I know you were my employer and not my friend, but you did save my life."

"You were one of my favorite hires, Carl. I was able to trust you, and you made me feel safe."

"I appreciate that, and I want to repay the favor."

"I'm not looking for someone to kill my wife."

"Whoa, hold on there. I never said I'd do anything like that." Carl looked at Beth and nodded toward the exit. She stood and left the restaurant.

"I'm here to fill in all the blanks for you," Carl said once Beth was gone. "Whatever you do with that information is up to you. I'm not here as a hit man, just as an acquaintance, so you can forget about your little revenge fantasies."

"Sorry, this whole situation is just so weird. Why don't you tell me what you have to tell me?"

"For the last four and a half years, your wife has been conspiring to take your hotels from you and rob you blind."

"That's ridiculous! I would've seen that coming a mile away."

"Did you ever wonder why she came back after she left you the first time?"

"She said it was because she knew she loved me," Richie replied emphatically. The words sounded hollow considering what Carl had just said.

"She loved you so much that she made you draw up a prenuptial agreement stating that she would only get two hundred and fifty thousand dollars in a divorce, and you signed it."

"Yeah, that convinced me that it wasn't about the money. She was willing to give all of that up just to be with me. So what's your point?"

Carl reached into the large yellow envelope and held out some pages so Richie could read them.

"This is your prenuptial agreement. See the date?" Carl said, pointing to the bottom line.

Richie looked at the date and remembered his attorney presenting him with a lot of paperwork the day he signed the prenuptial agreement. Jessica had spilled a drink and made a big deal about wanting to get home to change.

"See the date on the medical power of attorney? You signed it the same day."

"The same day? I never signed a power of attorney naming my wife as my advocate. I keep telling everyone that, but nobody listens."

"Yes, you did. The signatures match, and it was signed with the same pen. Good enough to stand up in court anywhere in the United States."

"I'm a little confused here, Carl," Richie said, as his head began to throb.

"Wait, there's a lot more. I've driven your ex-wife to meet Chris Powell on hundreds of occasions. You thought she was going to the spa or the gym, but in reality she was going to meet him at hotels."

"What! Why didn't you ever tell me about that?" Richie hissed.

"Oh, I tried, but you threw the nondisclosure agreement in my face, and that was the last time I ever brought it up to you."

Richie vaguely recalled reminding Carl of his nondisclosure agreement but didn't remember what the conversation had been about.

"The night of your attack, I was in the car waiting for you, as usual. I saw you and Jessica walk out of the side entrance, so I got out of the car and started to follow you onto the beach. Jessica saw me out of the corner of her eye and told me that you two were fine, that you were taking a stroll on the beach. I ignored her and continued to follow you because I had a bad feeling, but then you told me the same thing. So I went back to the car and sat. Twenty minutes later, I saw a red van racing out of a side street behind the hotel. It turned onto the highway and raced away. I heard someone screaming that someone was dead. I ran down and found you lying in a pool of blood with Jessica next to you, screaming hysterically. I've been in a lot of combat situations, and I knew if you didn't get treatment right away that you'd be dead. I put you in the car to get to the hospital as fast as possible. Jessica was hysterical and refused to come with me."

"Did you get a look at who attacked us?"

"No, but my gut says they were in the red van that fled just before the screaming started, so I did a lot of investigating. Jessica caught me watching footage of the van in the hotel security room, and she fired me two days later."

"How long was she in the hospital?"

"The ambulance picked her up a half hour after the attack. The hospital kept her for two days for observation. All of her wounds were superficial."

"I almost get beat to death, and she gets scratches. Figures."

"Come on. You have to see that was by design. Beth got her hands on some papers showing that you have a next of kin, a distant relative that you're probably not aware of. If you had died, they would have had a claim on your property, but since you didn't, the medical power of attorney kicked in, and your ex-wife could do what she wanted."

"You're saying she had me bludgeoned to steal all of my money? She had a queen's life and reported to no one. Why the hell would she need to do that?"

Carl pulled an envelope from his jacket pocket and removed some photographs.

"See, that was the question I had when I started to think that there was more than just an affair between her and Powell. Jessica thought she was playing Powell, but the whole time he was using her to get at the money. Everyone knew that you kept the company close because of your father. Everyone knew that regardless of the amount of money, you refused to sell because of your father."

"Goddamned right I would never sell it. I had offers of billions, and I turned them down. I'm still in shock that Chris Powell was fucking my wife." Richie drained his second beer and motioned for another round to be brought over.

"Well, I started to look into your friend Chris and found out that your accountant Louie was just as greedy. The phone records I found showed that they called each other all the time."

"So maybe they were discussing work. There's no way Louie was ripping me off. I refuse to believe that."

"Did they know each other well enough to fly to Vegas together and stay at the Bellagio for three nights?"

"I didn't think they knew each other outside of work, to be honest."

"Yeah, well, a year before your attacks, a little meeting took place between Chris, Jessica, Louie, and a little investors group from Nevada that specializes in buying up five-star hotel properties."

Richie's headache began to worsen, and he felt dizzy. A crimson rage filled his heart at the thought of his inner circle of friends and colleagues all plotting against him. Richie opened the bottle he'd been given upon discharge and popped a pill in his mouth.

"Hey, Rich, calm down. Your face is purple, and if those are pain pills, I don't think you're supposed to mix them with alcohol."

"'Calm down', he says. You just picked me up from the hospital after a seven-month coma and told me that my wife arranged the attack, stole all of my money, and was fucking my supposed best friend. I think I'm allowed to be a little pissed. Just wait until I get some lawyers on their asses. It's going to be a bloodbath."

"Sorry, Rich, but nothing I have can be used in court, and that medical power of attorney made it all legal."

Richie stood up from the table and threw down a fifty-dollar bill. He slugged down the remainder of the third beer and started to leave.

"Where do you think you're going, Rich?"

"I'm going to take care of this!"

Carl could see by the rage on Richard's face that he was going to do something irrational and possibly homicidal. Carl jumped up and informed the waitress to keep the change; he grabbed all of the paperwork from the table and went after Richie.

Richie was walking toward the highway when Carl grabbed his arm and applied his thumb to a pressure point. Richie yelped in pain and attempted to free himself from Carl's painful grip, with no success.

"Let go of me right now!" Richie screamed.

Carl applied a new pressure point and used a police come-along technique to get Richie into the vehicle. Once Richie was in the car, Carl threw the paperwork onto his lap before getting in and starting the engine.

"Look, Rich, I'm not here to piss you off and make you go kill somebody all half-cocked. I'm here to repay a debt. You helped me get my life back on track, so I'm doing the same for you. You would have spent months if not years trying to find out what I've just told you."

"So what am I supposed to do, just grin and fucking bear it?"

"What you do is up to you. If you look through the paperwork on your lap, you'll see that Powell set up the meetings with the investors group and stoked interest. When you showed no interest in the offers, the affair started, and your marriage magically repaired itself. The way I figure it, Powell slipped the power of attorney in there and told Jessica to bide her time. It could only be done by someone who knew all about your business, so Lou was bought off with an eight million dollar payday. The investors group pressured Powell to come through with what he promised, and he did… by using Jessica."

"So where is the money now? The eight hundred and fifty million?"

"The payment was made already. However I've learned of a second, equally large payment that is scheduled for two months from now."

"Second payment…. All of the paperwork says that they paid eight hundred and fifty million."

"Are you trying to tell me that *you* don't have any accounts hidden from Uncle Sam?" Carl smiled.

Richie looked away from Carl. "Okay, and…?"

"It seems your lawyer and your wife are trying to cheat Uncle Sam out of his fair share of the profits. The public sale price was eight hundred and fifty million, but as you know, that's barely a fraction of what your properties are worth. Your property sold for one and a half billion, which is still a small sum compared to the value. Some sort of agreement was put in place in Australia for the other half of the money. The investors group hosts an annual outing, and they invited their newest members on the cruise. They'll meet in Australia and make the transfers there. There's an anomaly in the paperwork, however. If something happens to Jessica, then Chris gets all of the money. He set himself up as her executor and power of attorney."

"Why is that an anomaly?"

"It was Powell's idea to split the payment up like this, and he's the one who insisted that they go on the cruise to Australia to do it."

"Good. I hope he kills the bitch."

"I've repaid my debt, Richie. I'm going to drop you wherever you want to go and then I have a job in South America to get to. All I can say is don't buy any stock in Venezuelan oil for a little while." Carl smiled at Richie and pulled out of the parking spot. Richie said that he wanted to go and see his old house, and then he would make arrangements to find a place to live.

The car pulled up to the gates of Richie's house, but unlike the thousands of times, before the gates didn't open. The two men got out of the car, and Richie looked at the sold sign, indicating that someone had bought the property already.

As he looked at what used to be his home, he experienced a moment of delirium and his forehead began to burn. Richie began to grind his teeth and turned toward Carl.

"What exactly is it that you do, Carl? I mean I know you did a little bodyguarding for me, but I've seen what else you're capable of, so tell me."

"Huh?"

"The security agency that you worked for was an overseas contractor that I never heard of. I know they had government contracts, but they never officially acknowledged you as an employee from what I could find. If it wasn't for my connections, I would have never been able to verify your resume. You're a mercenary."

"Excuse me? I just do security consulting, maybe a few side jobs here and there, but that's it," Carl said, putting on his sunglasses.

"What is this other job paying you?"

"I don't discuss that kind of thing. I think you're being a little irrational right now. Maybe it's the drugs. Now where do you want me to take you so I can be on my way?"

"Four million cash," Richie offered. "Two now and two when we're done."

"What?"

"You heard me. I have fifteen left from the fisting that bitch gave me, and after what you've told me, it seems there was more than one person fucking me over. So four million dollars is what I'll pay you for a special job."

"The use of mercenaries on United States soil is illegal, and I couldn't do anything illegal. I'm sorry, now let's go."

Carl got back into the car, and Richie stared at him through the windshield. Carl motioned for Richie to get into the car, and when Richie refused, Carl pulled away and left Richie standing at the gates of his old house.

Chapter 5

THREE days later, as Richie was lying on the couch of his new apartment, he flipped through the channels and stopped at a large fire burning on the screen. The reporter mentioned a terrorist attack on a Venezuelan pipeline that would stop shipments of oil by Hugo Chavez's companies for the foreseeable future.

Richie sat up and stared at the screen intently.

"Don't buy Venezuelan oil, huh?"

There was a knock at his door, and he jumped. Richie hadn't told anyone where he was living so he wasn't expecting anyone.

"Who is it?"

An envelope slid under the door. When Richie looked out the peephole, there was no one there. Richie retrieved the envelope and saw that there were no markings on the exterior. He removed a small piece of paper with a date and time written on it. Richie flipped the paper over to see if there was any more writing, and he found an address. It was the Mexican restaurant where he and Carl had met when he was released from the hospital. His phone rang, and once again, he was surprised, because no one had his phone number yet.

Richie went over to the phone and picked it up. "Hello?"

"Hey, Richie, it's Beth," said a familiar voice.

"Hey, how are you... how'd you get this number?" Richie said in a confused tone of voice.

"You gave it to me at the restaurant. I hope you got that gift I sent you."

"No, I didn't give you my number. I just got this phone yesterday, and what gift?"

"You're so funny, Richie. Hey, Carl said he's in the mood for tacos tonight, so meet us there at six. I'll talk to you later."

The line went dead, and Richie wasn't sure what to make of what just happened. Caller ID was showing all zeroes, so he didn't know what number Beth had called from.

Richie decided that he was in the mood for tacos and got dressed. He arrived at the taqueria at six o'clock sharp and had a seat in the same booth where he'd been seated several days prior. A young Latina came to the table. "Mr. Cosgrove?" she asked. When Richie nodded, the young woman placed a beer on the table. Richie began to protest that he had not ordered a beer, but the waitress walked away without acknowledging him.

A strange man walked up to Richie's table.

"Mind if I join you, Rich?"

"Do I know you?" Richie asked, feeling apprehensive.

"Relax. Carl said to give you this." The man handed Richie a note and walked away.

The note read *follow this guy* and was signed by Carl.

Richie followed the man to the back of the restaurant, past the kitchen, and into a back alley. The hair on the back of Richie's neck began to stand up, and he stopped before walking out the door.

The man kept walking, not bothering to turn around as he said, "You only get one chance at this, Rich, so make up your mind right now."

Richie's survival instincts told him not to go into the back alleyway, but he ignored them. A van drove up, and the passenger in the back opened the door and motioned for Richie to get in.

Richie got into the van and the door slammed shut.

"What the hell is this all about?" Richie asked.

Carl turned the front passenger seat of the van around and faced his former employer.

"It seems me and the boys have some free time on our hands, and the price sounded about right. Are you still looking to hire me?"

"Hire you for what?"

"You tell me, Richie."

"What kind of stuff do you do?"

"Before I answer, the little piece of paper you got under your door today... that is where you're going to bring the two million in cash. Understood?"

"Okay, but what do I get in return?"

"Well, after a little spitballing, the boys and I came up with several plans. Once we have your down payment, we'll tell you what your options are."

"What assurances do I have that you're not just going to take the money and disappear?"

"You saw CNN today. Does it look like we just blow smoke?"

"How in the hell did you know about me watching CNN?" Richie asked indignantly.

"How do you think this works, Rich? You think it's like the A-Team, and we have a little meeting and weld some shit together while I wear a lizard suit and smoke cigars? We're professionals, and we deliver exactly what we are paid for."

None of the other men in the van spoke. They just listened. Richie had dozens of thoughts echoing through his mind, but the image of the things he was going to do to Jessica sent adrenaline surging into his veins and he decided that he would comply with the demands.

"Okay, I'll be there with the money, but I'm not giving you shit until I know what you plan to do."

"Well, the two million is the fee for our planning and the little meeting. We can decide to walk away at any time without having to refund the money. If that's unsatisfactory, my colleague will stop the van and you can get out, but if you get out, that's it. There's no second chance."

Richie didn't like the idea of handing over two million dollars in cash without knowing what he would get in return, but he hated the idea of his ex-wife stealing from him even more.

"No need to pull over. Just drop me at my car, and I'll get the money for you. I do have one condition, Carl," Richie said authoritatively. "I want to be there when you take care of my ex-wife and lawyer."

"That's a pretty tall order, Richie. The guys and I would have to discuss that."

"There's nothing to discuss. Either I'm there so I can see the life drain out of both their faces, or I'll take care of this myself."

"Do you realize the risk of you being anywhere in the vicinity? If you got caught or something happened, the cops would be knocking at your door within an hour. You know too much about me so there's no way I can risk you getting caught. I'm going to have to pass on this job, Rich, if that's a nonnegotiable point."

"What if there were certain assurances in place?"

"Have you ever killed anyone, Richie? Have you ever seen anyone killed?"

"I've seen dead people before. I'm not squeamish."

"That's not what I asked. Have you ever looked into the eyes of a person whose life you just took?"

"No."

"So you've never seen the life drain out of a person's face or seen them go limp as they bleed out."

"No. I haven't."

"I don't think we could risk having you along if you aren't sure how you'd react to that." Carl looked around at the other men in the van, and they shook their heads.

"What if I upped the payment to ten million dollars?" Richie said.

"You're going to hand over two-thirds of what you have left?"

"Carl, you may be the best investigator and stalker I've ever seen, but I'm guessing you don't know how to hide money from your wife and the IRS," Richie said with a smile.

"Are you talking about the forty million you have spread out between the Cayman accounts and Switzerland?" The driver of the van peeked into the rearview mirror to gauge Richie's reaction to his words.

"Okay, I take that back." Richie sat back in his seat and put his hands on his lap.

"Look, it's not the money, it's the risk you're asking us to take by bringing an amateur into an operation."

"How do I prove to you that I want this more than you could imagine? I'm doing everything short of begging here."

"Give me a couple hours, and I'll be in touch. The boys and I have a few things to discuss," Carl said as he looked at his driver "Just lay low, okay, Richie?" Carl spun his chair around to face front.

Carl nodded at the driver and the van turned a corner. The side door opened and Richie saw that he had been brought back to the Mexican restaurant. He exited the van and went back home. Three hours after the meeting with Carl, he got a call from an anonymous number.

"Hello?"

"Rich, it's Carl. Come downstairs and meet me in the parking lot." The line went dead.

A knot formed in Richie's stomach. He was worried that Carl had decided to pass on the job and there would be no payback for what they had done to him. Richie grabbed his wallet and cell phone and went to the parking lot.

The van he had been in earlier pulled into the parking lot and drove up to him. The side door opened and Richie looked inside. The only occupant was Carl.

"What's up, Carl?"

"You going to get in or what?" Carl asked without looking at Richie.

Richie got into the van and closed the side door. He started to get into the front passenger seat, but Carl instructed him to stay seated in the rear so no cameras got pictures of them riding together.

"So what's the answer?" Richie asked as he buckled the seat belt.

"I talked to the team. Ten million might make this worth the risk, if we do some planning. However, there is one little detail we need to take care of first," Carl said as he pulled next to an apartment building and flashed his lights.

"What's that?"

"You're telling me that you have no problem taking a life, right?"

"I never said that. I said I didn't mind taking the lives of the people who destroyed my father's legacy. I'm not going to kill some random people to show you that I'm capable. I'm not a cold-blooded killer or a psychopath."

"That's what I wanted to hear, Rich. I don't enjoy killing, either. I only kill who I'm paid to kill or anyone that gets in the way." Another van pulled from behind the apartment building, and Carl followed them.

"I don't understand. What are you talking about?" Richie asked, even more confused than when had had woken up in a hospital bed.

"We looked at a couple options. We came up with a plan to ruin everyone who was involved in the sale of your hotels, but there's way too much money and power in play. We considered making them disappear, which was a very appealing option, but once again, anything inside the United States borders would be a massive headache. The third option is to dispose of them permanently, and that's the one we like."

"Okay, so what's the plan?"

"First, we're going for a little boat ride to discuss some details, and you're going to sell the rest of the guys on taking you along."

"You sure I'm coming back, Carl?" Richie said, chuckling nervously.

"If we killed you, we wouldn't get a penny."

"You seem to know everything about me, so I imagine it wouldn't be that hard to make me disappear and bleed my accounts dry."

"I'm not a thief. I provide specific services at the client's direction. The reason my team gets so much work is we're good at what we do, and we do what we say we will."

Carl pulled up to a dock with a small charter fishing boat moored to it. Carl put the van in park and told Richie to come with him. The men who followed him onto the boat untied the moorings, and Carl signaled to the man standing on the bridge to depart.

"Are we going fishing?" Richie asked in an attempt to lighten the moment.

"I love deep sea fishing. How'd you know?" Carl said as he opened the door to the cabin.

Richie entered the cabin and saw four men sitting at a table. One of the men was passed out leaning against the wall. He had acne, teeth the color of milk chocolate, and open sores on his arms and neck. The sleeping man was repulsive, and his hands and feet were bound.

"Who the hell is that?" Richie asked, unsure if the man was alive or dead.

"You don't recognize him?" Carl asked.

"No, should I?" Richie asked as the ship exited the no-wake zone and accelerated to full speed. Everyone shifted slightly as the bow of the boat lifted out of the water and sped along.

"I doubt it, you two only met once a few months back."

"What?"

"On the beach at your anniversary party. Come on, take a better look at him."

Richie had no recollection of the man, but he felt an indescribably uneasy feeling while staring at him. His headache grew exponentially, and he felt light-headed.

"Have a seat. You don't look so good," Carl said as he led Richie to a chair.

"Is that the guy who hit me?" asked Richie as his breathing grew labored.

"Hit you?" Carl asked as he pulled an envelope full of pictures out of his pocket. It was the same envelope that Carl had removed from his jacket pocket at the Mexican restaurant days before. Carl never had shown Richie what was on the pictures.

Carl spread the photos out on the table. "This guy and his buddy were hired to beat you into a coma."

Richie looked at pictures of naked Jessica and Chris Powell embracing. There were additional pictures of them engaged in sex, and pictures of Chris in court representing the passed-out, bound man.

"What the fuck is this?" Richie screamed as he picked up pictures of Chris and Jessica doing it doggie-style.

"Do I really need to explain? It's proof that this is real. Powell and your ex-wife were fucking. They hired this shithead and his buddy to take you out so that they could seize your hotels and make some money. If they'd killed you, then your uncle could have attempted to claim control of the hotels, so they tried to make you a vegetable. You told me that you want to be there to make the people who did this to you pay. Show me, Rich."

As an unfathomable anger and hatred filled Richie's heart, his headache subsided and a sense of euphoria came over him as he stood. Richie started to make his way over to the bound man, but the driver of the van stood in his way. Richie tried to push the man out of his way. The man refused to move, and Carl grabbed Richie by the shoulder.

"What the fuck are you doing? Let me go right now!" Richie screamed as he struggled. He felt the pinch of a syringe at his neck, and he passed out on the floor.

When Richie woke, he was lying on a bench inside the cabin. He rubbed his neck and sat up. "What the hell did you do that for?"

"This whole rage thing needs to be kept in check. There's a time and place for everything. We're fifty-one miles off the United States shoreline, so this is the place. The time is when I tell you, and not a second before. If you do anything before I say so, you become a liability that needs to be taken out. Do you understand me?" Carl asked, leaning down to stare Richie in the eyes.

"I think so."

"That's not what I asked. Do you understand me?"

"Yes, I get it."

There were now two men bound and seated at the table, awake and fully aware of their surroundings. The smell of fear was in the air as they looked around at the mercenaries.

Carl nodded at the driver. "TJ, is everything ready?"

"Yeah, boss, good to go." TJ stuck a syringe into each man's neck as a large man held them still.

"Sodium pentothal, also known as truth serum," Carl stated.

"What's that for?"

"Don't you have a few questions for these two?" Carl asked.

"Really?"

"Go ahead. That shit kicks in pretty fast."

"Do you remember me?" Richie asked the two men.

Neither man responded. This angered Richie.

"I asked you a fucking question, shit bags. Do you remember me?"

"I think I do. I'm not sure," responded the man who Richie had seen when he arrived.

"Do you remember beating my face in on the beach near Cosgrove's Resort?"

Both of the men's eyes widened. "Yeah," one of them said. "I remember that, you and that woman. Right?"

"Yeah, me and that woman," Richie responded snidely as his eye began to twitch.

"Hey, dude, it was just business. My lawyer said he'd take my case pro-bono if I did a job for him. I had to do it, or I would be in jail for the rest of my life. I'm sorry!"

"What about you, asshole? Are you sorry too?" Richie asked as he looked at the other man.

"Fuck you!" The man spit at Richie, but hit Carl.

"See, Richie," Carl said as he wiped the phlegm from his face. "The problem with dope fiends is that they build up a tolerance to chemicals. They tend to resist attempts to drug them much better than, say, your average third world dictator."

Richie rubbed the scar on his forehead that had begun to itch. As he ran his hand down the ridge of the scar, a scene flashed in his head of the spitter swinging a tire iron at his head. Richie felt the searing pain he'd felt that night and could hear the sound it made as it broke his skull.

"You son of a bitch, I remember you now." Another picture flashed in his mind: Jessica had let go of his hand and moved away just before their attackers emerged from behind a rock. Richie's anger could be contained no more. He erupted and jumped on the bound man who had spit at him. He repeatedly punched the man in the face and pulled him over the table to the floor. The man's eyes and mouth were wide open as the blood splattered against the walls.

"You smashed my skull in, and you have the balls to spit at me? You took my life from me, you motherfucker!" Richie screamed as he began to stomp on the man. Carl and TJ intervened and pulled Richie off.

"Let me go! Let me go! You're fucking dead, you piece of shit! You're fucking dead!"

"Calm down," Carl said. "In this kind of work, emotions can't be involved. It's not professional. Do you understand what I'm saying?"

Richie was hyperventilating while the man lay on the floor moaning in pain and choking on his blood.

"So what am I supposed to do?" Richie asked as he started to regain his composure.

"This man destroyed you, I understand that, and he's defiant and that enrages you even more." Carl calmly shot the man between the eyes with a small caliber weapon. The shot was deafening in the confined space, and Richie's ears rang.

"What the fuck?" Richie screamed.

"I could see that you were willing to kill that man. Now my question is, can you control the beast and do it the right way, or do you like prison?"

"Huh?" Richie said as he used his fingers to soothe his aching ears.

The other man at the table squirmed and screamed as he tried to escape his bonds. Two mercenaries grabbed him and dragged him over to Carl and Richie.

"This man had his friend beat you almost to death. He never touched you, but if it wasn't for him, you wouldn't have that scar on your forehead," Carl said as he reholstered his gun.

Richie's breathing was deep and slow as he wiped the blood from his hands and stared at the man who knelt before him. The man whimpered and begged for his life. Cries to spare his life and let him go home to his children fell upon Richie's ringing ears. Richie did not feel any qualms about what he was about to do to this man.

Carl handed Richie a heavy-gauge piano wire tied between two handles and made a motion to show how it was used.

Richie wrapped the wire around the man's neck and began to strangle him.

"What's your name?" Richie hissed in the man's ear.

"What?" the man asked as he coughed and gasped for air.

"What is your goddamned name?" Richie said louder.

"Daniel Gottfried, why?" the man asked as he coughed and struggled against the tightening wire.

"I needed to know what name your little bastards will be crying when you don't come home!" Richie said as he pulled the wire tight.

He held the handles as tight as his hands would allow as the life drained from the man and his body went limp. Richie held onto the wire long after the man had succumbed to the deadly grip of the cold wire. Carl looked at the rest of the men, and they nodded their heads in agreement. TJ walked over and removed the wire from Richie's hands, and the rest of the team began cleaning up. Carl threw a towel at Richie and told him to meet him in the bow of the boat.

Several minutes later, Richie emerged from the bathroom and walked out to Carl.

"The price is five million up front and five million when the job is done. The first payment is in cash, and the rest will be wired per our instructions. We'll take you on the job under the following conditions: You will do what you're told and when. If at any time we believe you are jeopardizing us, we will kill you and disappear. The job is over when we say it is, and that's all there is to it."

"Agreed. What now?" Richie asked as he stared at the ink-black sky lit only by a few stars.

"We clean up and head back to shore. Then you wait until the date on that paper, and we meet up. At that point, we'll fill you in on the rest of the plan," Carl said as he drank from a flask.

The boat's engine roared to life, and Richie heard two splashes from the back of the vessel.

TWO days passed excruciatingly slowly for Richie. He made the arrangements for the five million in cash. The other five was stashed in a new hidden account.

Richie placed the money into a rolling suitcase and went downstairs to his car, excited and nervous at the same time. He threw the suitcase into the trunk and got into the car, thinking about his ex-wife and his alleged best friend screwing him over. He stared into the rearview mirror and fantasized about them being tortured in the most sadistic manner possible. The thoughts turned Richie on in a way he had never felt before as he headed to the meeting point.

Carl was standing outside a warehouse with the large door behind him open. He motioned for Richie to pull into the building.

Immediately after Richie pulled into the large abandoned warehouse, the door creaked shut.

Richie exited the vehicle, and Carl asked, "Where is it?"

"In the trunk." Richie replied.

"Pull it out," Carl said.

TJ walked over to the car. As soon as the trunk lid unlatched, he opened the trunk and removed the bag. He placed the bag on a cargo scale, and it registered one hundred and two pounds.

"Looks like five million, boss." TJ opened the suitcase and looked inside at the stacks of hundred dollar bills. He nodded at Carl and secured the container.

"Let's get this party started!" Carl exclaimed.

Carl clapped his hands twice, and an overhead projector came to life showing a blueprint of a ship. The boat was the *Queen Mary 2*, and Carl began to explain what the team planned to do.

When the briefing ended, Carl turned to Richie. "Tomorrow morning, go to our favorite Mexican restaurant and wait near the service entrance. Here is a list of what you should do and what you should bring with you."

Richie took the list and followed Carl to a black BMW underneath a car cover.

"Hop in. I'll give you a ride home," Carl said as he folded the cover neatly.

The engine of the BMW purred to life, and they headed to Richie's residence.

Richie got out of the vehicle, and Carl pulled away immediately. Richie could not believe what he had heard at the briefing: these guys were more organized and connected than the government. As he walked up to his door and put the key in the lock, he was struck by a pang of guilt at what he was about to do. His head began to pound and his eye twitched a little. He went to the medicine cabinet, removed two white, oblong pills, and swallowed them without water. The pang of guilt quickly disappeared as he stared into the mirror at the scar that ran the length of his forehead. As he lay down in his bed, he no longer felt bad about paying back the people who'd scarred him and destroyed what he and his father built. He decided to get up early and pack.

The alarm went off at six in the morning, and Richie rolled over to silence it. He felt groggy from the pain medication and was about to go back to sleep when he saw Carl's list on the nightstand. After he showered, he followed the instructions, packing all of his fancy clothing in one bag and some other items in a smaller one.

He took the two bags to his car and went to the Mexican restaurant for his rendezvous.

AFTER CARL pulled into the rear of the Mexican restaurant, Richie stepped out and opened the back door of the van.

"Morning, Rich. How'd you sleep?" Carl asked after Richie secured his luggage in the rear section of the van.

"Like shit! If it wasn't for the painkillers, I would've been up all night. My palms are sweaty, and it feels like my heart's going to pump out of my chest," he said as he wiped his hands on the legs of his pants. The door slammed shut and Carl pulled away from the building.

"That's normal," Carl said. "Just don't let it interfere when we get on the ship."

"Easy for you to say. You've done this before."

"Something like that," Carl said cryptically.

TJ handed Richie a large yellow envelope and blew him a kiss. Carl and TJ chuckled lightly as Richie's face contorted into a confused mess.

"What's all this?" Richie asked as he looked at the pile of itineraries and identification documents.

"Well, since Richard Cosgrove is in Milan for the next month, Dennis Eckerd will be going on a cruise with his gay lover, Drew Montoya, aboard the *Queen Mary 2*," Carl said as he smirked at Richie in the rearview mirror.

"What are you talking about?" Richie said as he looked at the picture of two men kissing on the brochure.

"You have a doppelganger in Milan going on a spending spree and throwing a party or two with so-called investors. I have a few people in place on the ship to get you on board without having your picture taken. The only way I could get you on that ship was to list you with a large gay group that had a few cabins open up for this trip. They were the last open cabins on the whole ship."

"How many people do you have on the ship?"

"You just worry about staying in your cabin and not having your picture taken. TJ will be with you all day, every day. He is taking the role of your partner of ten years, and you're on your second honeymoon. That will keep you away from the targets until it's time to eliminate them. If TJ tells you to kiss him or suck his dick, you do it immediately. I don't give a shit what you feel or think about it. We're professionals, and we have a cover to maintain. Gay groups get certain concessions and access that normal cruisers don't, so this is the way it has to be. If you have a problem with it, you tell me now."

"I'm not a homophobe, but... suck his dick? Seriously?"

"Yes. Nonnegotiable," TJ said in a deadly serious tone of voice.

"TJ is the only member of the team that you acknowledge on this cruise. No matter who you see, you make sure that you do not approach or talk to them. You do nothing unless TJ tells you, are we clear?"

"I got it already." Richie scanned through his documents. There were some very convincing doctored photographs of his alleged wedding and vacations.

"Nothing will happen until after we stop in Hawaii. There are too many safety measures in place and the turnaround time for the ship would be restrictive to our operation if they discovered anything was wrong. Once we're underway to Sydney, I'll make the determination of when we go into action. We'll stick to the timetable we've laid out, but as the boys know, shit happens."

"Well, how do you plan to stop them from calling the Coast Guard or the Navy for help?"

"Not your concern, Richie, plans are in place as well as contingencies. You just stick to your lover here like glue. Now, what is your name?" Carl quizzed.

"Dennis Eckerd, and this is my lover of ten years, Drew Montoya. He's the wife in the relationship." Richie smiled at TJ.

"We'll see about that," TJ quipped back.

"Good, you have three days to learn the cover story and memorize it. Then we'll be on board the ship and headed to Hawaii."

RICHIE dug through more of the documentation and was amazed at the depth of the details Carl and his team had devised. He would have loved to know the rest of the plan, but Carl had made it very clear that he would know what he was supposed to and no more.

"Where are Chris and Jessica staying on the ship?" Richie asked as he leaned forward in his seat.

"They're in one of the owners' suites. You and your lover Drew here couldn't get any closer to the engine if you tried. I couldn't risk you running into your soon-to-be-deceased wife or anyone else that might recognize you, so you're going to have to rough it for a few days."

"Whatever. Just make it worth my while," Richie said as he leaned back in his seat.

Richie, Carl, and TJ loaded several bags and a large plastic pelican case onto the Gulfstream jet that was taking them to California. The flight took five hours, and they landed at a private airstrip somewhere in the desert.

Richie studied his cover story and his part in the plan intently. He obsessed over every detail since Carl and TJ would give him pop quizzes. A man Richie had never seen came to the building and quizzed Richie and TJ about their identities, trying to trip them up. Once Carl was satisfied that Richie was ready, the stranger left and was not seen again.

"So who the hell was that guy?" Richie asked as he ate the sandwich Carl had given him.

"He's an Israeli intelligence interrogator. I wanted to make sure you could stand up to someone like him. You may end up being questioned by security or law enforcement, and I can't have you breaking down and compromising me or my team."

"I just want that bitch dead, Carl. I don't care what has to happen. I want you to put her and Chris Powell in front of me. I want her to watch Chris die before I take her apart. I have nightmares about what happened to me on the beach. Until I saw my attackers on that boat, I couldn't remember shit about what happened. Now that I've seen the guy who smashed my face in, I can't forget."

"That's all well and good. You've paid us and we'll make sure you get your opportunity to make her atone for her sins. Just remember that I will not jeopardize my team to do it. No rogue shit out there. Are we clear?" Carl said, poking his finger into the table as if he were nailing his point to the surface.

"Yeah, yeah. I'm dead if I risk you. I get it!" Richie said dismissively.

TJ's eyes widened and Carl nodded. In one movement, TJ slammed Richie's head onto the table and placed a knife to his neck. The side of Richie's face was smashed into the sandwich he had been eating moments earlier.

"No, I don't think you understand me. If I nod my head, TJ will remove yours, and then we'll dissolve you in some acid and go home like nothing happened. All it takes is one look from me and you're dead."

TJ's blade began to draw blood as he applied more pressure.

"I got it, Carl, I swear!" Richie said sincerely as a half-chewed piece of sandwich flew from his mouth.

"Good."

Carl nodded at TJ, and the mercenary put his knife back in its concealed sheath. Richie touched his neck and felt the trickle of fluid oozing from his wound. TJ went back to eating as if nothing had happened.

The day the team was to depart on the cruise, Richie shaved his head and put in blue contact lenses. TJ wore a skintight tank top over ultratight jeans. He used makeup to shade his face in very specific areas.

"We'll be getting on the ship and even if they get pictures of us, ours will never make it to the database. Most people on board will barely see us, so I'm trying to make my face very undistinguished," TJ said when he saw his faux lover's confusion.

"If you say so… Drew."

Richie's clothing was more masculine-looking, but it was a far cry from the Brooks Brothers suits and Italian shoes he had worn to work.

When they were ready, everyone got in the van and headed to a secluded area near the docks. As the men unloaded the van, a small truck with the cruise line's logo approached. The truck stopped and two men exited to load the gear into the back. One of the men handed Carl two envelopes with the cruise line logo on them.

"Change of plans, boys," Carl said as he read a note from one of the envelopes.

"What's up, boss man?" asked TJ.

"It looks like we're going to have to board the ship through a back way. Department of Homeland Security operatives are at the port due to a heightened security risk, and we can't chance them seeing or videotaping us."

"Now what?" Richie asked.

"Calm down, we have backup plans for our backup plans."

The two men placed a duffel bag on the ground, and Carl instructed TJ and Richie to put on the uniforms inside. Richie asked no questions, quickly suiting up in the provided clothing.

"Richie, you and TJ are going to be porters. You'll ride with these two guys in the truck and let them do all of the talking. You got that, Richie? Make sure when these guys start to unload the truck that you grab our gear and take it on the ship. Once inside, our guy will take you where you need to be."

The four men got into the truck, and it pulled away. Richie's mind raced with thoughts of getting caught trying to sneak onto a ship. The truck drove up to a security checkpoint, and the guards asked the driver where they were headed. Richie observed the other three handing over their employee identification cards and followed suit.

The security guard looked like he should have retired twenty years ago. He gave the men in the truck a cursory glance as his partner did a bomb sweep underneath the vehicle.

"All clear," the man with the truck mirror shouted.

"See you later, guys," the old guard said as he hurried back to his chair and his newspaper.

"That's it? Department of Homeland Security is that guy back there?" Richie asked.

TJ shot Richie a look of admonishment, and Richie quickly closed his mouth and faced forward. The truck pulled up to a walkway attached to the ship. Men were loading equipment and luggage into the cargo holds. Department of Homeland Security dogs were walking around with their handlers. Richie and the other three unloaded their baggage onto a hand truck and strolled on board as if they belonged there.

As soon as they arrived at the top of the walkway, they were challenged by a younger security agent. He scanned their identification cards, and two of them failed to scan. The young agent glanced at TJ and Richie. A small bead of sweat formed on the back of Richie's neck, his heart began to race, and his stomach knotted. They were busted. He just knew it. *What would they do now?* he wondered silently.

TJ feigned annoyance at the delay of his workday as the two men who had transported them to the walkway were waved through the checkpoint.

A man wearing lieutenant's bars approached the young security officer. "Is there a problem, Holbrook?" he asked.

"These two IDs aren't in the database, sir."

"Did you run them manually?"

"I scanned them, and it flashed 'not found' on the screen." The young man scanned them again and received the same message.

Richie's fight-or-flight response started to kick in. He could feel his knees weakening, and the urge to run was becoming overwhelming. If he ran, he knew he would be caught by one of the officers on the dock. If he stayed, he most likely would end up detained for attempting to board the ship with fraudulent papers.

"Enter them manually," the lieutenant said. "We've been through this a hundred times, for Christ's sake."

TJ wasn't sweating it. From what Richie could see, the mercenary might as well be in the checkout line at the local grocery store. This put Richie somewhat at ease. As the older security officer typed in the numbers on the identification cards, TJ began making small talk.

"Man, it's hot out here, isn't it? I bet you could steam a lobster in my pants," TJ said in his best Jamaican accent.

The lieutenant stopped what he was doing and replied, "Thanks for sharing that, pal. From the looks of you and your buddy, I'd think it would be more like crabs."

TJ rolled his eyes, and the lieutenant continued to enter the data into the computer. The screen turned green and access was granted.

"You two have a nice day, now, ya hear?" the lieutenant said as he handed their badges back.

TJ grabbed some random bags piled near the door and nodded to Richie, indicating he should do the same.

Richie grabbed two bags and loaded them onto a cart. When the security lieutenant came over, Richie's ears began to ring and a headache started to form.

The lieutenant said two words as he walked past TJ: "Follow me."

Richie and TJ were led through several secure areas of the ship until they were in a storage room near the cargo area. The security officer locked the door behind him and then opened a small map of the ship with a route drawn on it in red.

"Listen carefully. In five minutes, the cameras in these parts of the ship will be down for maintenance," the officer said, pointing to the highlighted route. "You'll have fifteen minutes to get to your cabin before surveillance will be back online. Here are the master keys and the access codes to the system, including the secure cargo area. Here are the sea passes, as well. Instead of money, the ship uses onboard credit accounts for all transactions." The man opened the door and then left the room quickly.

"What do we do now… Drew?"

"Let's get out of these porter uniforms and into civilian clothing."

The two men known as Dennis and Drew changed back into the clothing they'd had on before the snag at the port. TJ handed Richie his additional documents and then looked at his watch. Exactly five minutes after the security officer left the room, TJ and Richie exited the storage closet and went to their cabin following the designated route.

They arrived at their inside stateroom without running into any crew or other passengers. The ship was still loading up cargo and preparing for the extended voyage, so passengers would not be embarking for at least another hour.

TJ removed a small communications device from his pocket and typed a short message.

Several hundred yards away, Carl received the text and smiled. The boys had gotten onto the ship without a hitch, and that was all he could hope for. The rest of the team had already signaled that they were in place, and now the last two pieces were on board. Carl grabbed his luggage and went to the embarkation area for passengers.

"CHRIS, honey, what time is our flight to LA?" Jessica asked as she stepped from the shower.

"I have the plane on standby, so we can head over anytime we want. The flight plan is filed for an eight o'clock departure, though," Chris replied as he watched the redheaded woman exit the shower. He continued shaving, watching Jessica's reflection in the mirror as she toweled off.

"I see you staring over there, mister!" Jessica scolded.

"After the things I just did to you in the shower, you're telling me that I can't watch you towel off? What a double standard!" Chris protested as he rinsed his shaving razor.

"You're such a horn dog," Jessica purred as she walked up behind him and wrapped her arms around him. Chris smiled at her in the mirror and then turned to give her a kiss. Jessica leaned in, gave him a short peck, and then moved away.

"So what's the plan after the cruise?" Chris asked.

"What do you mean?" Jessica inquired.

"Well, he's out of the coma now, so I'm guessing we don't want to stay in Florida. We aren't exactly poor right now, but in two weeks we're going to be billionaires, so where do we go from here?"

Neither one of them planned on sticking around after the rest of the money materialized. Chris had his sights set on keeping all of the money. Jessica planned to run off with the entire second payment and lock Chris out of the remainder of the legal funds as well. "Billionaires... wow, I just love how that rolls off my tongue." Jessica glowed as she said the word.

"Well? You didn't answer the question. Do we have plans after Australia?" Chris asked as he wiped away the shaving cream residue.

"We've discussed moving to DC, near your sister, or maybe California. There really isn't any need to map it out right now. Let's just get through this last piece of the pie and decide then."

"I'm just saying that it's a bad idea to stick around here too much longer. Sooner or later, he's going to come around, and considering what happened, I think we shouldn't be here when he does."

"If he was going to do anything, don't you think he would've done it by now?" Jessica said as she rolled her eyes.

"You think I'm being paranoid?"

"I think you should have spent a couple more bucks and had professionals take him out, instead of your drugged-out clients."

"Hey, that guy *is* a professional. I've been his lawyer for a long time, and I know his work. It's not my fault Richie's goddamned skull is so thick."

"Thick skull." Jessica laughed at the irony of that statement.

"What's so funny?" Chris asked, pausing as he removed his towel and put his underwear on.

"Well, if he didn't have such a thick skull and took his father's advice to heart, he wouldn't have had his face smashed in with a tire iron. So in essence his thick skull saved him and fucked him at the same time."

"You scare me sometimes," Chris said as he got dressed.

"Oh, stop, like you're Mr. Innocent."

"Can we change the subject, please?" Chris pleaded.

Chris and Jessica got dressed and finished packing their luggage for the cruise. As Jessica had the last of her bags brought down, Chris went into his home office and closed the door.

Chris logged onto his computer and made reservations for two on an airline out of Sydney, Australia, back to Los Angeles. He smiled as he thought about how much money he was wasting on two tickets when in reality he only needed one. He sent out a couple of e-mails and set his accounts to an auto reply that he would be away with his fiancée until next month.

The sadistic lovebirds got into a waiting vehicle while the driver loaded their bags. They smiled at each other and kissed briefly. Soon they would be on a cruise that would make at least one of them rich beyond their wildest dreams.

Chapter 6

W HEN Pat, Dean, Shawn, Brian, Greg, and Clay got off the plane in LA, they were met by representatives from the cruise line. Everyone was glad to get off the plane after the long flight and eager to board the *Queen Mary 2*. On the shuttle bus, Pat sat listening to Brian, Greg, and Clay chat about what they planned to do and how much time they would spend at the pool getting a tan. Dean looked over at Pat and smiled.

"Well, it seems the children are all ready to play," Dean said.

"Yeah, and I know what kind of playing Clay plans on doing with those two," Pat replied.

"Yes, I remember the stories from our trip to New York. Well, at least they'll be happy. And on top of that, Brian has stopped bitching about not being able to eat with us. He asked if we would eat with them in the main dining room, and I didn't hesitate to say no! Love them or not, I'm not giving up on the five-star food in the Queen's Grill to eat in steerage!"

Pat laughed out loud and said, "Sometimes you can be such a fucking snob!"

Dean smiled. "Yes, I can, especially at these prices!"

"We have to at least have breakfast or lunch with them once in a while. After all, we invited them to come along."

"Fine, I'll sacrifice a lunch or breakfast, but there is no way we're missing dinner."

The bus pulled up at the docks and porters unloaded the luggage. Any that had tags for the upper suites were whisked away, while those in regular cabins had to find a porter or carry the luggage themselves.

"Well, we'll see you guys on board," Dean said. "Why don't we meet on the upper pool deck after the lifeboat drill?"

"Why, where are you guys going?" Clay asked.

"We have a special check-in area, and we'll be in our suite in about ten minutes. So, see you there," Dean answered.

"Fucking snobs! Sure, see you there," Brian said with a laugh.

The detectives and their husbands went to the entrance that said, "Queen's Grill Check-in." They found a host of drinks and snacks available as they were processed. They were checked on board, given their sea passes, and escorted by their personal butler to their suite. As they followed the butler, everyone's heads were turning to marvel at the beauty of the *Queen Mary 2*.

They got in an elevator, went up to the eleventh deck, and entered their "penthouse" suite. Shawn whistled as he looked around at the plush surroundings. The interior was luxurious yet light, and the private balcony drew everyone's attention. The bathroom had a Jacuzzi tub that could fit two as well as a shower stall.

On the other side of the suite from the king-sized bed was the sofa where Hank and Shawn would be spending their nights. At 758 square feet, the suite was large enough to give the guys some privacy when asleep.

"Holy shit, Dean! We got all this for six grand? I'd say we got a bargain," Hank said.

"Yes, I'd say you got a great bargain on this one," Pat said.

Dean quickly changed the subject. "Let's see if they stocked our fridge with the booze I ordered."

Pat calculated in his head what the trip was really costing them and felt a little queasy. $34,000 just for the cruise, and that didn't include airfare home from Sydney. He decided he would bring this up later with his husband.

"Yep, fully stocked fridge," Dean said. "We have some time before the other guys get on board, if anyone wants a cocktail."

"I'll take a drink, that's for sure," Pat said.

When they had their drinks, they went out onto their balcony and sat down to enjoy them.

"What time do we eat dinner, and how do we dress tonight?" Hank asked.

"We can eat anytime between six and nine. But if we wanna catch the first show, we should eat at six. Tonight is just slacks and jacket. Tomorrow night is tuxedos," replied Dean.

The two detectives heard a noise and turned around fast to look into the suite. They saw their luggage had been delivered and their butler had started to unpack.

"I don't want him pawing through my underwear, honey," Pat said.

"I'll handle it," Dean said as he stood up.

Dean walked over to the butler and cleared his throat.

"Hello. I'm Dean, and I'd appreciate it if you would unpack the suit bags and send out any garments that need pressing. We'll take care of the suitcases ourselves."

"Very good, sir. Is your room comfortable?"

"Yes, this will do very nicely. I was wondering what happened to you once we entered the suite."

"I went to make sure your bags came up directly. Anytime you require anything, all you have to do is push the button on the phone marked 'butler,' and I'll be here quickly. If you need to ask for me by name, I'm Dong-yul."

"Is that Japanese?"

"No sir, Korean."

"Does it have a meaning?"

"Yes, sir. It means 'passion of the East'."

"Well, thank you, Dong-yul. We'll be eating at six this evening."

"Very good, sir."

Dean went back to his drink on the balcony.

"What's he doing?" Hank asked.

"*He* is Dong-yul, and he's unpacking our suit bags and attending to anything that needs to be pressed. We'll unpack our suitcases when he's finished."

"Dong-yul? What kind of name is that?" Shawn asked.

"It's Korean and actually very beautiful. It means 'passion of the East.' The fact that he's one of the hottest Asian men I've ever seen tells me that his parents knew what they were doing when they were picking a name."

"He is beautiful," Pat said as he admired the curve of their butler's ass.

They finished their drinks, unpacked their toiletries, and went up on deck to meet up with the rest of their party. After ten minutes, they found each other.

"Well, here comes the Queen's royal party now!" Greg said with a grin.

"Oh, stop it, we're no more royal now than we are back home," Dean said.

Shawn giggled. Clay frowned.

"It's a class system, just like on the *Titanic*! It's not fair," Clay whined.

"Not at all. If you could come up with the fare, you could be residing on our level as well," Dean answered.

"Yeah, well, who has that kind of money?"

"Oh be quiet, Clay, you got the third-person rate for our cabin just so you could come. I don't wanna hear any bitching because our friends are lucky enough to be in a suite. You can have visitors, right?" Brian asked.

"Yes, you can visit us anytime, and we'll even serve drinks on our balcony. The only thing you can't do is eat with us in the dining room. I'm sorry," Dean said.

"Look, we're not going to spend the entire cruise apologizing for being in the upper level suites. I'm sure there will still be plenty of excitement to keep you occupied," Pat said, getting a little hot under the collar.

Picking up on Pat's tone, Dean stepped in. "Look, since we're all together, why don't we go to the Commodore Club and have a drink?"

Smiles broke out on everyone's faces at the mention of alcohol. They headed up to the top to the Commodore Club, which looked out over the bow of the ship. A round was ordered, and everyone finally began to chill out a little. For Pat's immediate party, this was their second drink, and it turned out they weren't the only ones. Greg and Brian had snuck a large bottle of vodka on board, and Pat could smell that the boys had had a little warm-up party before they met up with them.

"I have to admit this is one beautiful ship from what we've seen so far," Greg said.

"Gotta agree. Can't wait to get to Hawaii and see the islands as we approach them. It should be very peaceful as we sail through the islands. I think we stop for one day and then on to Sydney," Brian said.

"That's right. We have nothing to do for sixteen days but relax and enjoy life. It's the kind of peace and quiet that Pat and Hank need," Dean said as he looked from one to the other.

"Yeah, well, we'll see," Hank said. "As long as none of us gets chucked overboard before we hit Sydney, I suppose the cruise will be a success."

Everyone smiled but Pat. After a tense couple of minutes, Dean cleared his throat and announced that it was time to get ready for the lifeboat drill. The men went to their respective cabins to await the drill, which went off ninety minutes before departing Los Angeles.

After the drill, they returned to their suite, and Shawn realized they'd been too busy drinking to plan the night's activities. He picked up the phone and called Greg and Brian.

Shawn informed them that they were all going to meet at the entrance to the Royal Court Theater no later than eight o'clock so they could sit together at the show. Dong-yul rang their doorbell with a tray of hors d'oeuvres that included chocolate-covered strawberries. He placed the tray on the table and passed out the napkins and silverware in what would be a nightly ritual.

The guys were starving and wolfed down the snacks like ravenous animals. Dong-yul smiled. "You sure are hungry men."

"Dong-yul, you have no idea about our appetites," Hank said, laughing.

"Oh, I see plenty. I see four men in one suite. I see four good friends, and it's my pleasure to serve you gentlemen." The butler smiled.

Shawn went over to the butler and hugged him. "That was awful nice of you to say, Dong."

"This not my first day at the rodeo. You can be comfortable around me, be yourselves, and enjoy all that ship has to offer. You need something, you ask. My job is to see to your needs." He smiled again as he picked up the empty tray. As he departed, he wiggled his tight little ass at the group.

"Well, I guess he just read our minds," Dean said, laughing so hard he fell down on the bed.

"What was with you hugging the butler?" Hank asked Shawn.

"Well, I wanted to show him we appreciate his acknowledging who we are and telling us to feel comfortable around him."

"Uh-huh, I think you just wanted to feel how tight his body was under the jacket. I know you, you little horny monkey," Hank said as he slapped Shawn on the ass.

"I'm going to take a shower, Dean. Care to join me?" Pat asked.

"Why, yes, I think showering before dinner is the right thing to do. We've been traveling since before the crack of dawn."

"And you guys, if you want, feel free to use the tub while we're in the shower," Pat said.

"Ah, damn, I was hoping the four of us could use the shower at the same time!" Shawn said with a devilish giggle.

"You'd enjoy being among all the man flesh too much, and we'd spoil you so you'd never be happy with just Hank again," Dean said.

"No, no danger of that. Hank is all the man I need," he said as he kissed Hank on the cheek.

Pat and Dean removed their clothes, grabbed a pair of fresh shorts each, and got into the shower. Hank looked at Shawn and asked, "Do you wanna use the tub, or wait till the shower is free?"

"Let's use the tub, and we can perv on Pat and Dean while we lie in luxury!"

"You dog. I'll put the water on, you get ready. I think I saw some bath salts in there that I'll add to the water."

Shawn heard the water come on and quickly took off his clothes. He didn't bother getting shorts. He was feeling horny and wanted to put on a little show for his husband and friends by walking nude from the bathroom to the dresser.

"Damn, you look good standing there!" Hank said as he took off his clothes. "The tub is filling quickly, so come on in."

Shawn walked into the bathroom and whistled at the guys he could see kissing through the glass of the shower. He felt the water in the Jacuzzi tub, and finding it the right temperature, he climbed in and waited for his husband.

Hank shoved his shorts down and got in behind Shawn so that Shawn could lie back against his chest. When he looked over and saw his friends kissing, he yelled, "Get a room, you two! Oh, that's right, you did!"

"You like watching, don't you? Should I start playing with your little twinkie?" Pat yelled back.

"Twinkie, my ass! I'm not a twinkie. I'm a young, slender, cut and defined young man with a buzz cut and a nice ass!"

"Yeah, a twinkie!" Pat and Dean yelled at the same time.

Shawn opened his mouth to shout something, and Hank put his hand over it. "Stifle yourself, Edith. They're just fucking with you," he said as he reached around and grabbed Shawn's cock. Shawn got hard almost instantly and turned his head for a kiss.

As Shawn and Hank were kissing, Pat and Dean got out of the shower, giving catcalls of their own.

Hank looked up. "What? You two just got off. I'm just getting a little horned up, that's all."

"Contrary to your erroneous conclusion, we did not just get off. We merely made out a little and got hard. We don't have enough time to do it right this minute, so when the lights go out tonight, the bed will be squeaking!" Pat said with a smile.

"At these prices, that bed better not squeak!" Dean replied.

Hank and Shawn went back to cuddling in the tub as the other two left the bathroom.

When Dean saw the clock, he called out, "We've got forty minutes until we have to be at the restaurant!"

"Fuck! Okay," Hank yelled back.

As Pat and Dean began to get dressed, they heard Hank and Shawn step into the shower to rinse off the bath salts. They quickly dried off to get ready. It was Pat and Dean's turn to whistle now, and it motivated Shawn to put on a show while crossing the room.

Twenty minutes later, the four men were dressed semiformally. They lined up and were impressed with how good their little group looked in their jackets and ties.

"I have to get a picture of this and one in our tuxedos tomorrow night," Dean said as he set up his camera and turned on the timer. He rejoined the others, and they stood, smiling, waiting for the flash. After the picture was taken, they all crowded around the camera to see how it turned out.

"Okay, I'd fuck me. I'd fuck me hard," Hank said.

"That one never gets old," Pat replied.

Everyone laughed, and they headed out the door. They found the Queen's Grill dining room and were surprised when the maître d' greeted them by name.

"Right this way, gentlemen. Your table is ready," he said as he led them to a table by one of the windows. Dean noticed heads turning as the four of them walked to the table and wasn't sure if it was because of how good they looked, or in surprise because four men were unaccompanied by women. They looked over the menu, and the feast began. By the end of the meal, everyone in the party was both full and pleased by the quality of the food. They had four courses followed by coffee, and every part of the dinner was perfect.

Before they got up, Dean called their handsome waiter over. After complimenting the meal and the service, he made a request. "Andre, could I have beef Wellington for dinner tomorrow evening?"

"Of course, sir. I'll inform the chef, and he'll be pleased to make it. Would anyone else care for that particular dish?"

Shawn said yes, which made Hank say yes. "We might as well make it four, then," Pat said.

"Excellent. It shall be taken care of, and may I ask what time you plan on dining tomorrow evening so that you may be served promptly?"

"We intend to be here each evening at six. If a problem comes up, I'll give you a call to inform you of our delay," Dean replied.

"Excellent, sir. The chef is very proud of everything that comes from the kitchen, and serving it fresh is important to him. Would garlic mashed potatoes and a vegetable suit you as side dishes?"

Everyone answered in the affirmative, said goodnight to Andre, and rose from the table.

As they were leaving the restaurant, Shawn said, "I didn't see beef Wellington on the menu."

"In this dining room, you can ask for anything, on or off the menu, and the chef will prepare it. I gave them twenty-four hours' notice as a courtesy. Beef Wellington is one of my favorite dishes. You won't find that being served in the Britannia restaurant for the regular passengers."

"Seems to me there are a lot of privileges for a mere three thousand per person," Hank said. "So how much did this cruise really cost, Dean?"

Put on the spot, Dean cringed, as did Shawn. "Oh, just a tad more, but that was my treat."

"You're evading the question. How much?"

"Ten thousand," Dean replied.

"You're shitting me! Twenty grand a couple and we paid you a lousy six thousand? Shawn, did you know about this?"

Trying to save Shawn, Pat cut in. "Look, let's not worry about money, okay? We're here. Let's enjoy the benefits of being on this level of the ship. Let's just go and meet the others and enjoy tonight's show. It's music from *Phantom of the Opera* with two of the original cast members."

"Fine, but we *will* pay you the additional fourteen thousand back over time," Hank said.

An awkward silence enveloped the group as they took an elevator down to the proper deck and met the other three members of their party at the theater.

"So, did you have a good dinner?" Pat asked their friends.

"Yeah, better than we get back home, that's for sure," Clay answered.

"The food is very good, and if yours is better, I can only imagine how great it tastes," Brian said as they headed for their seats.

"Let's sit in the front row. I wanna be able to really see any dancers. You know what I mean," Greg said.

"There are no dancers tonight. It's *Phantom*," Dean replied.

"You mean phantom as in ghosts and stuff?" Clay asked.

"No, as in *Phantom of the Opera* by Andrew Lloyd Webber."

"Oh," was the disappointed reply from Clay.

An hour and a half later, they left the theater with everyone but Clay having enjoyed the performance. He looked like he had lost his best friend.

"Hey, guys. I saw a notice that the gay group on board has booked one of the clubs for its exclusive use, which means they'll be dancing. Wanna head up there?" Greg asked.

The unanimous verdict was "hell yeah!"

When they arrived at the G32 nightclub, there was a sign that said, "*Closed, special event.*" Dean talked to a guy by the door and soon everyone was invited in to join the gay group in the club. Guys were dancing exuberantly together, and drinks were flowing.

"Now this is more like it!" Clay proclaimed.

"Yeah, I like this too. Let's dance," Shawn said, and Clay, Brian, and Greg followed him to the dance floor.

"Don't feel like dancing tonight, partner?" Pat asked Hank.

"Oh, I'll dance, but I need another drink first," Hank replied, smiling.

They sat at a table with a sofa back and ordered a round of drinks for everyone. After dancing for a couple of numbers, the rest of the group came to the table and were all smiles as they sipped their drinks.

"The music is perfect!" Brian exclaimed.

Greg agreed. Clay stayed in his seat but never sat still as he moved with the music. After the first round of drinks, everyone went out on the dance floor and really enjoyed themselves.

As the hour grew late, most of the group started to yawn, and when Clay proclaimed he was horny and down to fuck, everyone knew it was time to leave. Clay remained behind to cruise.

"Well, you have your own key, so just try and be quiet when you come in, unless we're going at it, in which case jump on in," Brian said as he grabbed Clay's basket.

Shawn smiled and mouthed the word "slut."

"See you guys at the pool in the morning?" Hank asked.

"Yeah, sounds like a plan. We'll save you some lounge chairs if we can," Greg said as they hugged each other good night and went their separate ways.

When they entered their suite, they found the bed turned down, and the sofa bed made up and ready for Hank and Shawn. Several chocolates were on each bed instead of the usual two. A note from Dong-yul read, "I hope you sleep well tonight."

"He is so sweet," Dean said. "We're going to have to leave him a nice tip."

"I agree," Pat said.

"Let us take care of that. It's the least we can do," Hank said. "And you—you would be getting a serious spanking if we weren't sharing a room with our best friends," he continued as Shawn stripped off his clothes.

"Don't let that stop you," Dean said, egging Hank on. "I promise, we won't watch."

"Shut up, Dean, and thanks for the support!" Shawn yelled.

The lights were turned out, and everyone crawled into bed, feeling frisky. But instead of making love like they had planned, all four were sound asleep in five minutes. It had been a long day with good food, alcohol, and entertainment.

Down below in the ocean-view cabins, Brian and Greg were making love like it was their last chance. Since Clay never came back to the cabin, they made the most of the privacy. After making love with abandon and then taking a quick shower, they fell into a deep sleep.

THE next day everyone woke up fully rested and ready for their first day at sea. Dean summoned the butler for coffee so that they could enjoy their first cup on the balcony in the fresh sea air. "Damn, this is living, boys," Pat said as he lay back in his lounge chair on the terrace.

"You said it, but I'm hungry. Are we going to order room service or go to the grill?" Hank asked.

"Either way you want it," Pat said.

"Anybody object if we have room service?" Hank asked.

No one objected, but Shawn suggested inviting the others to come up and eat with them. His suggestion was met with universal approval.

"I'll call them and see if they're awake yet," Hank said as he went back into the room.

Hank called and a sleepy Greg answered.

"Hello?"

"Hey, boy, you guys up yet?"

"Kinda. Don't know where that little slut is since he didn't come back to the cabin last night, but Brian and I are awake."

"You wanna get dressed and come up to our room for breakfast?"

"Yeah, that sounds good. Give us ten minutes?"

"Ten minutes! At least shower the sex smell off before you come to our palace."

"We showered last night, you prick. See you in ten minutes."

The line went dead.

Hank went back to the balcony. "Brian and Greg are coming up for breakfast, but Clay never came back to the room last night."

"Woo hoo, someone on the ship has a smile this morning," Shawn said.

"Yeah, not a big surprise with five hundred gay men on board," Dean said.

A short while later, the doorbell rang, and Brian and Greg arrived. They smelled coffee and wanted some, but there were no clean cups.

"Don't sweat it. We'll order more along with food. Look at the menu, tell me what you want, and I'll call it in to room service," Pat said.

When everyone knew what they wanted, Pat called down to room service and was told that it would be about twenty minutes until they had breakfast.

"So where do you think Clay got to last night?" Shawn asked Greg.

"He had his eye on a couple at the bar, and it looked like they were interested, so I'm guessing they went off somewhere to bump uglies. We left a note on his bed to let him know that we'd be back in an hour in case he comes back to the room while we're here. Speaking of here… *nice*! You fuckers are living like royalty while all we have is a damn window! Nice of you to invite us up for breakfast, though."

"I told ya we'd be inviting you here to do things," Pat said.

After breakfast arrived, everyone dug in and downed more coffee. When they had finished, everyone really looked like they were wide awake.

"Pool?" Greg asked.

"Yeah, sounds good to me," Shawn said.

"Okay, let's get changed, and we'll meet at that pool," Dean said, pointing to the pool they could see from their balcony.

After Brian and Greg left, the men in the suite changed into trunks except Shawn, who had the body for a Speedo. They put shorts on over their swimsuits and went down to the pool. The sun was bright, the seas calm, and it was a perfect day for some sun and fun.

Between the pool and the hot tubs on both sides, they stayed right through lunch, deciding not to enter the hamburger line at the grill. Around one o'clock, they had a round of drinks, and Pat and Hank noticed that a couple of older men watched closely when Clay finally rematerialized clad only in a very skimpy bikini bottom. The suit left nothing to the imagination, and even his friends stared at him.

"What? You'd think none of you had ever seen a bikini on a guy before. Are my balls hanging out or something?" Clay asked.

Pat, Hank, and Dean laughed; Shawn didn't. "No, your balls aren't hanging out," Shawn said, "but no one has to guess what you're packing because it's all on display. This is the *Queen Mary 2*, not some gay party barge going down the Hudson."

"You're just jealous because I got it." Clay dropped his towel, kicked off his sandals, and dove into the pool.

As they watched Clay, Dean observed, "If you think he was showing a lot before, wait till he gets out with that thing wet! No wonder the straight guys are staring."

"He is a little slut puppy, no doubt about it," Pat said and put his head back.

As predicted, when Clay got out of the water, his bikini became almost see-through, and once again, even the straight guys stared, not only at Clay but at the rest of their group as well. When some members from the gay group came down and took over the rest of the lounges, some people got up in a huff and left. "Well, guess they don't know what subtle means," Dean observed.

"Fuck 'em, who cares?" Pat replied.

"Well, it's almost four o'clock, and I've had enough for today. In fact, I think I might be a little sunburned. I'm heading in," Dean said. "Besides, Dong-yul will be by with our snacks."

Everyone else agreed, including Clay, and they returned to their cabins after agreeing to meet at the theater after dinner.

"What's playing tonight, anyway? I hope not more *Phantom* stuff," Clay whined.

"No, tonight is the ship's dance crew and singers. They're usually pretty good. We can even grab the front row if we're early enough, so that you can see all their *details*," Dean said.

"That sounds much better. See you tonight, then." Clay said.

WHEN the two couples arrived at their suite, Dong-yul was right behind them with a tray of hors d'oeuvres. As everyone peeled out of their bathing suits and went to shower, Dong-yul set out the food and utensils.

Dean was the first to shower, and when Dong-yul heard the water stop, he hurried into the bathroom with a towel. Pat peeked in as Dean opened the stall door and found Dong-yul holding a towel. Dean stepped out of the shower, and Dong-yul dried him off. Dean looked at Pat to gauge his reaction as Dong-yul handed him the towel and exited the bathroom. Pat came in and got into the shower next, as Dean finished drying off. When Dean was finished, he walked out to the bedroom and hunted through a drawer for a fresh pair of underwear.

"Dong, why did you dry Dean off?" Hank asked.

"Prior to coming to work for Cunard, I was employed at a very exclusive men's club in Seoul. It was the custom when a gentleman exited the shower to dry him off front and back. Of course, we did not dry the genital area without express permission from the gentleman. If you object to this service, I will not perform it. "

"It really was nice," Dean said. "Makes your skin tingle."

"I have no objection," Shawn said.

Hank just nodded and grunted.

The sound of running water stopped, and Dong-yul entered the bathroom to give the same treatment to Pat. Shawn then entered the shower, saying he would be two minutes.

Pat joined Dean in getting dressed while Dong-yul waited for Shawn to come out, and Dean explained the "special service."

"I don't give a fuck but if any of the others object, it stops," Pat replied.

"Nah, we don't object," Hank said. "I don't have an issue with it as long as I'm in the room."

The water turned off, and when Hank turned and saw Dong-yul working his way down Shawn's back, a pang of jealousy ran through him. He got into the shower and stepped out three minutes later, deciding to see how it felt. As Dong-yul dried Hank off, Hank watched Dong-yul in the mirror to see where his eyes were. The butler watched where he was drying and nowhere else.

"Here you go, Mr. Capstone. You do the front," Dong-yul said as he left the bathroom. When he was back into the main area of the suite, he asked if anyone wanted cocktails.

"No, that's okay," Dean answered. "We're going to the Queen's Lounge for a drink before dinner."

"Very good, sir, enjoy your dinner," the butler said as he left the suite.

Hank came out of the bathroom, naked but dry. "That was weird, if you ask me," he said.

"Not really," Dean said. "I stayed at La Costa Health Spa once, and they did the same thing. Only when you stepped out of the showers there, there were two young guys with towels who dried *all* of you."

"Okay, let's get dressed while we munch on these tidbits," Pat said as he picked up a cracker with caviar-covered cream cheese.

"Hey, Dean, I saw something in the room brochure that interested me," Pat said.

"What's that?" Dean asked as he sat down on the bed next to his husband.

"We can invite a ship's officer to dine with us in the Queen's Grill."

"What's so interesting about that?" Shawn asked.

"I'd like to meet the captain in person, to be honest," Pat answered.

"I think that would be cool too," Hank added.

"Well, what do we have to do?" Dean asked Pat.

"Just call this number and tell them you'd like to extend an invitation to the captain for dinner."

Pat, Dean, and Shawn looked at each other and saw they were in complete agreement.

"The captain of a Queen dining with queens. I like it," Shawn quipped.

"I always did have a thing for men in uniform," Dean said as he rubbed Pat's shoulder.

"I'll call the phone number and see if he's free one night this week," Hank said.

"Hello, this is the St. James and Capstone suite. We'd like to extend an invitation to the captain for dinner this week. ... Oh, he is? ... I see. Well, we don't mind joining them if there's room for four. Yes, that'd be great. Thank you. Bye."

"So we're set, then?" Pat asked.

"Yeah, we just have to share him with a straight couple the evening we sail away from Hawaii. That's another formal night, just so everyone knows."

"Ew, breeders!" Shawn gagged mockingly.

WHEN they were all dressed in their tuxedos, they took more photos before going to the Queen's Grill lounge, where complimentary drinks were served as they sat and looked out at the sea. The sun was going down, but the ocean was still very bright as they enjoyed two rounds of cocktails before going into the dining room.

They took the same table, and Dean ordered a bottle of white and one of red for the table. It was beef Wellington night, and Dean couldn't wait. Shawn and Hank had never eaten the dish before, but as far as Hank was concerned, it had beef in the name so it must be okay.

The wonderful staff of the restaurant made the food seem even better. The mashed potatoes were perfect, with just the right amount of garlic, and the gravy for the Wellington was exquisite. The dish was served with fresh green beans amandine along with soup and salad. With coffee and Bananas Foster for dessert, they were more than satiated.

"Did you enjoy your dinner this evening, gentlemen?" the maître d' inquired.

"Yes, everything was outstanding. Please pass our compliments on to the chef," Dean replied.

"Outstanding, sir, I shall. I see that the captain will be joining you on the evening we leave Hawaii. There will be two additional guests that night as well. When the captain dines here it is always special, so we bring out the finest china and silverware for the occasion. I look forward to seeing you that evening." He bowed and left.

Dean's and Clay's parties met up at the theater once more, and everyone had a good time. The ship's dancers were all young hotties with great bodies, and they danced their asses off on stage. They, along with the singers of the cast, put on a performance that lasted ninety minutes, and everyone was sorry when the show ended.

As they left the theater, they decided it was time to have a few more drinks and raise some hell in the casino. All seven men went into the casino to see if Lady Luck was with or against them. Pat and Hank knew that whether they won in the casino or not, they were going to get lucky later in the suite.

THE door to Jessica and Chris's suite opened, and Chris walked in. "Hey, you're not going to believe this, babe!" he said in a glee-filled voice.

Jessica sat up in the hot tub and took a sip of white wine while she enjoyed the jets of water spraying all over her body.

"What's up?" she asked.

"Alfred Patterson from the investors group just introduced me to the captain of the ship. I got to go up to the bridge and see how it all operates. It was pretty awesome," Chris said like a ten-year-old boy who had been allowed to sit in an army tank.

"Oh, for God's sake, you're like a big kid," Jessica said as she relaxed back into the hot tub.

"What can I say? I've never been on a ship this big. Boys and their toys, and all that." Chris was still beaming from ear to ear when the phone rang.

"I can't get a moment's peace in here," Jessica complained as she drained her glass. Chris had the urge to drown her in the hot tub right then and there but he restrained himself.

"Love you too, babe," he said as he reached for the phone.

"Hello? ... Yes, that would be great, Captain. ... I look forward to it." Chris was even more excited now than when he had walked into the suite.

"Who was that?" Jessica asked in an annoyed tone.

"It was the captain accepting my invitation to dinner."

"Oh, you two are dating now. How nice," Jessica purred.

"No, smarty-pants, I wanted to thank him for taking me on the bridge, and since a privilege of dining in the Queen's Grill is that we can invite a ship's officer to dinner, I invited him to eat with us the evening we leave Hawaii, and he just accepted."

"Well, it can't be any worse than eating with the jerks from the investors group," Jessica shouted as she turned the hot tub jets to maximum.

"For the money they're handing over in Sydney, I'll laugh at their lame money jokes any day."

Chris jumped face-first onto the bed and stretched out. Dollar signs and what to do with the money were all he'd obsessed about since he and Jessica had boarded the ship. A short nap was in order, and then they would get ready for dinner and tonight's show. Jessica had insisted on going to see the dancers in the theater tonight, and so Chris had acquiesced to her demands.

BY THE time most of the guys in the group were ready to leave the casino and go back to their cabins, some were up and others were in the loss column. Dean and Shawn were the big winners that night, on the slot machines, of all things. Hank's pride was a little damaged because he thought he was hot shit at craps, but the crap was on him as he lost almost a thousand dollars of the winnings he had accumulated. Pat had no luck, either; after bragging during dinner about how he was the blackjack guru, the money he'd allotted for gambling that night had been seized by the house.

After they said their good-nights and headed to their cabins, Clay did not wander off. Instead he went with Brian and Greg to their room. Pat figured that the three of them would be fucking like rabbits within twenty minutes of entering their cabin.

As the two couples entered their suite, they once again found extra chocolates on their beds and all the empty booze bottles replaced with full ones.

"He sure is working hard for his tip!" Dean said.

"I'll make him work for his tips," Hank said, chuckling.

"Oh? You like our butler?" Pat asked.

"Yeah. There's something about his ass, and how very fuckable it looks! Ouch!" Hank yelled when Shawn punched him in the arm.

"If there's any fucking around here, it will be me getting it, mister!" Shawn said in a low, sexy voice. "And if you somehow manage to nail the butler, I better be present."

"Don't worry, honey. It's not gonna happen, I promise. We're married now, and that changes everything as far as playing around with strangers."

"Hey, does that include us?" Dean yelled as they were getting ready to get into bed.

Hank snickered. "You're not strangers, and I'd feel bad because I'd ruin you for Pat."

The lights went out, plunging the suite into darkness. After a moment, the sound of kissing was heard as both couples began to get amorous.

"I'm gonna fuck you hard," Hank whispered into Shawn's ear.

"I hope so. My ass has been begging for cock since the theater," Shawn replied.

Shawn slid down on the sofa bed, and after finding Hank's hard cock in the dark, wasted no time in going down on it. He worked it up and down until he could go all the way down to Hank's nuts. Since it was dark, Hank kicked off the covers to give Shawn more room to work.

"I think they're going at it, and it's making me horny," Dean whispered to Pat.

"Yeah, that's the sound of a dick being sucked, and knowing Hank, it's his dick receiving the attention," Pat replied.

Dean kicked their covers off and followed the same course as Shawn. Pat wasn't hard, but it didn't take him long to get that way once he felt Dean's hot tongue hit the head of his dick and run over his balls.

Hank lifted Shawn up and turned him around so they could sixty-nine, and the sounds of sucking increased on that side of the room. When Shawn began moaning, the not-so-secret activity was out in the open. Shawn began to drive his cock down into Hank's mouth instead of passively allowing Hank to suck him. In response, Hank grabbed Shawn's head and thrust hard and fast. Pat pulled Dean off his dick and brought him up to sit on his chest.

"Face-fuck me, honey," Pat urged.

"You do love that, don't ya?" Dean said, smiling in the dark.

Dean moved up, stuck his cock in Pat's mouth, and began to rock back and forth, shoving his entire length into Pat's mouth each time. As Dean continued to thrust, Pat inserted a wet finger into Dean's ass and began to massage his prostate gland. Now, both Dean and Shawn were moaning, and Pat and Hank no longer tried to muffle the sounds of sex.

"I want your dick, honey," Dean pleaded. He fetched the lube and then returned to the waiting arms of his husband, stubbing his toe on a chair in the dark.

"Fuck! Damn, that hurts," he yelled.

"Hey, partner, take it easy on the poor man. I need him fresh for our sauna date later!" Hank said.

"Oh, be quiet, I kicked a fucking chair," Dean said.

"Are you all right?" Pat asked.

"I'll live, and you can make me feel better by doing what you do best."

"What's that? Catch homicidal maniacs?" Hank shouted again.

"No, what I should do to you. Fuck you up the ass!" Pat yelled back.

"Promises, promises!" Hank replied. Dean got back in bed without the hard-on he'd had when he got out.

"Damn, that hurt," he said quietly.

"Want me to make you feel much better?" Pat asked.

"Yeah, baby, do me."

Pat kissed Dean deeply, their tongues dueling for dominance. When Pat reached for Dean's dick, he found it fully erect once more. Pat went down on his husband to make him rock hard. He moved down to Dean's balls, licking slowly, taking each one in his mouth before releasing it.

When he was satisfied with Dean's state of hardness, he squirted some lube on his finger and massaged it into Dean's opening. Dean reacted by pushing down on Pat's finger, and Pat knew he was ready.

He coated his cock liberally with lube and got between Dean's legs. He moved them up over his shoulders and lined up his cock as Dean begged him to hurry and get inside.

Pat pressed against the entrance, and after a little resistance, his dick passed through and he continued until he was balls-deep in Dean's ass.

Dean let out a sigh to express his pleasure at being impaled on his husband's cock.

Hank and Shawn heard the telltale sigh, and Hank went into action. He moved Shawn off him, grabbed the lube he had put on the table next to the sofa, and greased himself up.

"Ride me, baby," he whispered to Shawn, who didn't hesitate to climb back on top of Hank and lower himself onto Hank's erection. After taking a moment to adjust to the fullness, he began to slide up and down Hank's dick. As he did, he played with Hank's nipples, which drove his husband extra crazy.

Hank grabbed Shawn's bouncing erection and began to stroke him furiously. Hank was super horny and wasn't interested in anything but quick, hot sex. As Pat thrust inward especially hard, Dean exclaimed, "Fuck yeah, fuck me, fuck me good!" Hank and Shawn were so into their sex they didn't even hear Dean yelling.

"Slow down or I'm gonna cum," Shawn warned.

Instead of slowing down, Hank stroked Shawn's dick even harder.

"Give me your cum all over my chest, you cute piece of ass you!" Hank responded.

Shawn let go and his climax made his ass muscles clench and release on Hank's cock, triggering Hank's climax as well. As both men grunted and moaned, Pat's climax was triggered as well, and Dean finished himself off by hand at the same time.

Within twenty minutes, all four horny men were satiated, and the air was heavy with the scent of sex. Dean popped out of bed first to clean up in the bathroom. When he came out, Shawn went in to do the same thing.

"Hey, partner, why don't you and I get together somewhere tomorrow to talk?" Hank asked.

"Yeah, it's about time. Besides, I feel so mellow right now, I'd even let you win an argument!"

Hank chuckled. "Okay, tomorrow, then."

Shawn brought out two warm, wet washcloths, tossed one to Pat, and took the other over to Hank. He wiped down Hank's cock and chest before throwing the cloth toward the bathroom. Pat cleaned himself up and dropped the cloth on the floor next to the bed. It had turned out to be a great night.

"You guys mind if I open the doors to the balcony so we can hear the water and air out the room?" Shawn asked.

No one had a problem with that, and the combination of their climaxes, the warm breeze, and sounds of the ocean put them all swiftly to sleep.

THE next day, after breakfast, everyone but Pat and Hank headed off to the pool for another adventure in the sun. Pat and Hank grabbed more coffee and went to a quiet corner and sat down. The bar didn't open until after lunch, so they were alone, and no one would be eavesdropping on their conversation.

"Okay, so what are we going to do with the work situation, Hank? End our partnership and maybe destroy the friendship?" Pat asked.

"Why should we end our friendship? I'm trying to get ahead and get back to the action. I wouldn't stop you from doing that."

"Are you really an adrenaline junkie? Is that what you need to be happy at work? Someone constantly trying to kill you?"

Hank sat back. "Maybe. Is that so wrong? Tell me you don't think narcotics are one hell of a problem and the cause of so many of the homicides that come through our office. By attacking drug pushers, we can lower the murder rate. I might even be able to prevent a few from happening in the first place. What's wrong with that?"

"Nothing. It's a much-needed bureau, without question. But why you? You're breaking up a winning team, Hank. We're viewed as one of the top—if not *the* top—teams in the detective bureau. We have solid reps everywhere we go. Name me a cop who hasn't heard of us. Hell, they teach some of our cases in the police academy!"

"So you don't like the idea of me going off to make my own way, or you just don't want to lose your partner?" Hank asked.

"Honestly, it's both. I don't want to see you make a career mistake, and I don't want us to break up. Aside from Dean, you're the closest human being to me. I love you and Shawn, and if you leave, we'll barely see each other. Is there some reason that you don't want to work with me anymore?"

"No, although getting stuck in your shadow sometimes is a little annoying. After all, you're the one who was the bait in both the motel homicides and the governor's arrest. You're the one who got the medal of valor, not me."

"Ah, now the truth comes out! Are you really upset because I got a medal for almost being killed twice?"

"Wait, we're getting way off the point. This has nothing to do with medals. This is about you acting like a child because I've got my own mind," Hank said.

"A child? Do you mean that?"

"Look, we're getting a little hot under the collar here, and I'm sorry, I didn't mean that the way it came out. I'm just frustrated. Have you given any thought to coming with me? I'm almost sure the chief would approve us going in as a team," Hank said.

"Narcotics? No. My future is in Homicide. Even though we end up looking at some sick death scenes, it's still a cleaner environment than the Narco Squad. Dealing with junkies and pushers and whores, not to mention the diseases they have. When I was in Patrol, a junkie drag queen made a pass at Rogers when he was printing her in the processing area, and when Rogers told her to shut up, she scratched him on the face with filthy fingernails. He asked me to leave the room, but I reminded him the room was under video surveillance.

"That class of people is at the very lowest end of society, and the chances of getting stuck with a needle or contracting hepatitis is higher than in any other bureau, but if you wanna go, then go. I'm not sure what the future will hold for us, but we can try our best to stay friends. Dean will be seeing Shawn every day, and I don't want our issues to interfere with their relationship at work."

"That's a little different than what you said the other day," Hank replied in an annoyed tone. The fact that Pat had made a veiled threat against Shawn's employment had made Hank furious.

"I was pissed and depressed. I love Shawn, and I wouldn't want any hardship to befall him because of this. Dean loves him too, and says he may have a management future with the bank. I wouldn't even begin to try and screw that up."

"Okay, well, I'm glad to hear that. I never told Shawn about your comment, by the way. So where do we leave this?"

"I guess that's entirely up to you. Tell you what. Whatever you decide, I'll support you. If it makes you happy to do this, then do it. I'll stand by you."

Hank got up, Pat rose to meet him, and they hugged. Pat felt like crying but was determined not to let that happen. They released each other and left the bar.

"You wanna go to the pool?"

"Nah, I feel like hitting the casino. Wanna join me?" Pat asked.

"Yeah, that sounds good. After the beating you took at blackjack last night, I'm sure you want to try and win back some of your money," Hank joked to conceal his sadness.

"Yeah. After seeing you shoot craps, you need to stay away from that table," Pat said with a laugh.

THAT night, they were attended to by Dong-yul and enjoyed another incredible dinner at the Queen's Grill. From there, they followed their now established pattern of joining up with the rest of the boys at the theater to watch that evening's entertainment. Afterward, they strolled around the deck, enjoying the warm breeze.

"Where's Clay?" Pat asked.

"He said something about going to work out or steam or something," Brian replied.

"Oh, really? Let's see if he comes home tonight. I hear the sauna is hopping at night."

Instead of joining the boys on their little jaunt around the top deck, Clay had returned to the cabin and changed into a bathing suit, pulling shorts on over it. He put on a T-shirt and sandals and went to the steam room, where he paid for a three-day pass. He wandered through the fitness club, and upon discovering the men-only steam room, he quickly disrobed, hung his towel on a hook, and then walked into the sauna naked.

When he looked around, he saw three other men already there. One elderly, one middle-aged, and one slightly younger. Two of them had decent builds, and the youngest was nude. Clay quickly checked him out, but the younger guy didn't seem interested in anything other than the steam.

Clay leaned back so that it was easier for the others to get a good look if they so desired. The elderly man got up and left the steam room. Clay noticed that both remaining men were wearing wedding bands, and his hopes of snagging a trick dimmed. The younger man got up and left, giving Clay a good eyeful. Disappointed that there was only one man left, who didn't seem interested either, he was about to get up and leave.

The middle-aged man spoke up. "Temperature is just about right, wouldn't you agree?"

Clay moved up to the top level of the benches so that he was even with the other man. "Yeah. I hate it when it's so hot that your lungs burn from breathing. This is just about right."

The other guy opened his towel, exposing his package to Clay's gaze.

"You married?" he asked.

"No, you?" Clay responded.

"Yeah. Wife and four kids who I love dearly, but they sure disrupt the love life. By the way, I'm Ryan," he said as he stuck out his hand.

"Hi, I'm Clay. How do they mess up your love life?"

"Well, the wife is always tired and never feels like doing it. I don't know how long it's been since I've had a good blow job," the man said as he spread his legs a little farther apart.

"That's terrible. A man shouldn't have to go more than a couple of days without getting his dick sucked… especially when it's one that as nice as yours." Clay looked directly at Ryan's cock.

"You like my dick? You think it's nice?" Ryan asked with a smile.

"Hell yeah, I like it. If you were gay, I'd be trying to get me some of that," Clay said as he gave his own dick a pull.

"Well, I'm not gay, but I wouldn't mind a blow job," Ryan said as he inched closer to Clay.

"You asking me to suck your cock?"

"It's there if you want it."

Clay didn't respond verbally. He just bent down and latched on. When the guy got hard, Clay had about eight inches to munch on, and he had a hard time going all the way down as the man got very thick toward the base. But to judge from Ryan's reaction, he was very happy to have a hot, wet mouth on any part of his dick.

Within five minutes, the guy shot a large load into Clay's mouth, and Clay swallowed it all. He continued to suck until Ryan's dick went soft, ensuring that he had gotten every last drop from him.

When Clay sat up and ran his hand over his mouth, Ryan smiled. "That was incredible. Only a man knows how to suck a cock that well. My wife has never given me head like that. I feel so… relieved."

"Good, I'm glad I could take care of that for you. Do you think you might be in need again before the end of the cruise?"

"Count on it, unless my wife begins to put out again all of a sudden. I don't cheat, and this was just a matter of a very urgent need. I would never let another woman go down on me, but with you, it's different. Do I owe you anything?"

"For blowing you?"

"Yeah. You provided a good service, and if you earn your living doing this, I'm willing to pay for it."

"Honey, I stopped charging for my oral talents when it almost got me killed. No, this service was on the house."

"Well, thank you again. Maybe we can meet in here around the same time in three nights?"

"Sure, if I'm not busy with my friends," Clay said.

"Fine. You have a good night," Ryan said as he used his towel to wipe his cock while Clay admired his tight ass. Clay's eyes followed the man as he walked out of the steam room, and he gave himself a tug.

Well, that was a pleasant surprise, Clay thought.

The only problem was that it left Clay as horny as hell, but not for long. When he left the steam room, he saw one of the men from the gay group walk into a shower stall naked. The guy looked down at Clay's cock and winked. Clay smiled, opened the door, and walked in.

Fifteen minutes later, Clay came out, fully relieved of his own load, dried off, and went to the cabin with a huge smile on his face. It had been a great night for Clay, and he filed it all away for future use as masturbation material.

IN ABOUT two days the ship would be in Hawaii, the one and only stop before Sydney.

When they got close enough for the passengers to see the islands, Pat and his little group sat on their balcony and watched the tropical beauty as they approached. While they enjoyed the scenery, they sipped drinks that Dong-yul had made for them. It was a good life indeed.

Chapter 7

CARL had finished his third day of surveillance on Jessica and Chris. He knew their daily routines better than they did. The fastidious work of his team enabled Carl to plan how and where he would get the targets separated and to the secure cargo area.

He typed a message on his handheld communication device: *4:30*

Within a minute there were six separate replies. The team had been informed that Carl wanted them to be on the private wireless network that had been set up by the advance party. At four thirty.

Carl kept his distance from Jessica lest he be recognized. On a few occasions, he had to make it look like he was interested in the other gay men on the cruise to throw off suspicions. On one occasion, Carl even left the bar with a muscle boy to avoid being seen by her.

At four thirty, the team logged onto the encrypted chat software and the briefing began:

SESSION OPEN (6 CHATTERS)

1: J.C. and C.P. are alone no security in sight. Routine is down pat, will continue as planned.
2: A.P. has two spooks following him around. Check on their background reveals they're corporate security agents. Changes needed. I'll have two additional targets and need one more operator.
1: 5 and 6 will assist. Pull video and conduct further surveillance. Additional will be dealt with prior to primary.

5: Roger.

6: Roger.

2: Roger.

4: R.C. is still secure. Wrench and cutters are ready.

1: Start clocks at 72 hours. Completion in 84 hours. Maintain current plan but note changes. Extraction on time. Keep your devices close. Any questions?

The screen flashed: SESSION CLOSED

Carl closed the software and switched on the feed from the ship's camera server. Chris and Jessica were in a nude embrace, engaged in sex yet again. Carl flipped to Alfred Patterson's room and saw that he and five other investors were meeting with an unidentified person. The two corporate security goons were seated near the doorway, paying close attention to the entrance. Carl could not tell if the two men were armed, but due to the cruise line's tight security, it was highly unlikely. Carl smiled as a thought popped into his head. He had just solved the problem of the two security officers, and it would be taken care of shortly.

The ship arrived at the island of Oahu on the fifth day of the cruise. The overhead intercom announced that shore excursions would begin in two hours.

One of the teams was assigned to follow Chris and Jessica if they got off the ship. They weren't scheduled for any sightseeing tours, but that didn't mean they wouldn't get off the ship to enjoy the island.

Carl opened the instructions to the Israeli communications disruption device and began to run through the preventive maintenance and services checks to ensure that the unit was still in working order. He had not used this type of device before, but knew it would prevent anyone on the ship from calling for help or broadcasting their position.

All communications would go offline an hour before Alfred Patterson would disappear. The ship's engines were then scheduled to become inoperable thanks to some sabotage to the software that ran the engines. The extraction team was scheduled to rendezvous with the ship in eighty-two hours and take everyone out of the area before communications came back online fourteen hours later. No civilians or crew members were to be harmed if it could be helped.

Patterson was on the boards of several weapons companies as well as the hotel investors group. Richie Cosgrove believed that Patterson had been at least partially responsible for his attack and wanted him to suffer as well. Patterson had placed pressure where it needed to be placed; that had been the tipping point for Chris Powell and Jessica Cosgrove that had caused the two conspirators to take drastic measures. So in Richie's eyes, Patterson was just as guilty as the drug-addict thug he had killed on the fishing vessel.

David Phelps was another target for Richie; David had facilitated the transaction's swift conclusion. He knew who to bribe to push the papers through the courts before Richie or his long-lost relative could make any noise about the sales.

Louie, the accountant, had been working for Richie since the days when the hotel chain consisted of three crappy little beach properties. At first Louie had resisted giving Jessica the information she had requested for the sale, however, he'd caved in when Chris offered him eight million under the table. Louie had disclosed everything that he knew about the hotels and where Richie kept his money stashed. There was almost nothing Richie owned that Louie didn't know about, save for two bank accounts Richie had set up on his own.

Richie had never trusted anyone enough to let him or her in on all of his secrets. His father had constantly reminded him how business partners would screw you in the end and that lesson had been wired into every fiber of Richie's being.

Richie's revenge plan was devised to look like a failed terrorist attack on a luxury cruise liner. Several very important weapons contractors were on board, as well as many aerospace engineers and investors, and the mercenary team members were old hands at this type of business. There was no reason it shouldn't work.

The materials Carl had brought on board consisted of the Israeli anticommunications device, a computer virus capable of seizing the engines, and a large binary chemical explosive device. The chemicals of the bomb were completely harmless until they were mixed. Once combined and triggered by an electrical spark, they would produce enough energy to sink even a ship the size of this one. Carl had rigged the detonator to abort if the ship's security failed; the bomb would only be used in the absolute worst-case scenario. Carl did not want to end the lives of a large number of innocent people. However, if they got between him and freedom, he wouldn't hesitate for a split second in killing them all.

The team's secondary mission directive was to harm no innocent people unless it was in self-defense. If everything went according to plan, Al-Qaeda would be blamed for attempting to blow up the *Queen Mary 2*. When the official investigators concluded their work, Richie's tracks would be covered thanks to the efforts of Carl's team and some very expensive bribes. There were very few ways that Carl could see the plan coming unraveled to the point that he would need to actually destroy the world's only true ocean liner.

DEAN'S group had decided to take a shore excursion and see a bit of Oahu. Pearl Harbor was in Honolulu, where they had docked, and none of the men wanted to miss seeing an important piece of history.

Pat, Hank, Dean, Shawn, Greg, Brian, and Clay all got in the security line to exit the ship. A large sign listed items that were approved for guests to take off the ship or bring back aboard, and others that had to be checked through security.

"Ugh, I can't believe we're not allowed to bring alcohol back with us. They charge way too much for the drinks on board," Clay complained.

"I agree. Ten dollars for a martini is outrageous!" Greg commiserated.

"Well, pretend you're going to prison, Clay. Shove a couple of gallon bottles of vodka up your ass and sneak them on board," Shawn said with a smile.

"Oh, sister, please! You're confusing my ass with that vacuous black hole you got going on," Clay said, winking at Shawn.

"Vacuous? Um, Clay, I don't think that word means what you think it means," Brian said. "Unless you were making a joke about Shawn's inane anus."

"Whatever," Clay said as they reached the front of the line.

They all presented their documentation to security and when they were all cleared, they proceeded down the walkway to the shore.

"Look at that water. It's amazing!" Hank looked down at the crystal blue water. It was clear enough to see the sandy bottom twenty feet down.

"Back home it's so murky, you're lucky to see one foot into the Potomac," Greg said as he put his arm around Brian.

Pat followed suit, putting an arm around Dean, and Hank and Shawn weren't far behind. Clay paid no attention to them. His sugar daddy had given him a strict limit of $20,000 to spend on himself, and he had mapped out the stores in Hawaii before the ship had even left port in California.

"Clay, I can't believe your boyfriend would let you go on a gay cruise without him. Where is he, anyway?" Dean asked.

"He hates cruises. He told me to go ahead with you boys and enjoy."

"How old is he?" Shawn asked.

Greg and Brian looked at Shawn as if he had just asked to bang their moms. "What?" Shawn's asked, confused by the disapproval.

"Never ask a sugar daddy's age," Greg said from the corner of his mouth.

Shawn attempted to change the subject before he ended up getting spanked again. "When do we get to meet him, I mean."

"He's always busy with work and stuff, but I'll ask him about doing a dinner sometime soon. You guys are always welcome to stop by if you call first."

"How'd you two meet?" Dean asked.

"Are you writing a book or something? I got some money to spend, girl, so let's go get some matching shirts for the white party," Clay exclaimed, dancing around like he was in a club.

As the boys continued their walk, a very well-to-do couple getting into a taxi caught Pat's and Hank's eyes. It looked as if there was someone following the pair.

Dean saw the look on his lover's face and shot a glance at Hank.

"Oh no you don't. I know that look, knock it off!" Dean said as he stopped walking.

"What?" Pat protested.

"What look, Dean?" Shawn asked.

"Not you, Shawn. These two are looking around for trouble. We are on a fabulously expensive vacation as friends. We aren't here to play *Die Hard,* so quit looking for shit, or I'm going to tie you both to a bed with blindfolds and ball gags." Dean pointed an admonishing finger at the two cops.

"Hot! Can I watch?" Clay said.

"Oh, come on, guys. Could we just have one normal trip, please?" Shawn pleaded as he stepped closer to Dean in a symbolic gesture of unity. "Otherwise, I'm adding a butt plug to that list of things to keep you in place!"

"Okay, okay! It's not like you can just turn off the cop sense, ya know!" Pat protested. "It's not easy to stop doing what you've done for five years almost every day. I mean, I catch you two reading the financial section while we're on the cruise."

"Just stop looking for trouble, buddy! When we get back to the ship, I'll show you trouble!" Dean said as he grabbed Pat's hand, and the group began to walk again.

"Yay, mommy and daddy made up!" Clay cheered as he clapped.

"Keep it up, son, and you're going to be getting a spanking!" Pat said.

Clay wagged his cute little ass at Dean and Pat. Greg stuck his foot out and touched Clay's ass with it. Everyone had a laugh, and they continued on to the Lanvin store.

As the group approached the store, Pat and Hank spotted the Waikiki Gun Club across the street.

"Look, Hank, they have the Smith & Wesson .500 Magnum available for test firing." Pat grinned.

"Screw that! I see the words 'automatic weapons'," Shawn exclaimed.

"Hey! I thought we were going shopping!" Greg said as the group changed directions.

"I'm with Greg and Brian. Could we just go shopping?" Dean said, rolling his eyes at the giddiness over firearms.

"I swear to God, those two are a handful," Shawn said, shaking his head at Dean.

"Let them go play with their guns. I'm going shopping. Who's with me?" Brian said.

Dean, Greg, Clay, and Brian turned to walk into the Lanvin store. Hank, Shawn and Pat went over to the gun club.

"Et tu, Shawn?" Dean bellowed.

Shawn threw his hands in the air as he walked backward with the group that had decided to go fire interesting guns instead of shopping for overpriced clothes.

Pat, Hank, and Shawn walked into the gun club and were greeted by a good-looking man wearing shooting glasses and a Glock T-shirt.

"Welcome to the Waikiki Gun Club. What can I do for you guys today?" the clerk said. Shawn squeezed between Pat and Hank, his eyes as wide as saucers as he stared at the automatic weapons.

"I see someone's anxious to get their hands on something that goes boom," the clerk said drolly.

"I've never shot a gun before, so when I saw the words 'automatic weapons,' I couldn't resist." Shawn was practically drooling.

"Well, safety first, sir," the clerk said as he handed Shawn a two-page form to fill out.

"What's this?" Hank asked.

"It's a liability waiver. If you're a convicted felon, you're not allowed to handle a firearm. By signing the waiver, you're stating that it's not against the law for you to handle a weapon. It also says that if you choose to handle a gun or you get shot on the premises that we cannot be held liable. Read it carefully, and then sign on the line at the bottom if you agree."

"Okay," Shawn said, signing the paper without even looking at it.

"I need your identification too… Shawn, is it?"

"Yep, it's Shawn, and here you go," Shawn said, handing over his Maryland driver's license.

Pat and Hank retrieved their police identification and driver's licenses. A placard on the wall stated that law enforcement would enjoy a 10 percent discount, so they figured they would take advantage of it.

The clerk took their ID and swiped all three licenses through a card reader. A beep indicated that none of three was a convicted felon, so they were able to rent guns.

"Prince George's County, Maryland. You guys are far away from home," the clerk said as he gave the IDs back.

"We're taking a cruise to Australia, and the ship stopped here for the day," Hank said as he placed his identification back in his wallet.

"That's a great cruise. The wife and I took it a couple years back."

"Um, can I have a gun now?" Shawn said, interrupting the exchange of pleasantries.

The three men smiled at Shawn's excitement, and the clerk turned toward the locked gun rack.

"How big do you think you can handle?"

"Oh, you'd be amazed how big he could take." Hank chuckled.

Pat slapped his partner on the arm and whispered, "Behave."

Shawn flipped Hank a middle finger behind his back as he stared at the MP5s and M249s.

"I've played *WarGames*, and I remember wondering about the SAW M249."

"That one is a thirty-dollar rental fee plus ammunition fee of twenty dollars for thirty rounds. Let me caution you that thirty rounds go very fast with this weapon. It fires twelve hundred rounds a minute," the clerk said.

"Ouch, that's steep," Hank said, as he winced at the price.

"I'll tell you what I'll do, officer, since he's your friend. Why don't I sell you the ammunition? I'll let you have one hundred rounds for forty dollars plus the rental."

Hank saw Shawn's face light up at the mention of one hundred rounds.

The clerk picked up on Shawn's excitement and started to pitch the specifications of the weapon to increase Shawn's desire.

"The M249 here fires twelve hundred rounds a minute, that's twenty rounds a second. When I did my tour in Afghanistan, this is what I carried with me. You could rip a car to shreds in seconds, and there's nothing like the smell that was all around you when you were done firing. Sure, the MP5 is cheaper to fire, and every Tom, Dick and Harry that saw any police movie wants to try it, but not many men could handle what this puts out. I'll even shoot a video of you firing it as a souvenir."

Hank could see that Shawn was sold on the weapon. He rolled his eyes at the clerk for laying the bullshit on so thick and handed the man his credit card.

"He'll take it," Hank said, gazing at his partner's smiling face.

"Thanks, but I can pay for it!" Shawn protested.

Hank winked. "Nope, this one's on me. I just want the video for later."

The clerk completed the paperwork and looked at Pat and Hank, "What about you two?"

"Automatic doesn't excite me that much. I want to try the Smith & Wesson .500 Magnum."

"Ah, a man who likes power. I get it," the clerk said as he ran Pat's transaction through.

Then it was Hank's turn, and it took him the longest to decide. Hank had been in the Army and had fired a lot of military hardware, so automatic and power didn't excite him quite as much as the other two men.

"I'm more into history, so I'm thinking either the World War II Sten gun or the Tommy gun."

"Well, if you want my opinion, go with the Thompson. It's a forty-five caliber fully automatic with a thirty-round clip. The Sten is just a very uncomfortable gun to fire, with the magazine on the side like that."

Hank thought about the gangster and war movies he had seen and decided he would use the Thompson submachine gun that had been favored by gangsters in the 1920s. The clerk ran Hank's transaction and handed each man a small yellow piece of paper.

"If it's okay with you, sir, we'd like to go one at a time," Shawn said.

"I'm short a range worker, so that's how I was going to do it anyway." The man hit a buzzer and motioned for the men to walk through a very thick steel doorway.

Pat, Hank, and Shawn walked into a secured room and were locked inside. After several minutes, a man opened the inner door, and they walked into the gun range. Each was handed a pair of shooting glasses and headphones to dull the sound of firing weapons. For the moment, they had the range all to themselves.

"Okay, gentlemen, Mike told me that two of you are cops. I'm guessing that means you know how to act on a range," the gun range employee said as he pointed to a large white sign that stated the range rules in large red letters.

"Yep, no problem, we got it," Pat said as he put his glasses and headphones on.

"Which one of you is Shawn?" the man asked as he grabbed the M249 squad automatic weapon from a bench.

"That would be me!" Shawn said like a giddy schoolgirl. He tried to hold back his excitement but it was impossible. The instructor smirked.

"Keep it pointed down range at all times. I'll load it and show you how to charge the weapon. Don't just hold the trigger back and fire away, shoot in three round bursts or the barrel will get hot as hell and you'll burn your hands."

The man extended the bipod on the end of the weapon and demonstrated to Shawn the correct posture and method of firing. "If you don't hold it like this, the gun will be all over the place while you're firing. Automatic fire likes to lift the front of the gun, so hold on tight. Got it?"

Shawn nodded, acknowledging the instructions he had been given. He walked over to the range master and watched as the man placed the green ammunition box on the weapon and fed the belt into the mechanism. Shawn bent at the waist and got behind the weapon like he had been shown.

Hank watched with erotic delight as his husband stood behind the machine gun and gripped it with such force that the muscles in his arms stood out in stark relief.

The range master yelled, "Fire."

The rifle erupted as Shawn pulled the trigger and the muscles in his arm vibrated with the staccato rhythm. A shower of brass casings and metal links fell to the floor. The sound of metal hitting concrete echoed throughout the chamber. The air became rich with the smell of freshly fired gunpowder. Hank closed his eyes and inhaled deeply.

"Cease fire!" the range master shouted.

Hank looked down range and saw why the man had told Shawn to stop firing. The target had been cut in half by Shawn's accuracy with the weapon.

"You still have about thirty rounds left, buddy. Nice shooting."

"Thanks," Shawn said with a big smile on his face.

"Want me to post another target, or do you just want to empty the can on the back stop?"

"Hey, Hank, you have to try this!" Shawn said.

Hank held both of his hands in front of his crotch to cover the massive erection caused by the testosterone in the air. The range master smiled knowingly.

"Relax," the range master said with a smirk. "You're not the first guy to pop a boner when someone fires this baby."

Shawn looked down at his partner's crotch.

"Put another target up. I want to rip some more shit apart," Shawn said with a crooked grin that showed his canine teeth. Shawn's body was pulsating with adrenaline, and he felt powerful. A feeling of powerless anxiety had been hanging over his head like a dark cloud ever since the night Keith Albright broke into the house and nearly killed him. Confidence flooded his body as he gripped the weapon firmly again and the range master yelled, "Fire!"

Pat and Hank fired their respective rentals with the accuracy expected of police officers before leaving the gun club to meet Dean, Greg, Brian, and Clay.

"Do my little warriors feel all manly now?" Dean teased.

"I'm pretty sure when they get back on the ship Shawn's going to be feeling something," Pat whispered in Dean's ear.

Hank heard what Pat had said and smiled. Shawn was, in fact, in some serious trouble when they got back to the bedroom. Hank put the video of Shawn firing the M249 in Greg's shopping bag and then they went to lunch.

AFTER lunch, they took a couple of cabs to the *USS Arizona* memorial. When they arrived, they saw a large circular viewing deck near the water and headed over to see what was on the plaques. A park ranger stopped the men and advised them to pick up their passes for the ferry ride to the memorial before they wandered too far. Passes went fast, and there was already an hour wait for the ferry.

"Do we have time to go out to the memorial itself?" Shawn asked as he looked at the rest of the group. Clay looked bored and was scouting the hot men walking around in shorts.

"Frankly, I'd skip dinner tonight to see this," Hank said. "As long as we get back on board before they set sail, I say let's go for it."

"I agree," Pat said.

Dean saw that they were intent on seeing the memorial; it seemed to mean a lot to them. Dean mentally wrote off tonight's dinner plans until he remembered who they'd invited to dinner tonight.

"You remember we invited the captain to dinner tonight, right?" Dean asked.

"Well, I'm sure if the ship leaves without us, we'll miss the dinner anyway," Hank said jokingly.

Greg and Clay saw that Dean was annoyed and volunteered to split off from the group and get the tickets.

"Hey, guys you can go look around while me and Clay go get the tickets," Greg said as he and Clay walked away from the group and got in line for the passes. The remainder of the group went to the viewing platform to see what the draw was. The circle was dotted with plaques and laminated photos that showed where each ship had sunk. White pylons with the names of the ships stenciled in black sat exactly where the ships had been moored during the attack.

"I remember learning about Pearl Harbor in high school," Shawn said while gazing out at the water. "It never really registered with me how big of an attack and loss of life this was until 9/11. Now that I see the harbor in person, I have a new perspective and it is truly amazing."

Hank moved over to his partner and put his arm around him. They walked around the circle hand and hand until they had read every plaque.

"Excuse me, guys." An obviously irritated man blocked Hank and Shawn's path.

"Yes?" Pat asked in a helpful tone of voice.

"I have my kids here with me, and they don't need to see that. I don't care what you do in your bedroom, but out in public it's another matter!" the man hissed.

The hair on the back of Hank's neck stood on end, and in an instant, hot rage filled his heart. He let go of Shawn's hand and took a step toward the bigoted homophobe. "Get away from us!" Hank hissed back.

The tourist sneered. "Fucking queers can't just keep it in the bedroom."

Pat stepped in front of the man as he started to walk away. "Are those your kids over there sir?" Pat pointed at the people staring at them.

"That's none of your business, tough guy. They don't need to see a display of your sinful lifestyle, so take it somewhere else. Now get out of my way."

The man attempted to walk around Pat, but the cop sidestepped and blocked him. Hank saw that Pat was becoming enraged as well, and the park rangers were taking notice also.

"Just drop it before there's a problem," Dean told Pat.

"Yeah, why don't you do what your little boyfriend says?"

Pat felt he needed to do something to strike back at this man, but a physical response could get him arrested and ruin the vacation. Just then Clay and Greg walked up with the passes for the ferry and stopped in their tracks as they sensed the tension. Brian whispered what had happened in Clay's ear.

"Oh for Christ's sake." Clay grabbed Greg and kissed him passionately. Then Clay broke the embrace and got on one knee, holding Greg's hand. Greg had no idea what was going on but he played along.

"Greg, I've known you forever, and I've loved you ever since the orgy in New York. I want you to make an honest man out of me, baby. Will you marry me?"

Greg fought back a smile and covered his face as if he were crying. "Oh my God, yes! A million times yes!" he cried.

Clay jumped up, and they kissed again, even more passionately. The man and his family stormed off and got into their rental car. Most of the crowd was not sure how to react until Pat and Hank began to applaud. The park rangers and crowd joined in, and the happy couple strolled over to the ocean romantically. The two boys couldn't hold it back anymore and laughed until tears rolled down their cheeks.

"What the hell was that?" Dean asked.

"Brian told me what the guy said to you two, and I decided that if he wanted his kids to have memories of gay men in Hawaii, we could give them one that they would never forget." Clay was smiling ear to ear as he continued to laugh.

"I love you three. We're never going anywhere again without you guys. The vacations just wouldn't be the same," Dean said.

An older couple walked over to the group and congratulated Clay and Greg. They wished them good luck as they walked away and intensified the inside joke. The men went to the ferry and were whisked away to the *USS Arizona* memorial.

As they walked the bridge that crossed over the battleship, they noticed that drops of oil would occasionally leach to the surface. A rusted smoke stack from the ship sat partially exposed from the water line. The boys asked a stranger to take their picture near the railing of the memorial, and they then all paused to reflect on the meaning.

After a half hour visit to the memorial, the men decided to head back to the ship in an attempt to make dinner.

Chapter 8

THE four men arrived in the dining room two minutes before their seating time and received a warm welcome from the maître d'. A blond man in his forties and a redheaded woman who could have been a model were already seated at the table with the captain and another man wearing the uniform of an officer.

The captain and the ship's officer stood up as the four men approached the table.

"Gentlemen, I'm Captain Samuelsen and this is my chief of security, Lieutenant Commander Michael Kaspersky. This lady and gentleman are Jessica Cosgrove and Christopher Powell." After everyone had shaken hands, they sat down.

"I hope we aren't in trouble, Captain!" Shawn said.

"No, why would you think that?" replied Captain Samuelsen.

"The chief of security is here to greet us for dinner. I thought maybe something was wrong."

"No, actually, Mr. Kaspersky had heard who my dining companions were and did a background check, as is required. He tells me that the two of you are quite famous detectives, Mr. St. James and Mr. Capstone."

Pat and Hank blushed.

"After a four-year tour in the Navy, I worked Metro for twenty years before taking this job," Kaspersky said. "As soon as I saw the names I double-checked to make sure that it was actually you guys. I wasn't going to miss the chance to meet you in person."

"Well, thank you," Hank said sheepishly.

The sommelier came to the table and presented the wine list as the busboys filled water glasses. A second wave of servers came out and placed trays of cheese and fruit.

"My security chief and I are not permitted to drink, but allow me to buy you a bottle of wine." The captain signaled and the sommelier brought over two bottles of Spätlese.

"That's not necessary, Captain, but we appreciate it," Pat said.

Dean shot Pat a look of fiery death. It was considered rude to turn down a gift from the captain of the ship. Pat quickly looked at the label of the bottles and apologized for his faux pas.

"So, Captain, that bridge of yours is pretty amazing. Who designed this ship?" Chris Powell asked. The rest of the table sat quietly as the captain answered.

Jessica rolled her eyes and slugged down her wine before anyone else had been served. She raised her glass to signal that she wanted more, and the sommelier filled it.

When everyone had been served their wine, they began to snack on the cheese and fruit.

"So Mr. Kaspersky, what did you do in DC?" Dean asked the security chief.

"I worked Patrol for about five years when I started out. My beat was down by the shipyards in Southeast DC, then I moved on to SWAT, which I loved."

"I thought about joining SWAT," Hank remarked.

"Well, it's very exciting, definitely a lot of action. When I started to burn out, I transferred into the boat patrol and got certified as a diver. That was one of the most boring assignments I've ever had in my life."

"Why's that?" Pat asked as he sipped from his wine glass.

"I just didn't like patrolling the Potomac as much as I thought I would."

The waiter came to the table and presented the appetizer menu, carefully explaining the preparations before he left. A wave of busboys cleared the cheese and fruit plates and refilled the water glasses.

"So where did you end up after boat patrol?" Shawn asked Kaspersky.

"I moved into Narcotics work, mostly interdiction stuff with very little undercover."

"I've been thinking of getting into Narco myself," Hank said.

With everything that had happened at the Pearl Harbor memorial, Pat hadn't thought about Hank's transfer once all day. He stared at Hank for a second and then looked away.

The wine had started to kick in, and Hank was feeling warm and loose.

Dean kicked Shawn under the table in hopes that Shawn would change the subject.

"Great work, very dangerous, though," Kaspersky said before he asked the captain if he had ever heard of the detectives before.

"I'm afraid not, but then I spend so little time in American waters."

"So, what exactly do you know about me and my partner?" Hank asked the security chief.

"Well, recently a guy who was killing prostitutes in Rock Creek Park got off on a technicality and tried to kill you. You guys killed him, though, didn't you?"

The captain stopped in mid conversation with Chris Powell and shot the security chief an admonishing look. Obviously he didn't consider body counts appropriate dinner conversation.

Chris Powell grabbed his wine glass and proposed a toast. "To our crew, may the voyage be a safe one."

Everyone raised his glass and took a drink, and Dean figured he would redirect the conversation.

"So where are you from, Captain?"

"Originally, I'm from the Netherlands, but since I got into this line of work, I found it was easier to live in the United Kingdom since the *QM2* usually sails from there."

"What made you become a captain of a cruise ship?" Dean asked.

"As a kid, I worked on my father's fishing boat. I grew up around the water and decided I wanted to be a captain when he died. After a few years of commercial fishing, I moved on to the merchant marine and ended up captaining a car carrier from Korea to the United States.

That got boring, so I joined up on a cruise ship as a third officer and worked my way through the ranks to captain."

"Sounds like this kind of work is in your blood, Captain," Chris added.

"It truly is. I can't imagine doing anything else."

"I know how you feel," Pat said.

"So, Mr. Powell, tell me about you and your lovely companion," the captain said as the appetizers arrived.

Dean's eyes widened as he remembered where he'd heard the name Jessica Cosgrove. The financial trade papers had covered Richard Cosgrove's attack, as well as the hotel sales, very closely.

"Of the Cosgrove Hotels chain?" Dean asked before Jessica finished her little speech of introduction.

"Well, not anymore. I'm retired now," she said with a smile.

"We're just investors at this point in our lives. I've been thinking of investing in a couple of different fields, and we decided that we'd come on a romantic trip together and relax," Chris said. He glanced at Jessica, and they smiled at one another.

Shawn wondered what Dean's fascination was with the Cosgrove hotels. He decided he'd ask Dean after dinner.

The security chief's phone buzzed, and he excused himself.

"Just like back home, you're never actually off duty," Pat said as he nodded understandingly at the security chief.

The security chief ended his call and came back to the table. "I apologize, but duty calls. It has been a real pleasure to meet everyone," he said as he waved goodbye.

"Hey, chief, one second," Hank said as he got up from the table to chase after the man.

"Yes?" the chief inquired.

"I would love to trade stories with you. How do I get a hold of you?"

"I'd enjoy that. If you want to do a middle of the night snack or something, I can meet you." Kaspersky handed Hank a card with a number on it and then hurried away.

When Hank returned to the table, Dean and Chris were in a heated debate about business law. Shawn listened intently to the dry financial details as Pat chewed and tried to look interested.

The meal went on for an hour, and near the end, the captain had to excuse himself to attend to a matter. Jessica and Chris had no intention of staying once the captain was gone and quickly said good night. They didn't say anything else, but it was plain that they didn't find the company of homosexuals to their liking.

"Did you really feel it necessary to bring up our previous honeymoon on this ship?" Pat asked Dean.

Dean had drunk several glasses of wine at dinner, and as the conversation heated up over finances, his tongue loosened to the point he revealed that the four men were married. He went on to complain that they didn't have the same benefits as married people so all of his money could end up in probate or going to his parents when he died.

"Those two were snobs," Dean said.

Pat cleared his throat and looked around at the opulent environment they were in while picturing Greg, Brian, and Clay eating with families and kids. His silent reproach didn't go unnoticed.

"Are we ready to get out of here?" Shawn asked.

"Yeah, let's go get changed and find something to do," Hank replied.

The men got up and went back to their suite to change.

CARL sat at the upper deck poolside bar looking down at Patterson and his two bodyguards. He pulled his hat down lower on his brow as a long-haired man wearing a T-shirt with an antiwar slogan walked over to Alfred Patterson.

The bodyguards immediately stood up to block the man's path to their employer. The long-haired man sidestepped them and feigned walking away before he pivoted on his heel and addressed Patterson.

"You warmongering old man!" he said, pointing a finger.

Alfred Patterson had become used to these types of people. He got up and attempted to walk away.

"You coward. You can sell missiles but you can't talk to me face to face? You fucking rich coward!" The long-haired man—who was in fact a member of Carl's team—was doing everything he could to call attention to himself. His second goal was to have ship's security respond so they would be close to him for the next phase of the plan.

"Excuse me, sir. You need to leave," the large black bodyguard informed the protestor.

"Mind your own goddamned business, lackey," the protestor said as he continued shouting antiwar slogans.

"Let's throw him in the pool and cool him off. Sound like a plan?" the white bodyguard said.

"Yep."

Carl's communication device beeped and three words were displayed on the screen: *Security en route.*

Carl knew that the guards would be there in less than thirty seconds. He removed his sunglasses to signal two more members of his team. One of the men headed toward the bodyguards as a secondary diversion.

"Hey, get away from my boyfriend," one of the mercenaries shouted at the bodyguards as he ran toward them.

Enough of a distraction had been created that no one would notice the person carrying out the primary objective.

The final participant in the plan walked over to the bodyguards' backpacks and pretended he was tying his shoes as he placed a handgun in each bag. The butts of both weapons were left sticking out so someone would see them. He then walked past the two men as a signal to his compatriots that it was time to disengage the targets.

"Fuck you, Patterson! Come on, let's get away from this murderer and his goons," one of the mercenaries said as they disengaged the targets and headed for the back section of the ship, where they had stashed a change of clothing.

The men used a master key to enter a secured storage room. They opened two bags with a gay cruise line's logo on the outside. Within thirty seconds, the men had completely changed their appearance and clothing. They took two large bundles of methamphetamines from the bags, ready to put the next phase of the plan into motion.

Two very flamboyant males exited the storeroom chatting about the steam room and working out in the gym. Anyone who saw them would never think that they were mercenaries or protestors.

Carl looked around for someone that he could use to alert the responding security guards and found a couple that had been watching the disruption. The woman looked disgusted, and the man was clearly an overprotective jerk. Carl went down the staircase and walked over to them.

"Wow, lots of action on this ship, right?"

The man looked at Carl as if he had two heads; the woman decided she would acknowledge Carl's existence.

"Unbelievable. I knew this would happen when I saw there was a group of gay guys on board," the woman whispered to Carl.

"I know. People just can't be decent toward each other anymore. They need to learn how to—are those guns?" Carl said, focusing intently on the bags with the handgun grips sticking out.

The man broke his hateful stare at Carl and looked in the direction Carl was pointing. It took him a few seconds to spot what Carl was talking about, but when he did see the guns, he grabbed his girlfriend and vacated the area quickly. Security emerged from the elevator the man and woman were heading for, and the man stopped one of the guards and pointed the bag out.

The security officer removed his radio from his belt and walked toward the bags. One of the two bodyguards escorting Patterson stopped and grabbed the bags. Security immediately ordered all three men to freeze. Tasers came out of holsters when the bodyguards failed to follow the instructions.

Patterson instructed his bodyguards to obey security, and they reluctantly stood down. Security led the two bodyguards into an employee elevator. The only thing people on the pool deck knew for sure was that two guys who were arguing got arrested by Security.

Carl went back to his cabin, satisfied that this part of the plan had worked as designed. It wouldn't be much longer before they could bring the master plan to fruition.

THE security chief made good time getting from dinner with the captain to his office when notified that two passengers had been found on the pool deck with firearms. There were no firearms permitted on board except for those stored in the armory in case of an attack on the vessel.

When the chief of security arrived at his office, two men were in handcuffs secured to the wall. On his desk were two forty caliber Glock 27 handguns with full magazines sitting next to them. The security chief picked up one of the weapons and saw that the serial number placards had been removed. He field-stripped the handgun and pulled the barrel from the upper receiver. The serial number normally displayed on the breech had also been obliterated. Chief Kaspersky looked at the two restrained men and shook his head. "Why do you two have guns on board my ship?" he asked as he reassembled the weapons.

"Those are not our weapons," the black bodyguard stated.

"Really? Then whose weapons are they? I would track ownership with the serial numbers but they've been rather thoroughly removed," Kaspersky said as he took a seat behind his desk.

"Fuck if I know. Ask your security staff where they came from, because we didn't bring them on board," the black male replied impatiently.

"Their sea passes say they're Roger Manor and David Enfield," the lieutenant said as he turned toward his boss.

"Okay, Mr. Enfield and Mr. Manor, if these aren't your guns, then whose are they?" Kaspersky inquired.

"I want my lawyer," Manor yelled.

"Oh? Is that right? Lieutenant, were we still in US waters when these were found?"

"No, sir, we'd been in international waters for a good hour when Officer Joshua Holbrook observed the two men acting suspiciously around a Mr. Alfred Patterson. A passenger stopped Officer Holbrook and pointed out the handguns in the bags these two were carrying, so they were taken into custody."

"So US law doesn't apply, does it, Lieutenant? These two aren't entitled to shit. Right?"

"No, sir, they're not."

"You planted those weapons! We work for Mr. Patterson as bodyguards! If anything happens to him, it's on your head!" Enfield bellowed.

The lieutenant looked at Chief Kaspersky and shook his head.

"The plot thickens. Two men who claim to be Alfred Patterson's bodyguards are on board but are telling me that they aren't armed."

"It's illegal to bring guns on board the ship, asshole. I'm not going to prison for it!" Manor replied to the rhetorical question.

"Take these fucking handcuffs off, and I'll show your ass why I don't need a gun!" Enfield blustered.

"Alfred Patterson, one of the largest arms dealers around, sits on the board of KENYO weapons research and development corporation. That man has a lot of enemies, so I'm going to check on your story and see if you really are bodyguards. Even if it turns out you are working for him and not here to do something to him, it is illegal to possess firearms on a cruise ship, and you will be prosecuted.

"Lieutenant, you and Holbrook speak with Mr. Patterson and see if this story checks out. Let me know if they really are personal security. Until we sort through this, I'll notify the captain of what happened. Put these two in the brig for now."

The security staff grabbed both men and led them to the brig.

Kaspersky secured the two weapons in his safe and then dialed the direct line to Captain Samuelsen.

"What can I do for you, Chief?" said the captain as he answered the phone.

"I'm reporting two passengers that had guns on deck. We detained them and the weapons are secured."

"How the hell did they get the guns on board the ship, Mister Kaspersky?"

"They are allegedly Alfred Patterson's bodyguards, so I'm guessing it was for security purposes. The serial numbers are scratched off the weapons, so tracking them back to a point of origin is going to be difficult. As for how they got on board... we'll have to investigate that, sir."

"See that you do. Do we need to return to port?"

"They weren't actively employing the guns, and they didn't draw them on our staff. An officer saw the butt of a gun sticking out of a backpack that belonged to the bodyguards. I'll put my staff on higher alert and send out some more plainclothes to be around Patterson, just in case."

"Confine both men to the brig until we have more information. Find out how those guns got on my ship."

"Yes, sir!" Kaspersky ended the call and began his investigation.

CARL reached his cabin and entered the room. He was pleased that the team hadn't needed to kill the bodyguards. Even though Carl killed professionally, he did not enjoy murder. He preferred to live and let live if circumstances permitted and that was how he led the team.

Carl pulled out his small communications device and typed the words *chat in five*. He then pulled out the small laptop computer and set up the virtual private network. The computer did not require Internet or any other type of relay device; it was a self-contained communications server that only communicated with the other devices slaved to it. All transmissions were heavily encrypted making it nearly impossible for anyone to read what was typed in the chat program without the proper keys. Any capable device with the proper encryption key within a one-mile radius could log onto the network when the host device was activated.

The device was powered up and at the five-minute mark the screen flashed a message in large green letters:

SESSION OPEN (6 CHATTERS)
1: Status of waters?
6: On ice for at least forty-eight hours
1: Good work 3 and 4
2: So are we a go?
1: Everything is on track. Keep an eye on the clock
4: The package is getting unstable
1: Advised. Take no action yet.

4: Roger that

1: 6, I need 3 and 4 in the areas we talked about.

6: Final sweep has been completed.

1: Okay. Continue as planned. 4 you and the package meet me on the bow tonight when they turn the lights off around 11:00 p.m. Wear the hat and glasses.

4: Roger

SESSION CLOSED

If Richie was becoming a liability, he would be eliminated, and the team would just await extraction at that point.

THE phone in the security lieutenant's office rang, and he answered quickly.

"Security."

"Hi, this is Hank Capstone. I'm calling for Chief Kaspersky."

"He's not in right now."

"I'm just doing a follow-up call. We met at dinner, and I wanted to see if he was free to meet up tonight. Could you just leave him a message that I called?"

"Okay, sir, I'll let him know that you called. Goodbye," the lieutenant snarled. What did this guy think he was... a secretary?

The lieutenant quickly scribbled a message and threw it on the pile of papers on the chief's desk. Returning to his desk, he placed his laptop in a lower drawer. He was glad that after this cruise he could get off this godforsaken tub and not worry about ship security again. Shortly, he would be able to retire in style and live a life of leisure.

"Hey! Hey! Yo, buddy!" Enfield shouted down the hallway to the lieutenant.

The officer rolled his eyes as he walked down to the holding cells to face Mr. Enfield.

"Yes?" the lieutenant said in a drawn-out, breathy voice.

"I want to speak to my consulate or a lawyer. You can't just hold me here indefinitely. I'm also hungry as hell."

"Look lieutenant, has anyone spoken to our employer yet?" Manor said in a calmer voice. "I don't mean to be a pain but this is a pretty fucked-up situation. You have to admit that."

"I'll see what I can do about food," the lieutenant said. "As for your consular official, it's a pretty long swim back to Hawaii, and the only appeal you have on a ship is to the captain, so fuck you and your lawyer, you piece of shit." The lieutenant grinned at the rude bodyguard and walked away.

"Fuck you, you scumbag. Let me out of this cell, and I'll show you who the piece of shit is!" Enfield screamed.

"Calm down, Enfield, they clearly have us by the balls here. I just want to know where the guns came from," Manor said to his agitated partner.

Enfield paced back and forth in his cell, punching the walls occasionally.

The lieutenant called the kitchen and requested one plate of food for the prisoner Mr. Manor. Prisoner Enfield could starve to death for all he cared.

"OKAY, I don't mind telling you guys I'm super pissed off! We're here on vacation, maybe once in a lifetime, and where are our husbands? We haven't seen shit since they took off after that security dude," Shawn moaned.

"I was just thinking the same damn thing. Everywhere we go, it seems they can't leave their cop personas at home. Here we are in the Pacific Ocean, and you'd think they'd be more interested in popping us in the butts again, but no. They're off doing God knows what!" Dean said in agreement.

"Gentlemen, I'm sure your men are fine and are doing well. I take care of you both while they're gone. Drink?" Dong-yul interjected.

"Hell to the yes! Make me a cosmo, please," Shawn answered.

"I'll have a scotch on the rocks, Dong-yul."

"At least we have a great butler. Glad someone is enjoying his service!" Shawn said, still annoyed.

Dong-yul walked from behind the wet bar with two drinks on a tray.

"May I do anything else for you? You maybe like to take shower or sit in bathtub? I can run water for you and assist."

"That sounds good. Would you run a bath? My friend and I can slip into it and relax," Dean said.

Dong-yul smiled. "Very good, sir, I do that at once," he said as he scurried off to the bathroom.

"You know he just wants to see us naked again," Shawn said.

"Yeah, so what? He's gay. We're hot. What's the harm of his getting a little extra joy from his dull job?"

A few minutes later, Dong-yul came out to the main room.

"You're bath is ready, gentlemen. I put bath salts in water, like you like. Shall I make you two fresh drinks to sip while in tub?"

"By all means, Dong. We might as well get hammered since we've been abandoned," Dean replied.

"Dong-yul take good care of both of you," the butler said with a smile.

Shawn and Dean walked into the bathroom, dropped their clothes, and got into the tub, one at each end. Dong-yul picked up their clothes after getting a good eyeful and removed them from the bathroom. He brought in two bathrobes and hung them from the shower door.

"Mr. Shawn, meant to ask, notice you have scar on otherwise fine behind. How it happen? Boyfriend rough?" Dong-yul asked with a raised eyebrow.

"Ugh. No, Dong, it's actually from a bullet. I was shot in the ass by a homicidal maniac that our husbands managed to attract to our home."

"Such a shame to mar such beauty. But Dong-yul happy you okay other than that!"

When Dong-yul had left the bathroom, Dean chuckled. "It seems your ass has a fan."

"I'll have you know, my ass has had many fans, and they usually don't dump it for work shit!"

Three minutes later, Dong-yul brought in fresh drinks and set them within easy reach of the men.

"You want maybe I should scrub your backs?" Dong-yul asked.

"No, we wouldn't want you to get your work clothes all wet."

"Oh, no problem, I take clothes off and be naked like you men, then it not matter!"

As much as both men would not have objected to seeing Dong's tight little ass, Dean drew the line.

"No, that wouldn't be good, Dong. We think you're hot, and we wouldn't trust ourselves with you being naked. You can go now, thank you."

"Ah, too bad. I come back in half hour and check?"

"Sure, Dong, you come back and dry us off, okay?"

The butler broke out in a broad smile and replied, "You bet, I'll be back to do that."

He pulled out two towels and placed them on the counter so that he could quickly attend to them. He also laid out a cloth bathmat for the boys to stand on.

"I'll be back. You wait for Dong-yul, okay?"

"Okay," Dean said.

When the door closed, Dean and Shawn laughed at how obvious Dong-yul had been.

"I think he wanted to do a whole lot more than dry our backs off," Shawn said.

"Of course he did. He's cute too, and if I wasn't married, I'd take him up on his offer. But he can dry us off as a cheap thrill. Again, no harm. Unless you object?"

"No, that's fine. What will I do when I have to start drying myself off at home?" Shawn asked and laughed as he grabbed his drink and sipped.

THE lieutenant sat down and typed authorization orders into the chief's computer. He was informing the security staff that certain cameras would be going down for critical upgrades. The officers' patrol rotations as well as the alert rosters had been changed to leave certain areas open and without surveillance. If anyone looked closely at the assignments, it would appear as if they were assigning additional resources to watch for exterior threats. The lieutenant smiled because even if these orders were questioned, it would look as if the chief of security had done the reassignments.

The explosive device had been put in place after the last bomb sweep. There wasn't another sweep scheduled until they docked in Australia. The communications disruptor was active and awaiting commands from the central terminal in Carl's room. The engine sabotage was a bit more difficult because the command server was not part of the security network. The lieutenant knew that if they did not shut down the engines far enough away from Fiji, help could be on board within hours. The extraction team wouldn't be able to approach a moving cruise ship to retrieve the team, so the entire plan hinged on his ability to shut down the engines and kill communications.

Any physical damage to the engines could strand them at sea for weeks, so a software problem was the way to go. Carl had provided the lieutenant with a computer virus to upload into the maintenance network; the lieutenant had switched an on-board network technician's key with the infected one. When he logged into the network for his daily inspection, it would instantly download the dormant virus. The swift-acting virus would cause the engines to shut down and give false readings to all test equipment. Diagnostic tests would indicate that the engines had seized, and the engineers would have to physically disassemble the housing units and pumps to find the problem. This problem would take even a great engineer at least sixteen hours to solve. The staff of the *Queen Mary 2* boasted some of the best engineers outside of the US Navy, so sixteen hours would probably be the outside edge of the window of opportunity.

A WAITER arrived at the security station and dropped off a food platter for Mr. Manor. The lieutenant took it to the holding cell and slid it through the opening designed for just that purpose. Mr. Enfield protested loudly at not being fed as well. The lieutenant walked away, smiling with perverse glee as he was cursed in two languages.

When Chief Kaspersky arrived back at the security station, he heard the commotion coming from the holding cells.

"What the hell is that all about?" the chief asked.

"Enfield is being an asshole, so I didn't feed him. His buddy got a nice steak, though."

"You are a sadist, do you know that?" the chief said as he took a seat at his desk.

"I try. So what's the story with them?" the lieutenant inquired.

"They check out clean for the most part. They're employed by Alfred Patterson, and as far as he knew, they didn't bring guns aboard the ship. They did apply for permission but were denied, so I'm not convinced of their innocence yet."

"Yeah, well, let them rot for a while! If Enfield gets out he's going to be nothing but trouble."

"I talked to the captain, and he's leaving that up to me, so if they're going to be dicks, let them sit for a night or two."

"That's what I say." The lieutenant placed his hands behind his head and leaned back in his chair. He'd been paid to get the bodyguards out of the way and that task had been accomplished.

Unbeknownst to the lieutenant, Carl had put a backup plan into place. When the two mercenaries had changed clothes and disappeared into the crowd, they detoured to the bodyguards' cabin and placed a large amount of methamphetamines there. If the men had gotten released, he would've tipped security off to the two "drug dealers."

At 10:30 p.m., Carl watched the stern of the ship as he waited for the lights to dim as per a request from the gay group. The entire deck had been reserved for the group, and Carl had learned that the stern would serve as the play area because it was out of the sight of the other guests.

None of it bothered Carl. Throughout his career, he had had to seduce men though he was not attracted to that type of activity. He was a true professional and did what needed to be done in order to fill the client's orders.

At eleven o'clock Carl, watched TJ and Richie walk toward the stern. Richie was a very attractive man in his thirties, and TJ had a sculpted physique that would make the statue of David jealous. The two of them had men cruising them from the moment they appeared on the stern. Carl took the elevator and walked to the area where he'd seen them disappear.

As Richie's eyes adjusted to the low lighting and he saw what the men were doing to each other, he quickly became uncomfortable and started to make sounds of disgust. TJ saw that Richie was getting noticeably nervous and knew that their cover would be blown very fast indeed if they didn't blend in. He grabbed his pretend lover and slammed him face-first up against the wall, bringing his lips as close to Richie's ear as he could without physically touching him.

"If you don't put a smile on your face, I'm going to stuff it with my cock. These men are watching us like hawks, and you look like you're going to puke. Carl will be here any second, so show me a smile and then nibble on my ear."

"What?" Richie said, astounded at the man's request. "I'm not doing that!"

TJ swung Richie around and pinched a nerve in his neck, which took him to his knees, and with one swift motion, TJ popped open his pants and let them drop. TJ gripped Richie by the hair and pushed his head into his groin.

"Now pull my shorts down and suck my cock, or you'll not see what the sky looks like when the moon reaches its zenith."

Horrified, Richie pulled down TJ's boxers and gasped at the size of his cock.

"I can't do this. It's huge!" he whined.

TJ took his cock in hand and hit a pressure point on the other man's jaw that made his mouth open. Callously, TJ shoved his dick into the gaping hole.

Carl walked up to the two men and shoved the back of Richie's head, forcing TJ's cock down his throat until he gagged. Richie resisted until Carl licked his ear and whispered, "Start enjoying this like all three of us are going back to my room to fuck or you're going over the rail, Richie. Do you know what happens when you fall over the side of a cruise ship that's going as fast as this one?"

Richie fell a chill down his spine and tried to relax as TJ pumped his mouth.

"You get sucked under the ship until you end up in the pods that propel it. Now come off TJ's dick, stand up, and put your arms around your boyfriend Drew here. I've got some stuff to tell you."

A small, twinkish man approached the trio and asked them if there was room for one more.

Carl winked at the twink. "Sorry, honey, we only like men. We don't fuck boys."

Clay scurried away in a huff with his nose firmly in the air. Richie felt as if he was in a *Twilight Zone* episode as he spit over the railing. TJ kept his arm around Richie and nibbled on his neck. Richie tried to look like he was enjoying it, but felt like he was being raped in prison.

"I want you to remember one thing, Richie. You wanted to be here. We could have done this whole thing without you, but you demanded to come along, so now you play by our rules. Nod your head if you understand," Carl said as he grabbed Richie's package.

Richie winced slightly as Carl's hand moved into his pants. He felt Carl push a piece of paper inside his underwear, and then he leaned in as if he was going to kiss Richie on the side of his neck not engaged by TJ.

"You're going to make the final deposit into that account right after you leave here. Everything is in place, and you will get your wish shortly," Carl said as he moved from Richie's neck up to his ear.

"That wasn't the deal, Carl. I said you can have the rest of the money after this is done," Richie whispered.

"Look me in the eyes, Richie. If I say something's going to get done, it gets done… *believe me*. If you refuse payment then the contract is cancelled and the penalty is severe," Carl said, nodding toward the ocean.

"Look, the bitch—" Richie's words were cut off as Carl quickly locked lips with him. The mercenary knew that Richie had been about to make reference to his ex-wife, and the number of men who had gathered to watch them play had gotten too big. Carl grabbed TJ and Richie's hands and pulled them away from the play area.

As the men walked away, Carl brought Richie in close as if to hug him. "Just wire the money and be ready. We make our move shortly, and after it's all done, we'll be extracted near Fiji. Don't do anything unless TJ tells you to. Unless, of course, you'd rather suck on TJ's cock for a while before we cut your throat. By the way, TJ will also be more than happy to fuck you up the ass in front of the entire gay group on this ship, so just keep that in mind."

"I got it!" Richie felt dirtier than he ever had in his life. He had never had any man licking and kissing him like that before, let alone taken a man into his mouth, and he couldn't wait to shower. When the men were out of sight of the gay group, Carl separated from the other two and disappeared. TJ led Richie to the business center so he could make the necessary preparations.

"What assurances do I have that you won't just kill me or take the money and disappear?"

"You have Carl's word. Believe me when I say that you wouldn't be here right now if it wasn't for him."

"What do you mean?"

"What the boss says goes, and that's all there is to it. Just transfer the funds. We'll take care of business and get the hell off the gay Love Boat."

Richie sat down at the terminal and logged onto his bank's website. The money was transferred into a trust account that would release the funds when a password was delivered. After logging off the computer terminal, Richie turned to see TJ shaking his head.

"What? I did what you asked."

"That was pretty smart, Richie. I saw you set up a transfer password. The money doesn't get released without it."

"So? That doesn't violate the agreement. It's just a safeguard."

"If Carl knew you did that, you wouldn't see morning."

"I'm not disabling that feature... Drew," Richie said, using TJ's fake name.

"Not a problem, you'll get what you paid for, you can be sure of that. I just hope you're ready for it."

Chapter 9

THE guys slept in and didn't bother going to breakfast. Dong-yul made sure that there was at least one pot of coffee delivered while everyone was still asleep. The butler smiled as he quietly brought in the tray and set it down. He looked around at Pat and Dean, entwined, and Shawn's fine, well-built, young body. Dong-yul drank in the sight before leaving as quietly as he had entered.

Dong-yul was gay and always delighted when he had gay guests to tend to. He made sure he took good care of "his" men. It also made him miss his homeland, where his former boyfriend lived. He had left him to take to the seas to make money to send to his family, and he was often homesick. Having kind, handsome men like these to take care of made him feel better.

Around ten o'clock the phone rang, waking everyone up. Dean grabbed the phone without opening his eyes and said, "Yeah?"

"Hey, it's Brian. You sound like you're half asleep. Are you guys still in bed?"

"Yes, Brian, we are. We had a lively night with dinner and the show afterward. How come we didn't see you guys?"

"Oh, ah, well, we decided to blend in with the gay group on the stern."

"You were all out whoring, you mean. I bet there are a lot of men waking up today with big ole smiles on their faces." Dean chuckled.

"Ha ha, we weren't that bad. Clay's trying to talk us into going to the steam room with him. Says he blew some married guy who was all backed up from not getting any. Said it was real hot."

"I'm sure he did. In case you don't know it, there are more things in this world besides sex."

"True, but can you name me many that are more fun?" Brian laughed.

"Not at the moment, but I haven't had my coffee yet. Hmm, there seems to be a pot of it sitting on the wet bar. Damn, Dong-yul is sneaky!"

"Are you guys coming down to the pool when you get your faces on?"

"More than likely. Give us an hour or so and we'll see you there."

Dean hung up the phone, got out of bed, and went over to the coffeepot to pour his first cup of the day. The other guys woke up, stretching and yawning. Dean poured coffee for everyone and served it to them in bed.

"Where did this come from? Hank asked.

"I'm assuming that Dong-yul was in here while we were all sleeping," Dean replied.

"Aw, that means he saw me naked!" Shawn moaned.

"He's seen us all naked. Just enjoy your coffee while I brush my teeth."

LATER that night, Louie, Richie's former accountant, and Chris, Richie's former lawyer, met for a drink in the ship's casino. They sat at the poker table with three other men, enjoying a slow-paced game of Texas Hold 'em.

"How's the wife liking the cruise, Lou?" Chris asked.

"She's amazed by the size of this ship. To be honest, it stung a little bit when I wrote the check. Twenty grand is a lot of money," Lou said as he folded.

"Don't be so cheap, buddy. You're about to be a very wealthy man. Get used to affording the best things in life," Chris said as he patted his business partner on the back.

The other three card players got into a betting war that caused Chris to fold his hand as well.

"I worked for the Cosgroves well over twenty years, and I was lucky to afford a pound of salmon. Soon I'll be able to buy ten pounds of caviar when I fly to Russia to pick it up." Louie managed a small grin. He still felt bad about selling Richie out for a very large payday, but his wife was insistent that he do it. When he worked for Richie Cosgrove, he made $200,000 a year. The lawyer had waved an eight million dollar payday in front of him and his wife and they'd seized the opportunity. The money was going to be disbursed after the final payment was made in Australia. After that, Louie and his family would never have to work again.

"After the payments are made, I'm thinking about throwing in with this investors group. This guy Patterson has his hands in everything; most of the people in his group are directors for a couple different Fortune 500 companies. Just think of the power we could have." Chris took a long pull of the scotch in his glass.

"This is my last hurrah," Louie said. "I'm not looking for any power. I just wanted to retire and make sure my kids were set for the future."

Chris was the dealer for the next round. He dealt everyone their two hole cards and put the deck down. The hand played out normally, the players unaware that one of their number was a mercenary. Heinrich's native German accent kept anyone from engaging him too deeply in conversation. He pretended to speak only broken English as he monitored the table.

Louie lifted the corner of the two cards that he had been dealt; he had a pair of queens and knew he would be betting heavily into the hand. Chris picked up his cards; he had a pair of aces. The undercover mercenary folded his hand so he could observe the two men and gather some intel on where they might be going tomorrow night. The place for the execution had been chosen, but the team needed to get the targets away from their groups. That was the opportunity that Heinrich was listening for.

The other two men in the hand matched the big blind bet, as did Chris. Louie felt the need to place a large bet to scare away anyone that might be bluffing their way through the hand.

"Three hundred, on top of the blind."

Chris whistled loudly. "Pretty confident in those cards, mister," he teased.

"Whip out some cash, big spender, and find out."

After the announcement of a three hundred dollar cash bet, the only two left in the game were Chris and Louie.

"All right, big guy, let's see what you got. I raise fifty more."

Louie matched the bet without batting an eye. Chris wasn't sure if Louie was bluffing. The man's face was unmoving, and he seemed to be extremely confident in what he was holding.

Chris discarded the first card and turned over three more. He smiled when the third card turned over was an ace. Louie took another peek at his cards and started to calculate the odds of Chris having a better hand than him. The odds were in Chris's favor, but Louie wasn't going to give up without a fight.

"I'm in for two hundred." Louie slid the chips from in front of him into the pot.

"What happened to three hundred Lou?"

"Oh, stop it. You lawyers are all the same! Talk, talk, talk. Let's see some action."

"Nervous?" Chris asked.

"Oh, please, I'll bet you the bar tab for the entire day tomorrow that I've got you beat. So I'll call all in."

"So... unlimited booze?"

"Yes, and if I win, same thing goes for you."

"What bar do you gentleman drink at? The prices on this ship are outrageous." Heinrich asked in a thick German accent.

"Well, if I win, we're going to the English pub on the promenade, I'll tell you that much!"

"Amazing!" Chris exclaimed. "That was my choice too. I hear they have a great thirty-dollar lager beer."

"You're a two-beer queer anyway. I'm all in as well. Let's see the cards already," Louie complained.

Chris turned over his two aces, and with the additional ace that came out on the flop of the first three cards, he had the highest three of a kind you could have in poker.

Louie leaned back in his chair and sighed as he turned over his pair of queens.

"I can taste the fish and chips already, baby. I wonder if they have champagne there," Chris wondered aloud as he discarded another card and flipped over the turn card.

It was a queen. "Uh-oh, is that sweat I see forming on your forehead, Chris?" Louie said.

"I have three aces, you have three queens. Last time I checked, aces were higher in this game."

"Are you going to talk or are you going to deal the last card so I can beat you already!" Louie said tersely. "I'll tell you what. I want to raise the bet. Are you game?"

"Interesting… I'm listening."

"Nope, you have to agree to this blindly. Either it's a raise or we play the last card right now, leaving the bet as is. I thought you had balls, Chris. After the last couple of months, I would've sworn on a stack of Bibles that they must be elephant balls. Did Jessica take them away or were they hers to begin with?" Louie could see he was getting to the lawyer, and it did his heart good.

"Fine, what's your raise, asshole?"

"Loser has to sit in the sauna naked all day tomorrow!"

"What the hell kind of bet is that? Why would I care about sitting in the sauna naked? I do that all the time at the gym back home."

"I'm guessing this is the first cruise you've been on that included a large group of gay men."

The other men at the table chuckled.

"What! That's a ridiculous bet. What is this—high school?"

"Hey, you're the dumbass who agreed to a blind raise. So play or fold?"

"You're a prick, but since I have three aces, I'm going to make sure I'm extra hydrated so I can stay there the whole time and watch you get hit on by men."

The man with the German accent pretended to be offended by the conversation, grabbed his remaining chips, and left. In actuality, the two thieves had just given him exactly what he needed, and there was no point in hanging around the scumbags any longer.

"And I thought Europeans were so open and understanding," Chris whispered to the remaining men at the table.

Chris dealt the last card, a six of hearts that made him the winner. He laughed. "Tomorrow is going to be the most fun day of this whole cruise."

Louie threw his cards on the table in a huff, pissed that he had let greed and his competitive attitude lead him into the shit again.

"I'll see you tomorrow afternoon," Louie said as he stood up from the table.

"Oh no you don't. You said all day, and I'm having mimosas with breakfast and making this an all-day affair."

"You would do that, you drunk," Louie said as he walked away to avoid more insult to his wounded pride.

IN TJ and Richie's cabin, TJ became more and more irritated at Richie for trying to password-protect the transfer of funds. He wanted to just kick the shit out of him, but then he got an idea that would punish Richie while providing hours of entertainment.

He pretended to get a message over his comm device.

"We gotta go sit in the steam room and see if one of our targets is going there regularly. If so, we'll hit him there another time," TJ said.

"Why do I have to go?" Richie snarled.

TJ smiled." Because we're lovers and we should be seen together. If you need another reason, it's because I said so. Now let's go!"

Still mumbling to himself, Richie went to the steam room with the mercenary. The locker room was full of gay men, and Richie didn't want to take off his clothes.

"Get naked now," TJ hissed, "or I'll tear your clothes off and throw you to these gay boys like a chew toy. Sound like fun?"

Richie grimaced but complied, and they entered the crowded steam room. TJ held his towel in his hand while Richie wore his wrapped tightly around his waist. One of the few men who weren't orally involved with a partner spoke to them.

"Hi, I've seen you two around. Are you together?" he asked.

"Yeah, sure are. Ten years now," TJ answered, letting his legs fall apart as he sat down.

"Your lover's lucky. You're hung like a horse!'

"He loves sucking my cock, right, honey?" TJ said.

"Um, sure, whatever you say."

"In fact, he likes to play a game. Want to watch?"

"Sure!"

TJ told Richie to get on his knees one level lower. At first Richie pretended he didn't understand. TJ grabbed Richie by the back of the neck and pulled him between his legs.

"Suck my cock, bitch," TJ said as he stroked his dick to get it hard.

"I will not!" Richie replied.

"See, this is where the game begins," TJ said to the round-eyed spectator.

Using his considerable strength, TJ forced his entire cock into Richie's mouth. Richie coughed and gagged on the length of it, but he couldn't break TJ's iron grip on his neck.

The rest of the men in the steam room gathered around to watch as TJ began to pound his cock into Richie's face. As Richie gagged and retched, TJ face-fucked him for over five minutes. After he pulled out, he shot his load in Richie's face. Richie gasped for air as cum dripped down his cheek.

TJ finished by wiping the head of his dick on Richie's tongue. "Good show, boys?" he asked casually.

Everyone clapped. "That was hot as shit, man," one of the onlookers said. "Your boy really acted like he didn't want your dick. Can you fuck him now?"

Richie got up and ran out of the steam room to throw up.

"He likes it rough. You should see how hot he gets when I take a belt to his ass!" TJ said.

The crowd made enthusiastic noises. "Can I?" the first guy asked.

"If you're a good boy, we'll see."

TJ left the steam room and took a shower right away. As he washed, he chuckled when he heard Richie throwing up in one of the stalls. He dried off, then got dressed before going over and pushing open the door to Richie's stall.

"One last thing, Richie. I was standing right behind you when you set up your password for that account. I've locked you out, and the money has been transferred already."

THE captain had ordered the security staff to search the bodyguards' rooms as part of their investigation. They discovered thirty plastic bags containing methamphetamines. The security chief was called to the room as soon as the contraband was found.

The chief of security arrived at the cabin to find his lieutenant sitting in front of a pile of small plastic bags.

"What do you have for me, Lieutenant?" asked the chief.

"During the search we found methamphetamines hidden in a book. Thirty individual bags adding up to a pound."

The chief of security had worked Narcotics in Washington, DC, and something didn't sit right with him about this. "Did you find any money?" he asked.

"About ten bucks," the lieutenant replied as he continued to log the evidence.

"Thirty bags of meth weighing in at a pound, so… about a half ounce per bag. It's currently going for seventeen hundred dollars an ounce, so the packaging just isn't right for a dealer or a smuggler."

"What do you mean, Chief?" Officer Holbrook asked as he paused in his search.

"For the most part, no one on board will have enough cash on them to buy even a single bag of this crap. We use sea passes, and dealers don't take credit. Yet it's packaged for sale, not for smuggling."

The lieutenant attempted to make a joke. "All right, so they're shitty drug smugglers!"

"A smuggler would package this so it would be easy to dump if he needed to get rid of it quickly. Thirty small bags mean you have to make sure to grab all of them. It just isn't smart."

"You heard those two in the cells. I don't think they have master's degrees," the lieutenant said, looking up from his clipboard.

"Holbrook, come with me. Lieutenant, secure this meth in lockup," the chief of security said as he left the room.

"This is a job for a newbie!" the lieutenant protested but was drowned out by the sound of the slamming door.

The security chief and Holbrook walked down the hall to the elevator.

"What do you need me to do, Chief?" Holbrook asked.

"I worked Narcotics for a long time, and this whole scenario isn't sitting right with me. Since you're my tech geek, I want you to pull the video from the hallway and elevator cameras. See what keys have been used to access that door in the last forty-eight hours. Don't look at the names. I want you to identify the key numbers, and let me know as soon as you're done."

"Yes, sir. May I ask what I'm looking for?"

"I'm not sure myself. I was a cop for a long time, and the one thing I learned was that if my gut said something was out of whack, I should investigate it." The chief looked up as the elevator bell chimed.

The elevator door opened on Pat, Hank, Dean, and Shawn. Pat and Hank recognized the security chief, and Hank greeted him.

"Hey, Chief, how's it going?"

"Keeping busy. You know how it is." The chief was polite, but clearly had something else on his mind.

"I called your office earlier and left a message for you."

"I didn't see anything on my desk, but that thing is a mess right now. Is everything okay?"

"All is well. I just wanted to get together so we could chew the fat."

"I have a question for you, if you don't mind."

"Fire away."

"How much does an ounce of meth go for in your area?"

Pat laughed. "Why, are you in the market?"

The chief smiled politely at the trite joke. "I just wondered. I've been off the street so long I thought I'd ask someone who might have more recent knowledge. "

"Well, we work Homicide not Narcotics, but from what I'm told, it's between fifteen and seventeen hundred an ounce."

"Have you ever heard of it being packaged in half ounces for sale?"

"Not really. A street dealer wouldn't carry that much weight on him because he'd get federal time if he was caught, and if he got robbed that's a big loss," Hank said.

"Thanks for the information."

"Need help with anything?"

Shawn kicked the back of Hank's shoe, and Dean's eyes shot daggers through the back of Hank's head. The security chief saw the reaction of Hank's friends and decided against involving the two celebrity policemen.

"Got it all under control, but I'll keep your offer in mind. I'm going to be having a quick dinner with the captain tonight. If I'm free after that, I'll meet you around nine on the promenade. We can talk then if you like."

The elevator pinged as it arrived at its destination.

"See you at nine!" Pat said as he shook the chief's hand on exiting the elevator.

The doors closed and Holbrook asked a question.

"Who were they, Chief?"

"Two of the best detectives I've ever had the pleasure to meet."

"You're not really going to involve them in our investigation, are you?"

"Never discount experience, because you'll never know everything. Second, no, I don't plan on involving them in one of my investigations. Third, just do your job and I'll worry about mine."

The chief and Holbrook arrived at the level where the security offices were maintained. Holbrook went over to a computer and retrieved the surveillance footage. The chief did some background on the two guests in his holding cells. The jailer asked the chief if he could take a short break, and he was excused.

"Chief, all of the footage in that section is blank," Holbrook said excitedly.

"What do you mean it's all blank?"

"There's a note that the cameras were down for a half hour for maintenance."

"Who ordered that?"

"You did, sir. It says they were out of service for critical upgrades," Holbrook said as he pointed at the approval codes.

"I never authorized that!" The chief was red-faced as he clicked through the different outages in the suspect area.

"Let me see who did the maintenance," Holbrook said, happy to finally put his community college computer classes to work. "I have something here, Chief." Holbrook enlarged a frame of video.

"Who did the maintenance?"

"The logs are blank, but it was your keycard that was used to open the bodyguards' room as well as the computer maintenance areas." Holbrook began to feel uneasy having the chief standing behind him. The chief seemed to be in the middle of everything that was going wrong.

"You don't move from this computer until you find out what else I allegedly authorized," the chief told Holbrook "If you move, you're fired. Am I understood?"

"Yes, sir." Holbrook's hands felt clammy.

"Relax, Josh. I don't know what's going on, but I didn't do it. Report to no one else but me, do you understand?"

"Yes, sir."

Chief Kaspersky walked down to the holding cells. He sat down on the bench across from the cell doors and faced Enfield and Manor.

"So where did you two get the meth?"

"Excuse me?" Manor replied.

"Fuck you, man! Now you're planting drugs! What kind of ship is this?" Enfield shouted.

"Enfield, you're not helping. Shut up and calm down!" Manor said calmly.

"We found thirty bags of methamphetamines in your cabin. I need to know what you thought you were going to do with it."

"Listen, Chief, I understand you have a job to do. I know we're at your mercy, and I wouldn't believe me, to be honest. But the guns are not ours, and we did not bring any drugs on board," Manor said.

"What about your employer?"

Enfield snorted and laughed loudly. The chief ignored Enfield and continued to address his questions to Manor.

"What about our boss? Are you asking me if he would stick guns in our bags and then hide his drugs in our room?"

"Is any of the stuff his?"

"No, and it's not ours, either. You tell me if either of us looks like a meth head," Manor said as he unbuttoned his shirt and smiled to show his teeth. Enfield followed suit and stripped his shirt while smiling. There were no injection sites on their arms and their teeth were pristine. Neither man had lesions from scratching at bubbles under the skin.

"Why would anyone set you up?" the chief asked as he stood up from the bench.

"We're here to guard one of the richest and most hated men in the world. With us out of the way, an enemy would have a chance to strike at him. Right now his back is probably being watched by his secretary."

"Sit tight, boys. I'm doing some more investigating before I decide anything."

"Like we have a choice?" Enfield shouted as the chief walked away.

After Chief Kaspersky was out of earshot, the bodyguards held a whispered conversation.

"You know Patterson's going to end up in the sauna again," Manor said.

"Yeah, the old bastard can't keep it in his pants. He's hooked up twice on this cruise already. Even brought one of them back to the room."

"What? When?"

"Second day out to sea."

"If someone is trying to get us out of the way, it worked. We need to get back up there, and soon, or we're going to be unemployed and most likely unemployable," Manor lamented.

"Well, Captain Rent-a-cop isn't going to let us out anytime soon. At least we still get our bonuses."

"True, the contract does say if we're incapacitated, we still get the hundred thousand sign-on bonuses."

Chief Kaspersky called the captain and filled him in on the events preceding the phone call.

"You're sure that they weren't selling the drugs on my ship?"

"Sir, to be honest, something doesn't smell right. I'm looking into it right now."

"Call me the moment you have something solid, Chief."

The chief terminated the phone call just as Holbrook recovered a frame of video that showed two flamboyantly dressed men on the same deck as the bodyguards' room. They were carrying gym bags as they exited the elevator.

"What am I looking at?" the chief asked.

"These two don't belong on this deck."

"How do you know they aren't just lost?"

"You need a special card to get into that elevator. Now, watch as they get back in five minutes later. See that?" Holbrook pointed at the gym bags the men were carrying.

"The bags are lighter," the chief said. "Something's missing from that caved in corner. Did they use the same keycards anywhere else on that deck?"

"Yes, the same keycard was used to deactivate the bodyguards' lock and a maintenance room on the pool deck level in the stern area," the young officer said, almost panting like a puppy dog.

"Good work, kid, disable that key and let me know where it's been used since."

"I disabled it as soon as I found out it was used in an unauthorized door. The problem is that it hasn't reappeared since."

"Pull up footage of the pool deck incident with our two guests."

"Once again, most of the cameras were out for maintenance authorized by your codes."

"We have a mole!" the chief said as he pounded a fist on the desk.

"Are you sure, Chief? Couldn't there be another explanation?"

"Just keep this to yourself. No one gets to see or hear it. I'm calling the captain."

The chief went into a separate room to make his call.

"Sir, we have a mole among the crew."

"What do you mean?" the captain asked testily.

"Someone has access to a lot of restricted areas on the ship, and the video surveillance keeps going off-line. Someone is using my authorization codes."

"Do you trust your security staff?"

"Yes, sir."

"You have my full permission to do whatever you have to do to deal with this. Any level one officers are to be issued sidearms as of now. All quick reaction force members are to be issued full boarding gear. If this is some type of terrorist threat, we need to quash it now."

"Yes, sir, I'll open the armory and call the staff up. Terrorism crossed my mind as well. Someone seems to have gone to a lot of trouble to take Alfred Patterson's bodyguards out of commission."

"Why would anyone do that?"

"He's the head of weapons research and development at KENYO arms, so it's not too far a stretch, sir."

"I don't want to panic the guests, so keep this as low-key as possible. We'll continue to Fiji and stop there."

"Yes, sir."

The call was terminated, and Kaspersky exited the room. The lieutenant was in the office, yelling at Holbrook.

"What's the problem here?" the chief asked.

"I found the little shit messing with the camera logs. He's fucking done when I get through with him!"

"I doubt that, since he was acting on my orders," the chief said, staring down his underling. "Holbrook, release the prisoners and inform them that they're free to resume their bodyguard duty. Bring them to me before they leave. Understood?"

"Yes, Chief."

"You're letting them go? They had a pound of meth and two handguns, and you're just letting them waltz out of here?"

"We found surveillance that showed the drugs were most likely planted, and as for the guns, we have them in custody so they're out of the equation."

"If something happens it's on your head and not mine!"

"Who do you think you're talking to? If I didn't need everyone on alert, and you weren't the armory officer, I'd lock your ass up for insubordination!"

The two bodyguards came in, and Enfield stared at the lieutenant like a ravenous lion.

"I'm real scared!" the lieutenant scoffed.

Manor put a hand on Enfield's shoulder. "We're free to go?" he asked the chief.

"For now I think it's more important that you protect your boss than rot in my holding cells. You're subject to recall, though, and if you cause the slightest trouble, I'm locking you back up until Australia."

"Understood, Chief," Manor said, and the two bodyguards left the room. Enfield stared at the lieutenant right up until the door to the security office closed, and then the two men hurried back to Alfred Patterson's side.

"Lieutenant, go to the armory and start issuing sidearms to all level ones and full gear to the boarding repel team. Holbrook, I see you passed firearms training so I'm promoting you to level one as of right now."

"Thank you, Chief!" The excited young officer shook Kaspersky's hand.

As the lieutenant left the room and headed to the armory, the chief put his hand on Holbrook's shoulder. "I'm giving you a gun because we have no idea who the mole is. You're the one with the most information, and I want you to stick by me until we resolve this. Now go get your gun… and congratulations."

Holbrook nodded and hurried purposefully down the hallway to retrieve a sidearm. The lieutenant was typing something on a small device but put it away quickly as Holbrook approached.

Chief Kaspersky called out the alert code over the portable radios and then went to the armory, collecting Holbrook on the way.

The armory's large waterproof steel door opened and the lights came on. This was the first time Holbrook had seen the entire armory lit up, and he was impressed. "Here's a bulletproof vest to go under your uniform shirt and here's your firearm," the lieutenant said as he signed a paper giving Holbrook custody of a forty-caliber Glock.

Kaspersky passed by and called to Holbrook to follow him.

"Grab a holster on your way out," the lieutenant said as Holbrook joined the chief.

CARL lounged in his cabin, watching the targets on the surveillance cameras. Heinrich had reported that Chris and Louie would be at the sauna together at midnight, and Carl was passing the time until the team could finish this job and be extracted. His communications device beeped, and he got up from his comfortable position to retrieve it from the table.

"Shit!" he exclaimed.

The screen read, *"Watchers free."* This was not good news for Carl's plan. He cursed again when a second chime rang out and the text read, *"Security on alert."*

Carl sent out a mass text message to the team reading, *"Chat ten minutes,"* before setting up his communications terminal and opening a program that showed the ship's position and speed. The screen also displayed the projected course shown next to the current course and position. It appeared that the captain was speeding the ship up. Carl needed information, and he needed it fast, or the plan could unravel and their extraction would not happen.

Carl booted up the chat server and the screen indicated that he was online with only five chatters—one was missing. Unfortunately, it was the most important one, the security lieutenant. Carl prayed he'd been delayed because of the alert.

SESSION OPEN (5 CHATTERS)
1: Status update: watchers free, security on alert.
4: Abort?
1: Negative. Contingencies in place. Extraction
will be ten hours earlier than scheduled. We
begin in four.
1: 5 and 6 I need A.P. as soon as it begins. Use
honeypot plan if necessary. 4 bring R.C. to the
designated cargo hold. 2 and 3, forget the sauna
meeting. Too late retrieve targets before dinner.
Then meet at the hold.
5: Watchers? Ice or incapacitate?
1: Use your judgment. Prefer incapacitate if
possible. Restrict collateral damage so
extraction doesn't get complicated.

NEW USER LOGGED ON (TERMINAL 4)
4: Sorry, alert had me tied up.
1: I need four security uniforms and four guns.
4: Impossible while we're on alert.
1: Make it possible.
4: Impossible sorry.
1: Everyone stay with the plan. The extraction is
changing. Meet in the place we set up.

Carl was extremely annoyed by the security lieutenant's inability
to provide uniforms and guns. The team had weapons on board, but he
would prefer that they use the cruise line's guns.

1: The plan has moved up by ten hours. Make
sure the cargo hold is open and that you have
J.C. there at the new time. Smalls will be left
alone. It will be too complicated to get him in
the hold.
4: I can handle that no problem.
1: I hope so. Listen up team. I will be batting
cleanup so make sure we're all on the same
page. Communications will be down
permanently in six hours. If you miss extraction
you will need to make your own arrangements.
Meet up at assembly area.
1: 2 meet me at my room for details.
2: Roger
3: Roger
4: Roger
5: Roger
6: Roger
CHAT SESSION CLOSED.

Carl ended the chat program and ripped out the communications
card. He pushed a red button that caused the machine to smoke
profusely and rendered it unusable.

All of the surveillance equipment immediately shut down, and Carl threw everything over the balcony. Now the only communication he had with his team was the small device on his belt, and that would go down, too, when he activated the disruption device. As Carl carried out the necessary steps, he thought about the bothersome security lieutenant. He hadn't completed the job he was paid for, and in Carl's world there were consequences for failure.

TWENTY minutes later, there was a knock on Carl's door. It was the security lieutenant, reporting as ordered. Carl opened the door, but the officer did not enter the room.

"Come in, please. I can't exactly give you a huge envelope of money in the hallway, can I?"

"If this is about the uniforms, Carl, I can't do anything about that. All of the guns are signed out too," the lieutenant said nervously as he walked into Carl's room.

Carl could smell the lie, but his hearty tone revealed none of his suspicions. "Hey, don't worry about it. I'm a mercenary, and we improvise, adapt, and overcome all of the time. It's just part of the job. So what put ship's security on alert?"

"The chief is playing this one close to the vest. All I know is that the ship sped up and we're making an unscheduled stop in Fiji."

"I need you to send a message to this number on the ship's satellite phone."

The lieutenant took the scrap of paper Carl held out. "I have a satellite phone in my office, so that shouldn't be a problem. What do you need relayed?"

"Give these coordinates to whoever answers; they'll give you a confirmation code. I want you to bring that back to me within a half hour."

"You mentioned payment?"

"When you bring me the confirmation code, you'll get the money. Make sure you get Jessica Cosgrove to the cargo hold an hour before extraction. You cannot be late. If you miss that deadline, I'll have you killed or hunt you down myself, but you will die, clear?"

"Crystal clear," the lieutenant replied as he left.

The security officer feared that he had fatally crossed the mercenary by refusing to provide uniforms to his men. In a panic, he went to his room to fetch four of his uniforms for Carl, but there was no way he could come up with five firearms.

The lieutenant left his berth for his office and relayed the mercenary's message from Carl. He received the code and returned to Carl's room with the number and the uniforms. For his trouble and his treachery, he received an envelope containing $50,000 as well as the number and password to an account that held $500,000 more.

An hour before the communications and engines were set to go offline, Alfred Patterson was lounging by the pool eyeing some boys. His meeting with Louie, Richie, and Jessica wasn't for two more hours. Plenty of time to ogle pretty boys while Manor and Enfield watched everyone who walked by. The bodyguards had told Patterson that going out in public right now was a very bad idea, but he had reminded them who signed their paychecks.

Patterson sat up in his lounge chair when a blond young man walked into his line of sight and did his best to get Patterson's attention. Patterson was riveted as the twink took an ice cube from his drink and rubbed it on his neck and chest. Patterson swallowed hard when the sexy blond circled his nipples with the ice cube. Water from the melting ice gleamed as it ran down the tight abs to the top of his red Speedo.

Patterson nodded to communicate his interest, and the boy winked at him before bending over to rinse his hands off in the pool. Patterson's guards saw the byplay and became concerned. When Patterson walked over to introduce himself, they followed.

"Alfred Patterson. My friends call me Fred," he said, extending his hand to the twink.

"I'm Oliver, and it's nice to meet you, Fred. I adore your sexy silver hair," the kid said as he ran his hands through Fred's hair.

"I appreciate the compliment, but don't do that in public again. I'm somewhat famous, and I don't like people taking pictures of me. Why don't we go to my suite where we can relax in my hot tub?"

The twink cooed, thrilled to have bagged some sort of celebrity.

The bodyguards' disapproval showed in the stiff set of their shoulders as they followed their boss and his pickup away from the pool.

"So what are you so famous for, Fred?" the young man asked.

"I'm rich."

"My favorite kind of famous. Will your boyfriends be joining us?" the twinkie asked, looking back at the large men behind them.

"They're my bodyguards, not my boyfriends, and I don't think they'd enjoy it. Besides, I want you all to myself," Patterson said as he patted the twink on the ass.

The men entered the elevator, and Patterson pushed the button for his floor and then placed his room key in the clearance slot. The doors opened two floors early, and two members of Carl's team got in, dressed as armed security officers. The elevator stopped on Patterson's deck, and all six men got off. Carl's mercenaries put a key into the slot that would hold the elevator on that deck until they released it. The two bodyguards looked back down the hall and saw that the elevator was still open.

The disguised mercenaries complained loudly that the elevator had gotten stuck again. One of them pretended to contact maintenance as they walked down the hall, passing Patterson and his security force. Patterson placed his key card into the door slot, the suite door opened, and then Patterson and his twink entered the room. The two bodyguards turned to check the hall again. They were startled to see the security officers standing in the doorway, but their surprise didn't last long. They hit the ground, unconscious, as Patterson chased his pickup toward the bathroom.

Patterson and his trick were so wrapped up in their grab-ass session that they failed to notice the bodyguards slumping over with hypodermic needles in their necks. The two mercenaries quickly dragged the guards away from the door and closed it as Patterson stopped by the liquor cart.

The twink had been paid a thousand dollars to seduce Mr. Patterson and get him back to his room. The twink was not supposed to enter the room, but it was too late now. The men only had one more syringe, and it was for Patterson, so disposing of the decoy would require another method.

The young man turned from peeking in the bathroom door and saw the mercenaries advancing. "Oh my God," he gasped.

"After what I paid for this room, that better be your reaction," Patterson said as he poured the brandy.

One of the mercenaries was already on top of the twink with a piece of wire around his neck when Patterson turned with the drinks in his hands. The glasses fell to the floor as he backed away in shock.

"Wha-what do you want?" Patterson stuttered.

The mercenary touched Patterson's neck with a stun gun, and he fell to the floor. After injecting Patterson with a strong sedative, he removed the syringe and capped it. The man who was strangling the twink felt the boy go completely limp, but held the garrote tightly for another thirty seconds to make sure the decoy was dead.

The man who had rendered Patterson unconscious went to the door and looked out the peephole. There was no one outside, so he retrieved the large cleaning cart from the hallway near Patterson's room. The mercenary allowed the cabin door to close as Holbrook approached in full security uniform. Holbrook looked the man in the eyes and nodded in acknowledgement.

"Are you holding the elevator for something?" Holbrook asked.

"Yeah, the boss needed us to restore the cameras. I'm just waiting for them to get back with the rest of the stuff that needs to go down."

"Well, hurry up, we're getting complaints about the elevator being stuck on this floor."

"Yes, sir," the mercenary replied as he walked away to grab the modified cart.

The man knocked on the door of Patterson's suite, and his partner opened it. "How are we gonna do this? The cart was made for one person, not four."

"Why did you kill the little one?"

"I paid him to take off after Patterson opened the door, but he came in for some reason. I didn't have enough syringes for both of them so I took him out."

"How long until the bodyguards wake up?"

"If I dosed it right, eight hours."

"Let's strip the bodyguards naked and put them in bed with the little one. If housekeeping walks in, they'll think it's a three-way and get the hell out."

"What about Patterson's staff? Won't they come looking for him if they don't hear from him?"

"His schedule is clear until a dinner meeting tonight. That's where we're grabbing the rest of the targets."

The men stripped the bodyguards and placed them in bed with the twink, arms all entangled as though they were cuddling. They wiped the room of prints and blood and then exited the room as if they were domestic staff, not cold-blooded killers.

They entered the elevator and used the override to go straight to the cargo-hold deck.

After they secured Patterson in a large steel shipping container, they went to the house phone and called Carl's room.

"We made the delivery."

"Keep the champagne on ice until the rest of us are there," Carl said.

"Will do."

"Reservations are for one hour from now, so I'll see you then."

Carl ended the call and dialed TJ and Richie's room.

"Dinner's ready. Get it while it's hot."

"Sounds good," TJ replied.

Carl pulled a briefcase from under his bed. There were several lines of Hebrew on the outside of the metal lid. He opened the shiny silver case and turned on a power switch. He typed in the command codes and set the communications jammer to activate in five minutes. The countdown began; Carl closed the case and then slid it back under the bed. When it was active, the device would stop all electronic and radio-wave communications in the area. The ship couldn't even be sure of its position, thanks to the device's ability to interfere with satellite communications.

Carl removed his communications device from his belt and typed one word: "*Go.*"

Chapter 10

THE security chief met with the ship's captain regarding a missing persons report. He informed the captain that he believed it had nothing to do with recent events, but a nineteen-year-old passenger had disappeared that afternoon. The chief assured the captain that he would check the video and make sure the boy hadn't fallen off the ship. He was crossing the pool deck when Hank and Pat spotted him. They jumped up from their seats and put their shirts on.

"I'm curious why he wanted to know about meth," Pat told his partner.

"He looks like he's in a hurry. Are you sure we should bug him?" Hank asked.

"Worst he could say is go away."

The rest of the group was getting drinks at the poolside bar, and Shawn turned around just in time to see Hank and Pat pursuing the security chief.

"You've got to be kidding!" Shawn exclaimed.

"What's up your ass?" asked Dean.

"They're going to hound that security guy again."

Dean spun around and his face turned to ice. "Guess they'd rather go play with the security guards than relax on vacation with us. You know what, Shawn? Screw them. The five of us will have fun without those glory hogs." Dean paid for the round of drinks and ordered another. He was intent on having a good time no matter what.

Unaware of their husbands' displeasure, Pat and Hank caught up with the security chief near the elevators.

"Can I help you with something?" the chief of security said cordially.

"Well, you know how it is when you're a cop and someone asks you a baiting question that bugs you for the rest of your day," Hank said.

"Sure, why?"

"What was up with the meth question? Was someone selling on board, or did you seize a huge stash or something?" Pat asked.

"I'm not really allowed to discuss that sort of thing with passengers," the chief said. He nodded toward the elevator to tell them that he could talk in there.

The elevator doors opened and the three men entered. The chief pushed the button for the floor he wanted before he said anything.

"We seized a pound of meth during a search, but the size of the bags didn't make sense to me."

"What do you mean, Chief?" Hank asked.

"Well, usually it's sold in grams, not ounces or half ounces, and from what I saw, it was bundled in eight hundred and fifty dollar bundles give or take a hundred. No one on board carries a whole lot of cash with them, so if you're selling it, why not weigh and package it in a more manageable size? And we didn't find a lot of money or any packaging materials in the room, which seems really strange to me."

"Could've just been a stash room," Hank replied.

"It was rented to Alfred Patterson and his staff, and they were all clean."

"That *is* weird," Pat said.

"Yeah, it was just one of those things that you look at and say 'this isn't right,' know what I mean?" the chief said.

"I know that feeling well," said Pat.

"Now I have to tie up some of my guys checking video footage for a missing person."

"Missing from this ship?" Pat inquired.

"It happens. People fall overboard... sometimes they have help."

"Anything else strange?" Hank pushed.

"Seized two guns off some bodyguards. They happened to be the ones that had the meth in their room."

"How'd they get the guns on board?" Pat asked. "Have you traced the serial numbers yet?"

"The serial numbers are scratched off, and we haven't figured out how they got them on board yet."

"Who has bodyguards aboard a cruise?" Hank asked as he glanced at Pat.

"Alfred Patterson, the guy who runs KENYO research and development group."

"Never heard of it," said Pat.

"They make military weapons. I think he's a financial bigwig too," the chief said dismissively.

The elevator pinged and the doors slid open. "Well, gentlemen, I wish I had more time to spend with you, but I'm a little busy right now. If I get free before we hit Australia, I'll come find you." The security chief moved away down the hall.

"Good luck, Chief, talk to you later," Hank said as the elevator doors closed.

"My God, are you going to ask him to marry you, Hank?" Pat said, smiling at his buddy.

"Bite me. He's a nice guy, and I'm interested in what happens on a cruise ship."

The elevator bypassed the pool deck and headed up to the penthouse suites.

"Hey, why didn't it stop on our floor?" Pat asked.

"I pushed the button for our rooms and not the pool deck. Oops," Hank replied as he tried to correct the mistake.

"Ass. We're going to be late. Dean and Shawn are going to kill us!" Pat complained.

"Let's get off at the next floor."

"We're nowhere near the pool deck if we get off there."

"I gotta take a piss, and there's a public restroom on every floor."

"You can't hold it?"

"I've had to go since before we met up with the chief. It'll take two friggin' minutes. You can go ahead and I'll meet you at the pool, if it's that important."

Pat pushed the button for the next floor, and the elevator car stopped. Pat and Hank exited, and Hank ran off to the restroom. The elevator doors closed, and Pat leaned against the wall as he waited for his friend. The doors to the elevator car next to them stood open. Pat saw a large metal cart and guessed that the crew was working on something. He turned his gaze on a bouquet of carnations on the table near the elevator and admired the artwork on the walls above it as he waited.

THERE was a knock at the door of Chris and Jessica's suite. Chris was tying his bowtie as he stared at the clock.

"She'd better get her ass back here, or I'm going without her," Chris said to the mirror as he turned to answer the door.

Two uniformed security officers stood at the door. Chris looked down and saw that they were wearing sidearms.

"Can I help you, officers?" said Chris.

"Alfred Patterson asked us to come by and escort you and Ms. Cosgrove to a new meeting area."

"Why didn't he send his secretary?" Chris asked apprehensively.

"I don't have that information, sir. Is Jessica Cosgrove here?"

"No, she had to run to the shop and get something. Let me just give his secretary a call and make sure there isn't a mix-up," Chris said as he walked toward the phone. The guards stepped into the room and closed the door behind them. Chris tried to fight, but he felt a pinch in the side of his neck and then he got warm and dizzy, like he'd had way too much to drink.

He fell to the floor, and one of the men in the security uniforms checked the hallway for unwanted company. He saw Hank but didn't see him as a threat. Grabbing the large metal cart from the open elevator, he rolled it into the room as Pat exited the bathroom and wiped his hands on Hank's shorts.

"You're gross. Get away from me!" Hank said as he playfully shoved Pat.

"Let's get to the pool deck before we get decked," Pat said as he called the elevator.

The doors opened up on an elevator filled to capacity. Holbrook exited the elevator and apologized.

"Sorry, that one is packed. I had to get off to get some air. Where are you headed?"

"Pool deck," Pat replied.

"Follow me. The freight elevator on the other end will get you there faster."

As the three walked past Chris's suite, one of the mercenaries looked out the peephole. "Looks clear," the mercenary said, and he opened the door. As the cart cleared the doorway, the mercenaries saw the three men walking away in the other direction.

One of the soldiers of fortune put a finger to his lips. "Just hold on until they're gone," he mouthed to his companion.

The second jerked a thumb at the door they'd just exited.

The first man shook his head. "No, just hold tight," he whispered.

Holbrook led the men to the freight elevator and put his clearance key in the card slot.

"I'll override it for you so you can go right to the pool without stopping at each deck."

"Thanks, Officer Holbrook," Hank said, patting the young man on the shoulder.

"Hey, what were your guys doing in that suite with the big metal cart?" Hank asked. "It didn't look like they were working on the elevator."

"Cart?" said Holbrook, and then he remembered seeing other security officers with a big metal cart.

"Yeah, one of your crew was pushing a giant metal cart into a suite," Hank replied, pointing toward the suite.

"That's weird. I'll radio dispatch and see what's up." Holbrook keyed up his radio to transmit and received a squelching noise.

"I hate these radios, every little thing interferes with them," he said as he tried shifting the direction of the antenna to get signal.

"I thought we were the only ones that had crappy radios. See, Hank? It's universal!" Pat laughed.

"Go ahead and hop in the elevator when it comes," Holbrook said. "If anyone asks, you just tell them you saw an open elevator and hopped on because you were lost." With a friendly wave, he walked away.

"All right, Holbrook, thanks again."

"This elevator is just as bad as the other one, it's taking forever," Pat complained.

"The kid thought he was doing us a favor. If we walk past him to get on the other one, he'll be insulted. Just sit tight for a few and we can hop on, you impatient bitch."

"Screw it! I'm taking the regular one. The kid will have to get over it." Pat walked away. Hank rolled his eyes at his impatient partner as he followed.

As Pat and Hank rounded the corner, they saw that the young security officer speaking to the officers with the cart. Hank noticed that the uniforms seemed tight on the pair with the cart, and then he saw Holbrook reach for his gun. Holbrook drew his weapon and pointed it at the two men as he ordered them not to move. When he tried to summon help with the radio, it failed to find a signal again.

"He needs help," Hank said.

"Are you wearing a vest? Because I don't think a T-shirt's going to stop bullets," Pat replied in a hushed tone as they ducked down. Hank saw one of the mercenaries peek from around the back of the cart with a silenced weapon in his hand.

"Grab the fire extinguisher behind you, Pat!" Hank whispered.

"Goddammit!" Pat said under his breath as he took down the fire extinguisher and handed it to Hank.

Pat squeezed his partner's shoulder as the signal to spring into action.

The mercenary's weapon coughed twice, and Holbrook fell to the floor. Hank discharged the fire extinguisher at the shooter and a white cloud filled the hallway. Everyone in the vicinity started coughing from the burning powder in their throats.

The second mercenary jumped up and fired at Pat and Hank. The lack of oxygen and the burning in his eyes severely compromised his aim. He missed Pat entirely and only managed put a hole in the hem of Hank's shirt. Pat jumped on the man and pummeled his face. The second mercenary rose from his crouched position, spraying bullets.

Hank kicked open the door of a nearby suite and pulled his partner inside. After Hank locked the deadbolt, they jumped behind the kitchenette counter and hoped the men wouldn't get inside. The only noise they heard was coughing and the rumble of the metal cart as the mercenaries beat a hasty retreat.

"What the fuck was that!" Pat asked as he coughed and rubbed his eyes.

"They were going to kill that kid, and I couldn't let them do that," Hank spat back.

"Not that, dumbass, the whole fire-extinguisher bit. You are banned from ever watching *Die Hard* again."

Pat grabbed the phone and then returned to the covered position with his partner.

"Hello, I need security. Chief Kaspersky to the Queen's Grill level right now. There were shots fired, and one of his men is down."

"Is this some kind of joke, sir?" the operator asked.

"Get me some medics up here right goddamn now," Pat growled, and the operator disconnected the call.

Pat threw the phone. "Useless bitch."

"What's wrong?"

"She thought it was a prank and hung up."

"We should go see if we can help that kid."

"Who'll help us when we go out there and they gun us down?"

"I think they're gone. You can wait here, but I'm going to check on that security guy."

Pat bit his bottom lip and sighed. "Let's go," he said, grabbing a paring knife from the counter.

"What are you going to do with that? Scratch them and hope it gets infected?" Hank said, looking at the small knife in partner's hand.

"It's all about size with you, isn't it?" Pat said as he shoved his partner toward the door.

Hank unlocked the door and opened it slowly. The air still hung thick with the smell of the fire extinguisher's contents. Pat crouched down to look, but the fake security guards were nowhere in sight.

Pat and Hank crawled over to Holbrook. He had taken three rounds to the chest, but was still breathing thanks to his protective vest. Pat grabbed Holbrook's radio and attempted to call in to security. The radio emitted a high-pitched squelch but did nothing useful.

"Let's carry him to the infirmary, otherwise he's dead," said Pat.

"Okay, grab his gun."

As Pat grabbed Holbrook's weapon, he saw some blood splatter on the wall where the cart had been.

"Holy shit! The kid got a shot off," Pat exclaimed as Hank lifted the boy in a fireman's carry.

"Look, there's a blood trail to the elevator that was locked open. Holbrook must've got them pretty good."

In the doorway of the suite lay one of the silenced weapons in a pool of blood.

"Hank, here," Pat said as he grabbed the weapon by its silencer and handed the bloody grip to Hank.

"Gross, give me your shirt so I can wipe this thing off."

"Wipe it on your own goddamn shirt!" Pat replied.

They called for the elevator, and when the door opened, Chief Kaspersky emerged. Seeing Pat and Hank covered in blood, carrying weapons and a half-dead security officer, he reacted instinctively: he drew his weapon.

"Don't fucking move!"

"Whoa, Chief, hold on, don't shoot!" Hank said quickly, pointing his weapon at the floor.

"We didn't do this, Chief," Pat said as he dropped the gun he was holding.

"Yeah? Well, it sure as hell looks like you did something. Put my man down right now!" the chief ordered.

Hank and Pat complied immediately, putting their hands in the air as the chief attempted to radio for backup. The radio squeaked again, and when he tried his cell phone, it failed as well.

"Chief, listen to me," Pat said. "Two guys dressed as security were doing something with a big metal cart in that room. Your guy went to check on it because something didn't seem right to him. We walked around the corner and saw him talking to them. You know how it is when you get that gut feeling?"

"We called the operator and reported this, and she hung up on me," Hank continued.

"It's true, Chief." Holbrook coughed up blood with his words.

Hank and Pat were elated to hear the boy's voice. It meant he was still alive for now.

A look of understanding crossed the chief's face, "You two called the operator?"

"Yes, why? Hank asked as his arms grew numb.

The chief holstered his weapon. "I was at the operator's station trying to figure out why we lost use of our satellite phones when your call came in. I tried to call one of my men, but the radios and cell phones aren't working, either. The operator said it was a prank call so I figured I'd come up here and check it out."

"Grab him and let's go to the infirmary fast. We can talk on the way."

Hank picked up Holbrook and lifted him over his shoulder once more, in the classic firemen's carry mode.

The chief inserted his override key into the slot and the elevator was on their floor within twenty seconds. The people already on board were aghast at the sight that had greeted them: three bloodied men and a security officer, two with handguns.

"I have a medical emergency, folks. Please exit the elevator immediately," the chief ordered.

The occupants complied, and the men got into the elevator car. The chief put his key in the interior slot to override the controls so the car wouldn't stop until they arrived on the deck where the infirmary was located. The ride felt like it took hours as the wounded guard's breathing became shallower with every passing second.

"Did you two get a good look at the shooters?" the chief asked as they sped toward the medical facility.

"I got a really good look at the one who shot your guard," Hank said as he felt a trickle of blood flow down his arm.

"You have to give the kid credit, Chief. He hit one of them before he went down," Pat said.

"He's a good kid and a great officer. Hang on, Joshua, we're almost there," the chief said, his deep emotions betrayed by his use of Holbrook's first name.

The elevator dinged and the doors opened. The chief ran out, shouting for medical attention for his man. The nurses came running with a stretcher, and Hank put Holbrook on it. Hank grabbed the kid's hand and said, "Hang on, it's not that bad."

Pat saw that his partner was covered in blood. He looked at his own hands and saw they were just as red. Both cops were relieved when chief came back with wet towels.

"I just got off the phone with the captain. It looks like we have a much bigger problem than we thought."

"What do you mean?" Hank asked.

"The engines just died. We're no longer under power and the only communications working right now is the hardwired phone system, which explains how you were able to make your 'prank' call."

"So radio the nearest country and call for a tow," Pat said.

"You're just showing your ignorance," Hank said disgustedly.

"This ship has no communications with its crew, no engines, no global positioning, no radios, no working cellular or satellite phones. I can only talk to my guys via a hardwired phone, and right now they're on alert, so no one is just sitting by a phone waiting for my call. We're dead in the water."

"What about using the ship-wide intercom to have your guys rally somewhere?" Hank asked.

Pat nodded in agreement.

"If I do that, I risk panicking the passengers, and the captain said to avoid announcing an emergency until we had to. We are out in the middle of the ocean with nowhere to go."

"You have two killers on board and a half-dead security officer and that's not an emergency?" Pat bellowed.

"If we announce an emergency, we risk putting the killers on edge and that could mean more loss of lives. This isn't Maryland, boys. Welcome to life at sea."

"Fine, but since Pat and I are the only ones who can identify the shooters, we aren't going anywhere," Hank said matter-of-factly.

"Damn straight, partner," Pat replied.

"Glad to hear you say that. The captain told me to use you if I needed to and gave me permission to arm you. Let's head to my office and get some security jackets and ammunition."

The men took the back stairway this time and ran to the chief's office.

TJ AND Richie were carrying a small duffel bag to the elevator when Richie spotted a bouquet of carnations on a table.

"Her favorite, next to roses," he said with a sadistic smile. His eye began to twitch and his head started to ache, a twisted mix of euphoria and nerves filled his heart as he thought about the payback he was about to deliver. Grabbing two carnations, he held them tightly as they waited for the elevator.

TJ continued to stare at the elevator and barely acknowledged that Richie had spoken.

The elevator door opened, and Carl motioned for TJ and Richie to get in with him. Not until the door closed did anyone speak.

"Your old accountant, lawyer, and Patterson should all be down there and waiting for us," Carl said without any emotion. "Smalls is off the table, so I guess he'll be getting a big promotion when he gets home, since he will be the lone survivor of the senior board members. We have one hour to deal with them and be on time for extraction. The money's all been transferred into my account, so we're good to go. The lieutenant has become a liability, TJ, so clean up that mess."

"What about the bomb?" TJ asked.

Richie's eyes widened, and he dropped the carnations. He opened his mouth to object to what TJ had just said, but he was cut off by Carl.

"Save it, Richie. The bomb is not going to detonate. I only kill who I have to. As of right now, I have no need to kill the thousands of people on this ship. This whole scenario should come off as a terrorist plot, and if something should happen to prevent extraction, it's the last bargaining chip we have."

"So you brought a fucking bomb on board a cruise ship? What if that thing goes off by itself or someone messes with it? That's four thousand people that didn't do shit to me that are going to die," Richie said.

"Concentrate on what you have to do, Rich. This is why you pay us. Guess how long it would take investigators to piece this together if they knew you were on the ship? A couple of days? The bomb is a distraction. This is what I do for a living, so just relax and focus on your ex-wife."

Richie stared at Carl as his migraine increased. He raised his fist to punch Carl in the face and TJ grabbed him by the neck.

"No!" Carl shouted.

TJ held pressure on Richie's throat for a moment longer as a warning that he could've killed him. Then he let Richie go and shoved him toward the wall.

"Rich, cut the baby shit and let's get this done already. Your ex-wife is the target, not us, so save the rage for them. You're here sucking face and cock to pay her back for stealing from you and your father. She destroyed your life, and I'm here to help you get payback. If you forget that again, you're on your own," Carl said as if scolding a child.

Richie took a deep breath and bent over to pick up the carnations. For the remainder of the silent elevator ride, Richie's head whirled with a series of images: the attack that put him in the hospital; TJ groping him as Carl threatened him; TJ making him suck his dick in the sauna. All of this happened because he was too stupid to see Jessica for what she was. Hatred and rage swelled inside of Richie, and he knew where it would be directed.

They arrived at the cargo deck and Carl used the master key to access the secure area where the steel containers were kept. As Carl approached the designated container, he saw the lieutenant tending to one of his men.

"TJ, take Richie inside and let him play with his friends," Carl said.

TJ signaled to Richie that it was time to go inside the container. Richie dropped the duffel bag and entered, with TJ behind him.

When the door was secured, Carl spoke to the wounded man. "Did you get Patterson?"

"Yes," replied the man in the bloodied security uniform.

"What happened to you?" Carl asked as he looked at the man's chest.

"One of the security guards made us as fakes and tried to arrest us, so we took cover and shot him. He got me as he was falling over." The man coughed and winced in pain.

"He's dead, and if it wasn't for two passengers that decided to play hero, this would've been cleaned up. We had to get out of there fast, so we took off with Patterson and left the guard."

"Lieutenant, do you know if they found the guard yet?" Carl asked.

"Communications are all down. I can call the infirmary on a ship phone, but the nearest one is in the cargo office. This is going to be a fucking mess, Carl. I have to go with you guys when you extract, otherwise, sooner or later, someone will figure out that there's a mole," the lieutenant said.

"Very true, go make that call and get back here immediately."

The lieutenant ran to the cargo office a quarter of the ship away. Carl watched his man slowly dying.

"It's up to you, Heinrich. We both know you're not going to make extraction, and even if you do, we don't have a doctor standing by," Carl said, shaking his head. It saddened him that he was about to lose such a good man, but he knew there was no alternative, and Heinrich was a good soldier who knew he could die at any time.

"It's been an honor, Carl. Make sure my family is taken care of."

Carl teared up, and he wiped away the wetness as he handed the man a small black pill. "You have my word."

Carl stood up as the man put the ampoule in his mouth. There was no need for Carl to watch the man bite down on the cyanide. His men knew the risks when they accepted a mission, and only this fact made Carl feel slightly less sad.

Carl went into the steel shipping container and saw three hooded and bound men seated on the floor. All of them were gagged and drugged as well. "Okay, Simon, wake them up," Carl said.

"Is Heinrich going to be okay?" Simon asked.

Carl shook his head, and Simon sighed as he removed a small bottle from his pocket. He filled the syringe with a medicine to counteract the anesthetic that had been administered to the prisoners.

"I don't see a woman in the mix, Carl! Where's Jessica?" Richie demanded.

"She's on her way. Just deal with these three for now." Carl leaned over to Simon and whispered in his ear. Simon shook his head, and Carl straightened back up.

Simon removed the hoods as the three men woke up from their drug-induced sleep. Richie stared at Carl for a long moment before Carl looked down at the prisoners.

"Well?" Carl asked.

"I want Jessica here for this," Richie growled.

"If you don't get your ass moving, I'm going to be one lighter for the extraction, I swear to Christ!" Carl spat out as he grabbed a weapon from Vincent, a member of the attack team.

Alfred Patterson's eyes widened as he adjusted to his surroundings and realized what was going on.

Chris Powell saw Richie standing over him with an ax and raw hatred in his gaze.

Richie's eye was twitching uncontrollably, and he was grinding his teeth. His hands twisted around the ax handle, and he flipped it around to the flat side instead of the edge.

"Patterson, you fucking snake!" Richie delivered a blow to Patterson's head that put him on his back. Louie and Chris tried to stand but were quickly put back on the ground by the mercenaries.

As Richie was screaming at Patterson, the lieutenant returned out of breath,

"Security Officer Holbrook came in with gunshot wounds to the chest. He's in surgery right now, and if they don't get a helicopter to evacuate him to Fiji, he's dead."

Carl continued to watch emotionlessly as Richie delivered another blow to Patterson.

Richie dropped the ax and jumped on top of the man, pummeling his face until it was no longer recognizable as human. When Richie was sure the man would never move again, he stood up and was almost overcome by a wave of dizziness. When it receded, his head was pounding even harder.

"Holy shit!" the lieutenant exclaimed, his horrified gaze riveted on Patterson's remains.

Carl turned to face him, "I understand you're not used to this kind of stuff. That's why you had no part in the wet work. Did you manage to clear the escape corridor?"

"Yes. I changed the op order and assignments. The quick reaction team is busy guarding the bow and the outside of the bridge. The armed guards are all in positions that make it very hard to spot an approaching vessel coming from the stern. Patrols were rerouted to keep everyone out of your way until you get to extraction point."

"Is the rappelling gear from the rock -climbing wall waiting for us?"

"Yes, it's all set up."

"Good, meet us there in twenty minutes, and make sure none of your guards are anywhere near the place," Carl said as he patted the man on the shoulder.

"Okay." The lieutenant turned and walked out of the steel container.

To avoid a ricochet, Carl waited until the man was clear of the doorway and then fired two muffled shots into the lieutenant's head. The officer fell on top of the dead mercenary and didn't move again.

Richie was now blood drunk, shouting wildly at Louie as he beat him. "You fucking asshole! I trusted you, and you helped them! Why would you help them?"

The wooden handle of the ax had broken during the assault on Patterson so Simon provided Richie with a wire garrote to execute Louie. Richie's hands were sore and bleeding, and when he could no longer swing at the semiconscious man, he wrapped the wire around Louie's neck and pulled until Louie was dead.

While Richie was delivering the deathblow to Louie, Carl whispered to the three remaining mercenaries. He informed them that Jessica had not been found and that they would be extracting immediately after Powell was killed. If Richie had a problem with that, he was to be killed as well.

Richie let go of the garrote's handles and stood up. He was splattered with blood and out of breath but found the strength to kick Chris in the face, knocking him to the ground.

"When does Jessica get here?" Richie wheezed.

"We aren't doing that here. Finish Powell off. We have to move."

Richie saw a gleam in Carl's eye that he didn't like, but all of the mercenaries in the steel box were armed, so he knew better than to defy him. Richie turned his attention to his ex-counselor and former best friend.

"You're the worst one of all, Powell. We went to high school together, and you were best man at my wedding. You were fucking her for four years! I'm taking my time with you, wife-fucker. Your death is going to be slow and painful," Richie said as he pulled out a large knife.

Chris's eyes welled with tears, and he began to scream through his gag as Richie made the first slice. After several minutes of torturing the man responsible for his downfall, he finally delivered the deathblow and released Chris from his agony.

Carl opened the duffel bag and pulled clean clothes for each man.

"Just in case we run into someone. We don't need any screaming about blood-covered guys roaming around," Carl said as he stripped.

"Wait, I'm not changing yet. I still have Jessica to kill," Richie said.

"Rich, do you see my dead guy out there? Do you see the dead security guard? We have a wounded guard and two passengers who can identify Simon. Sorry, but we're aborting and heading to extraction."

Richie saw TJ tightening his grip on his weapon as he looked at Carl. Richie knew that if Carl said the word, he would be dead.

"Fine, but I want a refund of two million."

"All sales are final."

Richie glared at the mercenary leader—jaw clenched, breath whistling through his teeth, the copper taste of blood on his tongue— and teetered on the edge of madness. However, he still had a shred of sense and his survival instinct made him back down. Despite the wreckage of his enemies on the floor behind him, he felt a most unsatisfactory emptiness. Telling himself to bide his time, he meekly followed Carl's orders and waited for an opportunity to settle this score.

AS THE mercenaries exited the container, one of them pulled a note from a Ziploc bag and pinned it to the lieutenant's jacket. In Arabic, it read:

Allah Akbar. The demon Alfred Patterson has made weapons to destroy my people. He is with Allah now for judgment. All of the Infidels on this ship will be judged when the fiery tongue of Allah engulfs it.

THE security chief gave Hank and Pat bright yellow jackets labeled 'Security' on the back and sleeves before they went to the armory for ammunition. Pat and Hank were astounded by the amount of weaponry carried on the ship. Most of the gun racks were empty due to the alert, but there was still plenty of ammunition to be had.

The phone in the armory rang, and the chief answered, "Hello?"

"Chief, this is Officer Dunds from the holding area."

"I'm kind of busy. What is it, Dunds?"

"Sir, did I do something wrong?"

"I don't have time for this. Shouldn't you be out on watch?"

"I came when they called alert and the duty roster had me listed as the jailer."

"I don't put my snipers inside when there's an alert. Who the hell authorized that?"

"You did, sir."

The chief was supremely annoyed that someone was still issuing orders in his name—the same someone, presumably, who had terminated the camera surveillance and issued keycards.

"Stay put until someone relieves you, Dunds, I need someone I can count on by the phone," the chief said as he hung up.

"What's up, Chief?" Pat asked.

"Someone has hacked my password and made a bunch of changes in my name."

"What kind of changes?" asked Hank.

"They turned off cameras, issued master key cards, and changed the duty roster."

The chief had just resecured the armory when he heard the phone ring inside. He rolled his eyes and walked quickly to his office, accompanied by Pat and Hank. Dunds was sitting at the desk cradling the phone. He hung up when the chief walked in.

"Were you just trying to call me again?" the chief asked.

"Yes, sir, the bridge called. Holbrook has gone into surgery, but if they don't get communications back to call in a helicopter, the doctors say he'll die."

"Call engineering, that's their department. I don't know shit about electronics. Is that all?"

Hank was listening to the exchange of words when he discovered the bullet hole in his shirt. He lifted the shirt to show Pat as he shook his head.

"One other thing, sir. The bridge also said they have a warning light for an unsecured cargo hold door in secure area C-12."

"I'm aware that it's a secured area, thank you, Dunds." The chief motioned for Pat and Hank to follow him.

"Where are we going?" Pat asked.

"That alarm is hardwired because it's a secured area, and it's a door that's sealed to prevent us sinking if we spring a leak," the chief said as he quickened his pace toward the staff elevators.

"So we're going to check on an alarm?" asked Hank.

"I don't usually answer these calls, but I can't get hold of anyone but Dunds right now."

As the elevator raced downward to the cargo hold, Pat and Hank drew their weapons. The chief shook his head.

"I told you it's been a while since I've been on the road. This elevator car is a pretty good kill zone." The chief drew his weapon and went to one knee.

Pat and Hank stood to the sides of the elevator as it arrived at the cargo hold floor. The doors opened revealing nothing out of the ordinary. The three men maintained their tactical stances as they exited. The chief tried the door marked C-12 and found it was secured.

"False alarm, I guess," the chief said.

The men smiled at each other and chuckled before the chief went to the alarm panel, swiped his card, and typed in a code.

"Hold on. Someone did make access, then exited and went back in again within the last ten minutes."

"Who's allowed in there?" asked Pat.

"Definitely not civilians, and no individual guard is allowed to make access by himself. It's against protocol."

"What the hell is in this place? Nuclear warhead storage?" Hank joked lamely.

"We store gold, expensive cars, diplomatic cases, sometimes, pretty much anything of value."

"This is a big cargo hold. Three of us aren't going to be able to search it."

"Never mind. My lieutenant is the one who made entry."

"He has high enough clearance to get in by himself?" asked Pat.

"The two of us have the only cards capable of single access."

"What about the captain?" asked Hank.

"Well, of course. The captain runs the ship so he has a master key."

"I think we should see what he's doing in there," Hank said.

Pat stared at his partner like he'd lost his mind. "Three of us clearing a huge cargo space by ourselves? You're acting like this is routine police work, Hank," he griped.

"There is no such thing as routine police work. It's your call, Chief. If you want backup, I'll go in with you," Hank said, knowing his partner would always back his play regardless of how irresponsible it might be.

"Yeah, Chief, your call," Pat said as he stared daggers through Hank.

"It's unusual that anyone would come down here during an alert. I should see what he's doing at least. Thanks for the offer of backup," the chief said as he entered the code to open the door. With the swipe of his card, the door beeped that it had unlocked.

Pat put his hand on Hank's shoulder and gave it a squeeze. Hank nodded his readiness at the chief, and they entered the cargo bay.

CARL heard an electronic beep and then the sound of the heavy metal door opening. He raised his finger to his lips as footsteps echoed through the chamber. There was no more time to clean up the scene or hide. It looked as though they were going to add a couple more security guards to their tally of kills.

The mercenaries took up an ambush position across from the bloodied bodies. If the men searching the chamber came to check on the corpses, they would be joining the deceased. Carl held Richie in the steel container to minimize the risk of his team being exposed by an amateur.

Pat and Hank followed the security chief as they skulked along in a three-person stack. The security chief covered the front of the stack,

Pat covered all firing positions from above, and Hank covered the rear and sides. As they snuck along the containers, listening for any sounds, the hair on the back of Hank's neck stood up and he had an odd feeling.

A heavy, all too familiar scent hung in the air. The smell got stronger, and then Pat stepped in a shiny wet spot and slipped. He threw his hand out to catch the side of a container and was able to prevent a fall. Pat looked down and was not surprised to see that he had stepped in blood spatter. He gripped the chief's shoulder and stopped. Hank paused and looked at Pat, who was pointing at the ground. All three men saw the blood and knew this was no longer a case of "what if."

The mercenaries heard Pat's misstep and got a bead on the enemy's position. If the security staff continued on the same course, they would end up behind the ambush. The mercenaries moved swiftly and silently to new positions. When Carl looked out the container door, he saw that his men had changed positions and signaled to Simon to ask why.

Using hand gestures, Simon told Carl that at least two men were coming from the other direction. Pat, Hank, and Chief Kaspersky were now headed directly into the jaws of the wolf.

Inside the container, Richie's head was pounding, and he was sweating profusely. As he looked around at the bodies on the floor, he again became resentful that Jessica was not among the dead. Spotting Chris Powell's bloodied sea pass, he snatched it up. The card had a room number on it, and Richie was convinced he would find Jessica there. Richie lunged at the distracted Carl and grabbed his gun, firing several rounds that ricocheted around inside the steel container. The mercenaries jumped from their positions to see if a security force was engaging them from another direction. Carl slipped on the blood from the gruesome murders Richie had committed and fell, hitting his head on the floor.

Richie ran from the container toward the exit. Gunfire erupted between the mercenaries and the chief's group. Pat and Hank jumped to the sides of a container for cover, while the chief engaged the threats from a prone position. Hank knelt and returned fire. One round found its mark, striking TJ in the head and filling the air with a red mist. TJ was dead before he hit the floor.

"Nice shot!" Pat exclaimed.

"Look behind him—it's the shooter from the hallway!" Hank yelled back.

Pat rose, took aim, and fired. Two of the rounds struck the shooter in the chest and then Pat jumped back behind cover.

"Chief, get over here." Hank grabbed Chief Kaspersky's ankle and pulled.

The chief rolled over to Hank's position. "One down, one dead, and I count two more besides the guy who ran!"

The two remaining mercenaries were running low on ammunition. A sustained firefight in the cargo area was not a contingency that they had planned for. Simon was bleeding from his chest as he leaned into the steel box Carl had taken cover in. "Boss, we need to get the hell out of here; ammo's low."

Carl threw Simon another full magazine. "Get to the extraction site if you can!" Then he dove out of the steel case and ran down the empty aisle. Simon and his two remaining men continued to take shots at the three men in security uniforms.

"Go! I'll hold them off," said Simon as he realized that he would not be making it to the extraction point. The remaining two mercenaries followed Carl's route.

Hank saw the men running away and moved into a better firing position. He fired and hit one of the men in the back. The mercenary fell to the ground, twitching.

Pat saw Simon reloading his weapon using only one hand and moved in with the chief. The two men crept up to Simon, pointed their weapons, and shouted, "Don't move!"

Hank heard the commotion through the severe ringing in his ears and went to help his partner. His gun was out of bullets, and he was not thrilled about a hand-to-hand confrontation, but he would be there to back Pat.

Simon raised his weapon and fired. One of the rounds struck Kaspersky's protective vest, knocking him backward. Pat and the chief emptied their weapons into the mercenary, and he slumped to the floor.

Pat picked up the dead man's weapon to see the caliber. "It's a nine millimeter, fucking useless!"

"They're all nines," the chief said, scouring the bodies for ammunition.

"I saw at least three run toward the exit. Let's go!" Hank said, taking the dead man's weapon. The chief and Pat were right behind him.

"Isn't somebody going to hear all this gunfire and come see what's up?" Hank asked as they ran to the doorway.

"You can't hear shit down here!" the chief answered.

RICHIE pushed the emergency exit button and the cargo hold door opened. A screeching alarm announced that someone had opened the door. Carl saw the door open and fired at Richie; Richie felt the heat of the bullet as it passed by his head. Hurriedly, he closed the door and ran to an open elevator.

The elevator doors closed just as Carl opened the cargo-bay access door. Pat and Hank were not far behind Carl and the remaining mercenary. Carl heard their footsteps and heavy breathing as he closed the door behind him and ran to the stairs. He forced open a door and closed it just as Chief Kaspersky and the cops emerged from the cargo bay.

"The elevator door is closed, but the car is still on this floor," Kaspersky whispered.

Hank took up a position directly in front of the elevator doors. Pat and Kaspersky moved to the sides.

Richie frantically hit the elevator buttons, but the car refused to move. He knew if he opened the doors that Carl and what was left of his team would be there to kill him. He panicked and tried to access the roof panel, but it was bolted shut. Richie had no weapons, and it was just a matter of time before the doors were pried open.

Kaspersky grabbed the emergency elevator door key, a slim metal rod that would open the exterior and interior doors in case of power failure. He put the rod in the door and nodded at Hank and Pat. They acknowledged that they were ready, and Kaspersky opened the doors. Richie Cosgrove stood before them, unarmed and bloody from head to toe.

"Get on the ground right now!" Pat shouted.

Richie immediately fell to his knees and put his hands in the air. "Thank God, you're here!" he sobbed.

"What happened to you?" asked Kaspersky.

"They were going to kill me. They killed three other guys in there." Richie was able to produce tears with no effort.

"Why do they want to kill you?" Hank asked suspiciously.

"They called me an infidel and said that I was a homosexual and needed to die."

"I don't know, Chief. I'm not totally buying this," Pat said.

Chief Kaspersky handcuffed a protesting Richie and placed him against the wall, "Can you two watch him? I have to make a call."

As the chief picked up the phone, a message came over the intercom: "Attention, all passengers. Please return to your cabins immediately. This is not a drill."

The chief dialed the bridge.

The man who answered identified himself as the captain. Chief Kaspersky informed him of the situation and asked for a six-man security team in C-12.

"What the hell did we get ourselves into here, Hank?" asked Pat.

"Some serious craziness, and here I thought P.G. County was bad!"

"Okay," the chief said when he returned from his phone call. "We have reports of a man with a gun running down the halls with another male. The software that runs the engines was tampered with purposely, and the captain says someone's jamming all communications."

Three security officers emerged from the stairway and ran over to the chief.

"Sanderson, take this man to my office and hold onto him," the chief ordered.

"Yes, sir!" said Officer Sanderson.

"Give me some ammunition, and you two stay with us."

"Shouldn't we be finding the guy who ran out of here?" Hank asked. "What if he shoots more passengers?"

"First I need to check out what the man from the elevator said."

"What part?"

"He said there were three more dead men in the container. I want to see if they're anyone of importance."

The chief locked and loaded his pistol and then handed Pat some ammunition.

"I'm good with the nine," Hank said, holding up the weapon.

Officer Sanderson grabbed the handcuffed man and took him into the elevator.

"Let's go see what kind of damage we did," the chief said as he opened the secure lock again.

The five men walked over to the blood-splattered area where the gunfight had occurred. Chief Kaspersky saw his dead lieutenant in front of an open container with a note in Arabic stuck to his shirt.

"Anyone here read Arabic?" asked Kaspersky.

No one did, so Kaspersky folded the letter and placed it in his pocket. The lieutenant had been a prick and wouldn't be missed as far as the chief was concerned. Pat observed a fat white envelope in his jacket pocket. Pat leaned down and grabbed the envelope; he opened it and saw $50,000 inside.

"Wow, you security guys get paid well!" Pat said. As he showed everyone the contents of the envelope, a small piece of paper fell from between the hundred dollar bills. Hank retrieved it and examined it.

"Sir, we have three men in the container that were beaten beyond recognition," said a security officer as he gagged. "One guy is carved up like a Sunday roast. There were also discarded security uniforms."

Pat, Hank, and Kaspersky looked inside the container and saw the god-awful mess.

"Hey, Pat, didn't that guy on the elevator say he was a hostage?"

"Yep."

"I count three hoods, three tied up men, and no extra rope."

Pat's turned to Kaspersky. "He wasn't tied up, and I didn't see any marks on his wrists either."

"Well, he's in custody now, so don't worry. We can have a chat with him when we go back to my office."

RICHIE sat in the security office with his hands cuffed behind his back while the security officer read a magazine. On the floor near Richie's foot was a paper clip. A security officer from one of his hotels had shown him a video on the Internet during an excruciatingly boring third shift as a night clerk. The video showed exactly how to open a pair of handcuffs with a paper clip. Richie had practiced every time he worked with the security guard until he'd able to master the technique. It sure was going to come in handy now. "There's a bomb on the ship," Richie blurted out.

"Yeah, right!" the officer said as he flipped through the magazine.

"I'm serious. The terrorists were talking about a bomb when they had me in that container. You have to do something or this ship is going to blow up!"

"Where is this alleged bomb?" the guard said as he lowered his magazine.

"They didn't exactly tell me where they put it. You need to go tell someone! I'm handcuffed. Where am I going to go? We're all going to die if you don't do something, asshole!" Richie stood up and turned to prove to the guard that he was still handcuffed. As he sat back down, he pretended to miss the chair and fall to the floor. The guard came around the desk to help him and gave him a stern look.

"Stay here. I'll fucking shoot you if you move."

The guard went into the main office, where the phone was. Richie straightened the paperclip he'd picked up when he faked his fall. He then used the lip of the keyhole to bend the thin metal into a lightning bolt shape. After working the paper clip for a few minutes, the handcuffs opened and he removed them. Richie kept his hands behind his back as he waited for the security officer to return. The door opened, and Richie peered down the hallway at the vacant front desk.

"Aren't you going to search for the bomb?" he asked the guard.

"Nope, I get to babysit you until the boss gets back."

As the guard walked past, Richie jumped up and unsnapped the guard's holster. He removed the guard's weapon and placed the muzzle at the base of the guard's skull.

"If you scream or struggle, you're dead. Nod if you understand."

Richie could feel the security officer shaking as he held the weapon to the man's head. The guard nodded but did not move any other muscle in his body.

"Where's your partner? Is he out there at the desk?"

The guard remained silent, afraid uttering a single word.

"I asked you a question!" Richie spat in the man's ear.

"You said if I said anything, you'd kill me." The guard whined.

"Where is your partner?" Richie asked again.

"He tried to call the chief in the cargo area and the phone was busy so he went to find the chief. You said there's a bomb on the ship, and they're going to look for it."

Richie's eye was twitching and his head throbbed even more than it had in the cargo hold. His nose was bleeding. He felt blood trickle down his lip and heard it drip on the floor. He pulled the trigger and the front of the guard's head exploded onto the wall. The man fell to the ground without making a sound, and Richie pointed the weapon at the doorway, awaiting a response, but none came.

Richie put the handcuffs in his pocket and wiped the blood from his nose. He placed the weapon in the back waistband of his pants and covered it with his shirt. Slowly he walked to the front of the office and saw no one waiting for him. He left the security office and went to the elevator. The only thought in his mind was that Jessica must die.

PAT and Hank helped the security officers dig through the pockets of the dead men, looking for clues to help them identify the deceased and shed light on the killers' motives. Their clothing held no clues, but inside of the steel container, one of the security officers found two sea passes and gave them to the security chief.

"We have ID on two of the dead guys," the chief said to Pat and Hank. "None of the shooters have anything to identify them."

"Why would they be down here, Chief?" Hank inquired.

"I don't think they wanted anything from down here, to be honest. The only thing I can figure is that they wanted privacy to kill those men in there."

"Yeah, but look at the injuries. That was personal. Look at the one that got skinned. That's hatred," said Pat.

The entrance door to the cargo hold beeped, and Officer Dunds ran up to the group of men.

"Holy shit! Look at this mess!" he exclaimed.

"Dunds, what are you doing here?" the chief asked.

"That guy you sent up to the office said there's a bomb on the ship," he said, panting like a dog.

"They're going to blow up the ship!" Pat said as thoughts of Dean raced through his mind.

"We need to get everyone off the ship, and quick!" Hank said to the chief, thinking of Shawn and his friends.

"Hank, we have to call the guys and tell them to head to the lifeboats," Pat said as he ran to the hallway where he'd seen the phone.

"Wait, let's think about this for a second," Hank shouted.

"Think about what?" Pat replied.

"Why leave a note if you're going to blow up the ship?" Hank asked.

"You wouldn't," the chief replied.

"They expected to get away and for security to find the note. We fucked that plan up," Hank said.

The security chief started to piece together the events of the past twenty-four hours.

"Someone changed the alert and duty rosters, killed the cameras, stopped the ship, and jammed communications. I agree with Hank that the bad guys are expecting to get away," said Kaspersky.

"You have guards all over the place. How could they possibly expect to get off the ship without anyone seeing them?" Pat asked Kaspersky.

"Dunds, where is your normal sniper position?" the chief asked.

"I would be covering any approach from the stern, Chief," Dunds replied.

"Can a helicopter land back there?" Hank asked.

"No, our pad is on the bow, and the nearest island is way out of range of any helicopters I've ever heard of," replied Dunds.

"Dunds, is there anyone at the security office right now?" asked the chief.

"Yeah, Sanderson is there with the prisoner."

"All right, come with us!" Kaspersky shouted as he broke into a trot.

Pat and Hank followed the chief and Officer Dunds back to the elevator.

"Where are we going, Chief?" Pat asked.

"If we announce abandon ship, they might blow the bomb early. If Dunds was going to watch over the stern, I'm thinking they wanted a blind spot to get off the ship unobserved."

"How could you get off the ship from there? Wouldn't the fall kill you if you jumped?"

"Not necessarily. If you hit the water from that height, you might get bruised, but you only get sucked under the ship if the ship is in motion."

"What about rappelling down to the water?" Pat inquired.

The elevator opened and the men got into the car. Officer Dunds's mouth opened as something connected in his mind.

"The activities director called this morning. He said someone stole some rock-climbing gear. You can definitely use that to rappel down the rear of the ship."

"All right, let's go check out the stern. Stay close and don't shoot into any crowds of people. The decks should be cleared by now, but sometimes passengers can be a pain in the ass about doing as they're told. No offense."

"None taken," Pat and Hank replied in unison. The elevator doors closed and the car ferried them away.

RICHIE arrived at the deck where Chris and Jessica were staying, his heart racing like a Formula 1 car. A sense of euphoria enveloped him, and the headache instantly disappeared. As he approached the room, a crimson rage filled him like helium in a balloon. Blood ran from his nose and dripped onto his hand as he took the key card out of his pocket.

For a moment, Richie's thinking cleared, and he knocked on the door instead of using the keycard. As he heard footsteps approaching, he smeared blood across the peephole.

"Who is it?" Jessica asked.

"Mr. Powell sent me to escort you to dinner, Mrs. Cosgrove," Richie said, attempting to disguise his voice.

"One second; I need to get my sea pass."

Richie heard the woman walking away from the door, and he stepped to the side so Jessica wouldn't see him and slam the door. The footsteps returned and the door opened.

Richie grabbed Jessica by the throat and threw her back into the room. Jessica flew ten feet and fell to the floor. Richie slammed the door and locked it. As Jessica regained her bearings, she looked up at her attacker, and a cold chill ran through her.

"You fucking bitch!" Richie screamed as he lunged at Jessica.

"Richie, what are you doing? Help! Help!" Jessica screamed at the top of her lungs.

Richie jumped on top of Jessica and wrapped his hands around her throat. Jessica made choking, gurgling noises as she dug her nails into Richie's eyes. He screamed in pain, releasing his grip on her neck.

Jessica shoved him away and got shakily to her feet. Richie grabbed her leg and she fell to the floor. She screamed for help, and Richie placed his hand over her mouth as he removed the gun from the back of his pants. He placed the muzzle of the pistol to Jessica's temple and pressed it hard against her skull.

"You feel that, bitch? If you scream, you're dead. Nod if you understand me."

Jessica nodded in agreement, and Richie removed his hand from her mouth but kept the muzzle pressed against her head.

"Go sit on the bed," he ordered. He stood up and walked over to the bed with Jessica. His hands were shaking with rage, and he was dizzy again. "How long did it take you to dream up this little scam, huh? Did you laugh while my skull was smashed in? What did it feel like fucking Powell behind my back, knowing that you were just there to bleed me dry?" Richie asked, not expecting any answers. "I loved you with all my heart. I did anything you wanted, and you repay me by fucking my best friend and trying to have me killed?"

"Richie I'm—"

Richie hit her in the face with the gun. "Don't you dare tell me you're sorry. You're not sorry about what you did! You're sorry you got caught! You're sorry you're going to die by my hand! I loved you, and now I'm going to kill you."

Richie placed the weapon in Jessica's mouth. She grabbed the barrel and struggled to remove it, kicking Richie in the groin. Richie didn't even flinch. He was completely focused on Jessica when he pulled the trigger and watched her body fall to the bed and roll onto the floor.

It was done. Jessica was dead. Richie sat down on the floor and stared at her body. He watched as her fiery red hair became matted with blood and gore. The euphoria he had felt faded, and reality came flooding back in when he heard a knock at the door. He considered firing blindly at the person on the other side, but caught sight of himself in a mirror. The looking glass reflected the image of a crazed and bloodied man pointing a gun at a complete stranger. As Richie looked at the reflection of the man he had become, a wave of nausea overcame him and he vomited on the floor. The person outside the door said that they had called for security.

Abruptly, Richie experienced such severe pain in his head that he fell to the floor. As he rolled over, he saw Jessica's open eyes and mouth, the necklace he had given her for their anniversary sparkling in the light. Richie closed his eyes and saw the face of the man he had strangled to death on the ship, the face of Alfred Patterson as he smashed his skull in with an ax, the face of his friend and accountant Louie, and finally the face of the man he'd thought was a friend for life—Chris Powell. Richie shuddered as the memory of cutting the flesh from Chris's back replayed in his head.

Richie could not stomach the remorse and guilt that he felt. He had become a monster. The feeling that he had been betrayed did not fade; it remained and was layered on top of the guilt of murdering the woman he had loved and shared his life with.

Richie crawled next to Jessica and lay behind her corpse. He couldn't live with what he had done. The pain in his skull increased until it felt as though the plates of his skull were being pried apart.

Richie placed the muzzle of the gun in his mouth and pulled the trigger. He died instantly and all his pain ceased.

THE elevator arrived on the deck where Pat and Hank had boarded the ship. It was the only opening on the rear of the ship that someone could rappel down or jump from. There were no security officers in the area, so Pat and Hank knew they must be in the right place. Then a green flare discharged from the stern area.

"What's a green one mean?" Pat asked as the men ran toward the source of the flare.

"I have no idea," replied Kaspersky. "We don't have green ones on board."

Hank was the closest to the outer railing, and he could see a smaller vessel approaching the ship at a high speed.

"I think their ride is here!" he yelled.

A shot rang out and Officer Dunds fell to the ground, hit in the leg. Pat stopped to drag the man out of the line of fire as rounds flew past them. Hank returned fire with the chief.

Carl gave his weapon to the last remaining mercenary and instructed him to engage the men in a firefight while he finished securing the ropes to the railing.

Hank was determined to stop the man in any way possible. They needed to know where the bomb was, and the man getting ready to rappel off the ship was probably the only person who knew.

Hank continued to fire as the mercenary charged at him. Pat dropped the security guard and ran after Hank. Pat threw his empty gun to the ground as he ran. Hank's gun locked to the open position as it fired its last round at the mercenary. The mercenary's weapon also ran out of ammunition, but he had another magazine. As he began to reload, Hank leapt at him and he dropped his weapon. Pivoting on his heel, the mercenary grabbed hold of Hank, and using the impetus of Hank's lunge, sent him flying over the railing.

"Hank!" Pat screamed as he watched his partner disappear from sight.

Chief Kaspersky saw Hank go overboard as he raised his weapon and fired at the last mercenary. The bullet struck the man in the chest and then Kaspersky was out of rounds. Pat pounced and wrapped his hands around the throat of the man who had just killed his partner and best friend. The man's eyes rolled back into his head, and he fought for air as Pat's grip tightened.

Pat's eyes filled with tears, and his hatred for this man gave him strength he had never had before. The man's neck snapped, then he drew his final breath and went limp. Pat continued to squeeze the man's throat until he no longer had the strength to grip.

Kaspersky ran after Carl as he jumped over the railing and rappelled toward the waiting vessel. The chief had left his knife in the office, and the knot on the railing would not budge with a man's weight on it.

"Fuck!" the chief shouted.

Pat grabbed the rope and swung it back and forth as he tried to shake the man loose. Pat needed to hurt this man in any way possible, and he remembered that he still had the paring knife in his jacket pocket. As Pat tried desperately to cut the rope, he saw someone swimming toward the waiting vessel. His eyes bugged out and his heart soared when he recognized Hank. It appeared his partner hadn't died from the fall after all, and was in fact doing his best to get to the ship.

One of the men on the extraction crew saw Hank and opened fire, but Hank dove under the water and disappeared. Pat jumped over the railing, flying past Carl. Pat reached out but was unable to get a grasp on Carl or the rope. He brought his arms together over his head and entered the water as cleanly as possible.

Carl disconnected his carabiner from the loop of rope on his Swiss seat. He fell the last eight feet to the deck.

"Cease fire! Cease fire!" Carl ordered as he landed with a thud.

Hank came up to the surface and saw that Pat had joined him in the water. The men on the ship stopped firing, and the man who had rappelled down the side was grabbing something from the deck.

"Oh shit!" Hank exclaimed as he saw several security officers appear at the railing of the cruise liner with weapons. The security officers opened fire at the strange vessel, nearly striking Pat and Hank.

"Cease fire!" the chief shouted. He would prefer that the mysterious gunman escaped than be responsible for the deaths of those two hero cops.

Carl looked at the two men in the water and then up at the security officers pointing guns at him as his ship got underway. As he sped off, he threw life jackets and a flotation ring toward Pat and Hank. Pat and Hank grabbed the ring and clung to it; neither had the strength to tread water until they were rescued.

The security staff rescued the two off-duty cops and took them to the infirmary, where the captain of the ship was talking to the chief of security in a very loud tone of voice. Pat and Hank could hear him from the treatment room and hoped it didn't have anything to do with them. They were in enough trouble already. When a nurse entered, they asked him if there was a discount for frequent visitors, because their partners were going to beat them mercilessly when they found out what had happened. The nurse smiled and asked them to wait there for a few more minutes.

"That kid has balls, Hank," Pat said, nodding at Holbrook, the young security officer, who lay in a glass intensive care unit just across the hall.

On cue, the *Queen Mary 2* sprang back to life, communications, engines, and all other systems coming back on line twenty minutes after the terrorists fled the ship.

The security chief ordered a sweep of the entire vessel, starting on the lowest deck, where the engine room was located, and working up to the highest to locate the explosive device the terrorists claimed to have planted. The bomb was soon located and carefully carried to a lifeboat. The dinghy was lowered into the sea and sent one hundred yards from the ship, then the bomb was dropped gently over the side. After waiting a few seconds, the lifeboat sped back to the mother ship and was retrieved from the ocean.

Satisfied that there was no longer any danger to the passengers, the captain announced that passengers were free to move about the ship except in restricted areas. The bars were reopened, as well as the casino. When the ship was underway, the passengers calmed down and return to their briefly interrupted vacations. The crew began the extremely difficult task of cleaning up various crime scenes, after they'd been photographed. The bodies were stored in a freezer specially built for such a need. And so the danger passed and things went back to normal.

DONG-YUL returned to Dean and Shawn's suite and assisted them out of the tub, drying each one off, including their fronts. As he ran the towel over Shawn's genitals, Shawn rolled his eyes at Dean. Dong-yul wrapped Shawn in a fluffy robe and then helped Dean out of the tub. Dean wasn't surprised when Dong-yul dried off his chest, stomach, crotch, and legs. Dong-yul helped Dean on with his robe and then wiped down the bathroom.

"Look, the ship's moving again," Shawn said as he walked out on the balcony.

"The engine problem is fixed, it seems," Dean said. "I wouldn't be surprised if our husbands were down there turning wrenches. They've been gone for hours."

"Did you hear something like gunshots while we were in the tub?" Shawn asked.

"Gunshots? That's it, you're cut off from the cosmos," Dean replied.

"Can I get you anything else, sirs?" Dong-yul asked.

"No, Dong-yul, you've been great. Thank you for your service. Any idea where our husbands are?" Dean asked.

"No. You want me to make calls to try and locate them?"

"That would be great!" Shawn replied, forgiving Dong-yul for touching intimate areas with the towel. The wind blew through their hair, drying it, as they finished the last of their drinks.

"Excuse me, sirs." Dong-yul came out onto the balcony.

When the boys turned, they saw grave concern on Dong's face instead of the pleasant, horny look that he pulled off so well.

"What is it, Dong-yul?" Shawn asked sharply.

"I find your husbands. I'm sorry to tell you that they're in ship's infirmary. They helped out the ship's security and were injured. That's all I know. Come, I'll help you dress."

"For fuck's sake! This is supposed to be a vacation, and they get injured on the *Queen Mary 2*?" Dean yelled as Dong-yul pulled out underwear and socks so fast they flew through the air. By the time they had put those on, Dong-yul had shirts and jeans ready. When they put those on, they found pairs of shoes lined up for them to step into.

"You go now. I straighten up in here. I pray everything all right for my men," Dong-yul said and gave a little bow of his head.

Dean and Shawn flew into the infirmary so quickly that an armed security officer drew his weapon in surprise.

"Whoa, cowboy, we're related to Detectives St. James and Capstone. Where are they?"

"You mean Pat and Hank?" the young Filipino asked.

"Yes, them! Where are they?"

"Your names?"

"Dean and Shawn, their husbands!"

"Husbands?" the security guard responded, looking confused.

They rushed past the guard and found their husbands, who pulled their blankets over their heads when they saw them.

"Just what the fuck have you two been up to? We're on a luxury cruise. How could you get involved in some bullshit that got you injured? How are you injured?" Dean asked as Shawn tapped his foot with a look at Hank that said, *"You're not getting laid for a year, mister."*

"We fell overboard. Well, Hank fell overboard. I jumped," Pat answered.

The doctor came in and Shawn was on him like lightning.

"What are their injuries, and when can they leave?"

"They mainly have bruises. There's nothing broken. They drank some sea water so they may vomit a little more, but no bullet wounds," the doctor answered calmly.

"Bullet wounds?" Dean shouted. "So it *was* gunfire we heard while we were in the tub!"

The doctor continued as if he hadn't head the outburst. "As for when they can be released, I imagine they can return to their cabins now."

"We're in a Queen's Grill suite with a butler. We'll be fine," Shawn said.

"Where are their clothes?" Dean asked.

"I'm afraid they were covered in gasoline from the speedboat, so they've been isolated as a fire hazard. We can loan them robes, however."

"Oh my God, unbelievable. You two, put on these robes, and let's go!" Dean said.

Epilogue

PAT and Hank didn't hear the end of it all the way to Sydney. Shawn and Dean were quite upset, and on the final night, it became clear just how upset, when no conversation was taking place at dinner. Things were getting grim when the captain entered the dining room and approached their table.

"May I join you for a brief moment, gentlemen?"

"Of course, sir, please," Dean replied as a waiter drew up a fifth chair.

"I cannot tell you how much you helped Cunard Lines, the *Queen Mary 2*, and the crew and passengers of this ship. I think a large thank-you is in order for the bravery and dedication that you showed when you had absolutely no obligation to risk your lives. I've had a full report on your heroics from my security chief, and I've contacted Cunard. They've agreed to give you a full refund for your cruise. Therefore, gentlemen, you are guests of the line. Whatever you wish, you have only to ask."

"That's mighty generous of you, Captain, thank you very much!" Hank said. "But how could we not offer assistance when over four thousand lives were at risk in the middle of the Pacific?"

"It's in our blood. It's what we do," Pat added.

"Wait, there's more. You four gentlemen are invited to be our guests once again in the finest suite on board, the Queen's number one. It is two levels of beauty and luxury and it is yours for the same period as this cruise. I understand you are married couples, so naturally all four of you are to be comped. I hope it makes up for the verbal beating you took from your husbands, detectives. The ship's doctor tells me it was quite severe."

"You can say that again!" Shawn chimed in.

"That's very gracious of you and Cunard, Captain. I think I can speak for all of us when I say we'll take you up on your offer," Pat said.

"Does it have to be the same route?" Dean asked.

"No. Anywhere the *QM2* sails, you have fourteen nights on board in the number one suite. Please call this special number when you are ready for a vacation without murder and mayhem," the captain said as he handed Pat a Cunard business card that read "corporate headquarters."

"I hope this makes up for the ruination of your vacation this time," the captain said as he stood. "Now, forgive me, I must go. There is a lot to do yet with police officials and entry into Australia. The police may want statements from you as well, but for now, enjoy your dinner. Good evening, gentlemen."

As Pat and Hank's group was disembarking at the end of the cruise, they were met at the security desk by Chief Kaspersky.

"Gentlemen, I hope the cruise wasn't too boring for you."

Shawn and Dean glared at the security chief. He smiled at them before extending a hand to Pat and Hank.

"Thank you. If it wasn't for you two, God only knows how many lives would have been lost. I reviewed some videotape near the cargo elevator where Holbrook got shot. Where in the world did you come up with the idea for a fire extinguisher as a weapon?" The chief laughed.

"Too much television, Chief," Hank replied.

"How is Holbrook?" Pat asked.

"It was touch and go for a bit, but he's going to be all right. I'm putting him in for promotion if he chooses to stay on as security. The Aussies are going to want to have a word with you before you disappear." The security chief handed Hank a small video disc with the words 'fire extinguisher guy' written in black marker.

Hank shook his head. "I hope this doesn't end up on YouTube."

The seven men shook hands with the security chief and left the ship, but not before Dong-yul gave them all a tearful goodbye and a kiss for his three hundred dollar tip. After interviews with the Australian police and security services, Pat and Hank's party was driven to the airport, where they were put on a plane at the expense of Cunard. They had booked Hank, Pat, Dean, and Shawn into first class, and Shawn was overjoyed. The rest of their party hadn't been needed by the authorities and had caught their regular flights, which were in coach. Shawn couldn't wait to tease his friends about the upgrade.

"This is more like it! Maybe you getting involved wasn't such a bad thing," Shawn observed after they took their seats.

Dean punched Shawn in the arm and said, "Quiet, junior, or did you forget our husbands were shot at? I'm starting to understand why you get spanked so often!"

"Sorry," Shawn said.

"Good evening, Detectives St. James and Capstone," said the handsome flight attendant. "I'm Steve Foster, and I'll be your purser. It's a pleasure to have you flying with us today. I do apologize, but unfortunately our air marshal came down with something, and we can't replace him before the flight takes off. Would you be willing to act if needed?"

"You have no idea," Dean said at the same time as Shawn bleated, "Don't you dare, Hank!"

"Absolutely. It would be our pleasure," Hank and Pat said at the same time.

"That's very kind of you. I'll let the captain know."

Shawn and Dean looked at their husbands in horror.

"I want a divorce," Dean said, pulling a sleeping mask over his eyes.

"That's not a bad idea," Shawn replied as he got busy reading the movie selection list for the long flight home.

Pat looked at Hank and shrugged. Hank smiled.

"Been a real fun time. I think I need a vacation from this vacation," Pat said and chuckled.

TWO days after landing on US soil, Pat and Hank returned to work. When they walked into the station, Capparell greeted them with a smile.

"I got a weird call from a Chief Kaspersky about you two."

"About us?" Pat feigned innocence.

"Just said you helped him out in a pinch and wanted to let us know how valuable you two are."

"That was nice of him," Hank said as he approached his desk. Stacked on top were three fire extinguishers. Rodriguez turned on the wall video screen. Hank appeared on the screen running down a hallway in a Hawaiian shirt, shooting a fire extinguisher. The men in the bureau laughed and applauded Hank's shenanigans.

"If I ever see Kaspersky again, he's a dead man," Hank said as he sat down and removed the fire extinguishers from his desk.

Underneath the fire extinguishers was a letter congratulating him on acceptance to the Narcotics bureau test in three days. Pat saw the letterhead and his stomach dropped; Hank was going to transfer after all.

Lt. Capparell walked over to Pat and Hank's desks and sat on the edge of one. "Well, boys, Durkin got kicked upstairs. He's now Lt. Durkin of Patrol, and his party is next Saturday at five. Good luck on the test, Hank."

Hank crumpled the letter of congratulations and threw it in the garbage. "Lieutenant, if I need any action, I'll go on vacation with this knucklehead. I'm good right here in Homicide."

"Oh? Who said I still wanted you? After all, you'd look kinda silly carrying around a fire extinguisher in your holster."

"Really, Hank? You're staying?" Pat asked, not knowing whether to laugh or cry.

"Yeah, if this cruise taught me one thing, it's that together we can take on anything. I was thrown off the *Queen Mary 2*, and you jumped off into the water, and we both survived. You just don't break up a team like ours!"

Everyone applauded again as Pat shed a tear of joy. He couldn't wait to share the good news with Dean.

"Okay, who's up?" the lieutenant said. "We just had a triple shooting in a Hyattsville apartment, and it's a messy one."

"We'll take it," Hank said. "We're getting used to messy."

JOHN SIMPSON, a Vietnam-era Veteran, has been a uniformed Police Officer of the Year, a federal agent, a federal magistrate, and an armed bodyguard to royalty and a senior government executive. He earned awards from the Vice President of the United States and the Secretary of the Treasury. John has written articles for various gay and straight magazines. John lives with his partner of thirty-five years and three wonderful Scott Terriers, all spoiled and a breed of canine family member that is unique in dogdom. John is also involved with the Old Catholic Church and its liberal pastoral positions on the gay community.

Visit John's website at http://www.johnsimpsonbooks.com/.

ROBERT CUMMINGS is a police officer in Pennsylvania with fourteen years on the job; he also served nine years in the Army National Guard. After a year and a half tour in Iraq, Robert came home and became interested in writing after he was consulted by a well-established author on a work of police fiction. Robert enjoys biking, hiking, and as much travel as he can afford.

You can keep an eye on his progress or leave feedback at: http://www.facebook.com/#!/profile.php?id=100002732291489.

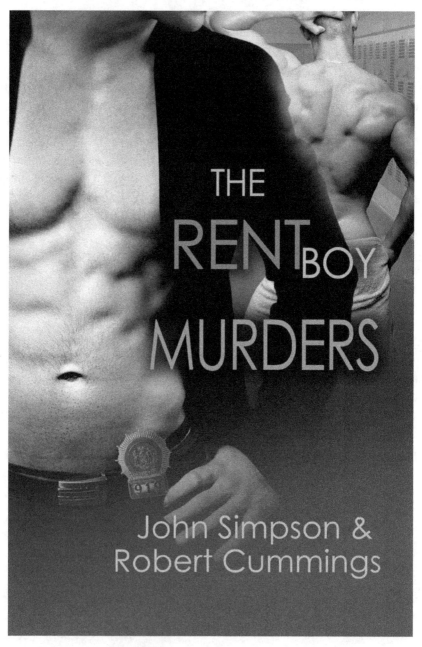

Murder Most Gay from JOHN SIMPSON

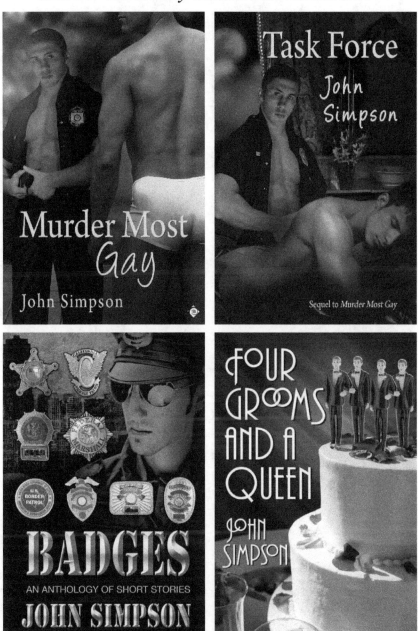

Also from JOHN SIMPSON

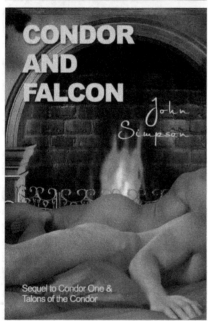

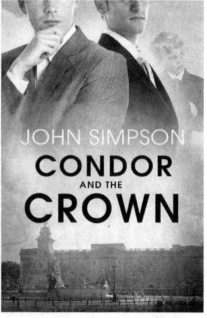

http://www.dreamspinnerpress.com

More from JOHN SIMPSON

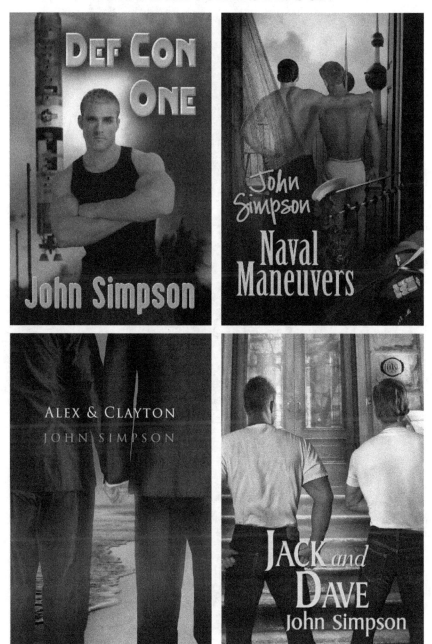

http://www.dreamspinnerpress.com

Romance from DREAMSPINNER PRESS

Good
to Know

D.W. MARCHWELL

http://www.dreamspinnerpress.com

CPSIA information can be obtained
at www.ICGtesting.com
Printed in the USA
LVHW092156030619
620048LV00022B/1049/P